THE
END
of
Summer

This edition was published by The Dreamwork Collective
The Dreamwork Collective LLC, Dubai, United Arab Emirates
thedreamworkcollective.com

Printed and bound in the United Arab Emirates
by Al Ghurair Printing & Publishing
Cover and design: Kasia Piątek, kasiapiatek.pl
Text © Salha Al Busaidy, 2022

ISBN 978-9948-8778-3-7

Approved by the National Media Council
MC-02-01-6163804

The content of this book is deemed appropriate for ages 21+ according
to the age classification system issued by the Ministry of Culture and
Youth, United Arab Emirates

Salha Al Busaidy

THE END

of

Summer

THE
DREAMWORK
COLLECTIVE

This book is for my hilarious, artistic, sarcastic and much missed nephew. And for my beloved niece, who found him.

Dear Reader,

I would like to issue a trigger warning here. I wouldn't usually, as I am Old School (OK, maybe just "old") and back in my day, we just let people be triggered, feelings be damned.

However, when we know better, we do better, and I do understand that this novel tackles difficult topics, especially subjects that are culturally sensitive, and some that may be very uncomfortable to read. Please note that this is a work of FICTION. Yes, I wrote it as a way to deal with my nephew's death and many of the characters and anecdotes are based on inspiration from my family. But, just because this novel is written in the first person, please do not confuse Summer's voice with mine. Or Summer's family with mine!

Summer has been through a lot; she is a troubled twenty-two-year-old. She swears a lot and her opinions and views are a result of her life experiences and trauma.

I also feel that I should mention that, despite only living in Oman for four years, I have nothing but love and respect for the country and its people. I am also not advocating drug use – I am trying to shine a light on its abuse, and the fact that young people today are struggling with identity and cultural conflicts, and we need to listen more.

If you, or anyone you know is struggling with addiction, trauma, abuse, depression or thoughts of suicide, please reach out to someone or use one of the resources at the back of the book. Do not suffer alone. Please.

Now, having said that, dear Reader, find a quiet spot, suspend disbelief and please enjoy The End of Summer.

Salha x

My family

Baba's Family

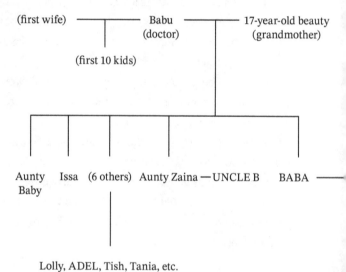

Mama's Family

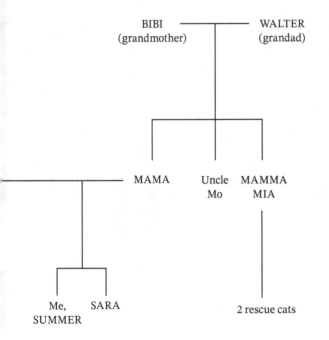

BIBI ——————— WALTER
(grandmother)   (grandad)

MAMA   Uncle   MAMMA
             Mo   MIA

Me,   SARA
SUMMER

2 rescue cats

1 September 2016, 12.08 p.m.

Oh, fuck! Fuck! What the...? Okay, get up! Clean up this mess! Shit, shit, shit, shit!

As is evident by my eloquence, blind panic is the first thing that hits me when I come to. And *what* a mess!

Clothes, upturned handbag, cigarette pack, rolling gear box, hash block, papers.

Needle.

Spoon.

The parents are out of town, so they won't witness the carnage here in the bathroom, but there's no need to advertise to Sara that I got completely wasted last night. And she's bound to find out. We share this bathroom. Not that she'll judge me. She knows what I do, but I don't want my little sis asking to tag along every time I go out either. I don't want her keeping an eye out for me. Or pitying me.

Or asking me for drugs.

Woah...

I still feel pretty high.

Really high.

I *must* still be high; I'm having what can only be described as an Out of Body experience. Or is it Outer Body experience? I'll have to look that up.

(I feel like one of those morons you read about on the Buzzfeed compilations, the ones who love the smell of their boyfriend's 'colon', or who think their granny has 'die of beaties'.)

Okay, I am.

Definitely.

Still.

High.

My thoughts are crystal clear and actually, so is my head, but I am literally looking *down* at my own body.

And I look like shit. Sitting on the floor by the toilet, half-dressed in last night's clothes and half ready for bed, my pyjama bottoms wrapped around one leg. My minimal makeup is still on but is really doing nothing for my complexion. Oh no, is that a little puke on my chin? Real classy.

Wait, did I drink last night?

Surely I have learned from disastrous past experiences that I mustn't drink and do other stuff simultaneously.

The cigarette I lit is in my hand, but I didn't smoke any of it and the entire length of it is ash. An undisturbed cigarette skeleton.

Well, that took some skill!

I must have lit it and immediately passed out. Lucky it didn't start a fire on the flammable bathroom rugs that Mama insists on decorating with. Chintzy, lacy, furry kitsch! You know, the kind that have matching toilet seat covers? I never understood the purpose of those. Warming the seat? In Oman, where it's almost 50 bloody degrees!

Shit! There's Sara knocking on the bathroom door.

Okay, I have to get up, quietly, chuck that needle, clear up the rolling papers and the spoon, and splash some water on my face. Wash that puke off.

Except I can't move.

She's banging on the door now. Okay, keep completely still. Play possum.

(I don't know what possums look like.)

She's calling.

'Summer? Summer! Open the door, I need to pee!'

Silence. Shuffling. Distant shuffling. Returning.

Oh no! The trick I taught her. She's got a coin and she's unlocking the door from the outside.

She walks in, stands in the doorway in her cute pyjamas, and looks down at me.

Okay, this is weird. She's looking down at me, and I'm not looking *up* at her.

But I can see her.

She bends down and moves me.

Oh dammit, Sara! You disturbed the perfect ash curve! I wanted a picture of that. In black and white; that would have looked cool—the ash in focus and my fingers slightly blurred. A new photo for my portfolio.

She holds my other hand and touches my face. Ugh, this hangover; I can't feel a thing.

She sits by me for several minutes and we say nothing. We do that a lot, so this is nice. And just about all I can handle this morning.

She walks out and gets her phone. Too late to take the bloody picture now.

'Hello, Bibi?'

Wait! What the hell is she calling our grandmother for?

'Bibi... Summer is dead.'

12.17 p.m.

Hilarious! Right? What is she on about?

Obviously it's not true. Because I am blatantly right fucking here.

I am watching everything that's going on.

But my eyes aren't moving...

And now I'm starting to slowly freak out because I can't move my body. I can see it, sitting by the toilet, which is where I sit to smoke a joint sometimes, under the extractor fan. But I can't move it.

How can I be moving in closer to my own body? How is this even possible? I come really close and look at my face. Slightly open, downcast, unfocused eyes; eyes that were probably willing the cigarette up to my lips. My head lolling heavily to one side, and my lips, powder blue, parted by a swollen tongue.

And a little puke.

Okay, think, think.

I *can* actually think, so that must count for something, right?

I think, therefore I am...

I can't physically feel anything though, and I can't move. And I look like death.

Yeah, exactly.

Death.

So, if I'm looking at my physical body, what am I? Floating eyes? A ghost?

I have the sensation that you get just as you fall asleep, the ataraxy that Mamma Mia says comes beyond deep meditation.

A light buoyancy, a weightless floating, an empty stomach-ness, like the plunging descent of a roller coaster, and a very keen sense of everything. Not a sense of just yourself, not just your breathing or heartbeat, but everything in the universe all at once. The terror of migrants fleeing, the elation of new parents, the drum roll of thunder a continent away, and the frolicking of fucking dolphins. I feel as if I have been one with all of creation this entire time, but I just couldn't tell.

I feel like a guru or a sage.

I sound like a tree-hugging hippy.

I feel as if I know the answers to everything. Everything except what happened last night.

I should be panicking, but I can't detect a heartbeat to quicken. My occasionally asthmatic breath should be ragged. I should feel like I want to puke, but even though I can feel everything in the bloody universe, I can't feel myself. I should be absolutely terrified. I know what I have read about Death and The Grave. I know the Quran and its Teachings and The Day of Judgement.

Oh shit...

Heaven. Hell.

My mind is racing and thoughts are tripping over themselves.

Have I been good? Good enough? What *is* good enough?

I can't die yet, because I haven't had a chance to make Peace; my peace with God, with my parents, with myself.

I haven't travelled everywhere I want to go. Uncle Mo was going to take me diving. I'll never get to my roots in Zanzibar.

I can't cry. I want to fucking CRY!

I have too many questions. Am I *really* dead? How did I die? What the fuck happened last night??

I can't die. I'm not done here.

I have to go back and finish my degree.

I want to be brave enough to exhibit my photographs.

No, I can't be dead.

PLEASE.

Please, no...

I'm still a bloody virgin!

12.18 p.m.

Sara is on the phone to our grandparents, Mama's parents. Sara seems incongruously calm as she sits on the edge of her bed, holding the phone tighter than necessary in her lap with one hand. The other hand is picking at the lace that borders her duvet cover. Sara fiddles with things so she doesn't bite her nails, which is maybe her only bad habit. I have many.

Bibi is on speaker and is clearly in shock on the other end of the line, but she's had to deal with death her whole life, so she's being quite pragmatic.

She asks Sara if she's sure and if she's done all the correct tests to tell.

Yes, Bibi.

She asks Sara if she's okay.

Yes, Bibi.

She says they'll be there as soon as possible and that they love her very much.

I love you too, Bibi.

Bibi and Grandad say that they are going to call our parents who are in England. Finalising the divorce.

Finally finalising.

It's been a long time coming; the two of them have been a domestic disaster for years with their seething, snide resentment permeating every corner of our household.

I remember visiting my Indian friend Nehal's house when I was at school. Her parents were wealthy, and they had a sparkling clean mansion with at least seven members of staff. But their house always smelled of cooking, garam masala, fried onions, sizzling garlic; delicious, but stale.

Well, that's what it felt like in my house. We all seemed happy to the Outside, to the Family, but at home the stench of their misery was in the fabric of the sofas and curtains. Fogging up the windows so you couldn't see through the constant awkwardness. Staining the carpets, so you never knew where to tread. Oozing an acidic path into the way I viewed men and marriage. Rotting the way I viewed confrontation (or the absolute, anxious avoidance thereof!).

I figured out when to leave a room as soon as I felt tensions rising. I learned how to avoid taking sides, not by being diplomatic but by mumbling and being noncommittal. And I dodged bullets of blame like a video game ninja.

They had been fighting for as long as we could recall, never coming to an understanding between them during their twenty-three years together, always on opposing camps in every verbal war they waged. They left unresolved arguments like corpses on the battlefield of our house; no victor was ever declared, no treaties made, let alone reparations, and Sara and I were scantily prepared triage nurses, gormlessly holding Band-Aids while looking at blown-off legs. Cannon fodder for the next battle.

This was all worsened by them saying they had to 'stay together for the girls'. Selfish cliché bullshit. Sara and I would be a lot less screwed up if they had divorced years ago, like normal parents, when we were young enough to bounce back.

Long before the Edinburgh Episode.

In our culture, you must respect and revere your elders. You must also, by penalty of certain death, NEVER talk private family business outside the house. What happens within your family unit is no one else's business. And that's why we didn't talk about how uncomfortable life was at home, not even to our own parents. We never told them how it pained us to hear raised voices or the breaking of kitschy figurines as they were flung against walls (to be fair, we had mixed sentiments about their demise). But, worst of all, when each parent spoke ill of the other to us:

'You know very well, the problem with your mother is...'
'Well, your dad doesn't believe that we women should...'

And on it went.

And because we felt so awkward inside but weren't allowed to verbalise it, those feelings boiled inside me and would belch out in the occasional teenage tantrum and rebellion. (To be fair, in my culture a 'tantrum' may be a little *sotto voce* backchat.)

My parents would look at each other in surprise at my 'outburst', shocked at my insolence and wondering where on earth it could have come from. They would yell about how little respect I have, that we didn't speak to our elders like that.

Or deflect to the state of my hair.

Or my grades.

Or my side of the room.

I would run off and lock myself away and smoke. A fag or a joint.

Or scream, or cry.

Sara on the other hand, would shut down. When confronted, she took on a hollowness. A Stepford robot-ness that made her seem simultaneously perfect and completely vacuous. She endured the blames and accusations with the grace of a swan, but underneath the surface of her still waters, I knew her heart was paddling like mad.

My sister and I are screwed up in different ways. Sara says she wants six kids. I always made fun of her for wanting to be a baby factory, but as the ultimate optimist she wants to prove that marriages can be happy. I, on the other hand, am quite adamant that I will have none of it.

Well, I *was* quite adamant.

But now, if the option is off the table, do I wish I could go back and have a chance to breed? I'm observing my reactions carefully. I think I'm actually trying to bargain with God: Please let me live! I'll be good, get married and have babies.

It's a big bargain.

The only way to guarantee fucking up a child's mind is to have a child...

Of course, my Nostradamus-style announcement to anyone who would listen, that I would *never* have children, was met with the same reaction from everyone, expressed in a variety of different ways: incredulous scoffing, eye rolling, comments about my youth and how I would change my mind, disbelief and dismissal. No one took me seriously. Is motherhood a foregone conclusion for all women in my world? Is there no choice in this matter? Looking around, everyone was marrying and breeding. Admittedly, there isn't much else to do in Muscat, but just because you *can* procreate doesn't mean you have to.

Sometimes it seemed like we were just livestock for breeding. What if you preferred to travel, have a career? What if you had no maternal instincts and knew you wouldn't be a good mother?

The mentality in this culture is that good, God-fearing girls got married and had kids. Good girls *wanted* to. Ergo, I'm not good?

I *wasn't* good?

My limited life options here made me feel claustrophobic. I didn't want to have kids who I couldn't protect from all the shit that could happen to them. I couldn't imagine giving life to someone and see them getting hurt by the world. That would be a burden too great to bear.

I wonder how my parents lived with it.

Look, it's not entirely my parents' fault. There is nature, there is nurture. There are things that happened in my life that it seems I will *literally* be taking to my grave.

I told Mamma Mia part of my secret when we were stoned once. But despite her insistent pushing, I couldn't tell her the whole story, so now not a single person in my family will ever understand who and why I am.

(Who and why I *was*?)

If I had broken down my emotional barricades, they might have understood, but I simply couldn't take that risk; the risk of them knowing me, blaming me, hating me.

And so they never knew me. They couldn't know me. And that was my armour, my justification, my excuse.

And I kind of wish I had told them, and maybe they might have loved me anyway...

How long will it take my parents to get here from London? Will they fight the whole way? And blame each other for events that led to my death. Perhaps they will hold on to each other and wonder if their actions caused this, or maybe they're completely oblivious to their effect on us.

I don't even know if their divorce is final. Maybe they will be forced to fly back as two single people, in awkward emotional handcuffs. Or will they go through this as parents and as a married couple? What if this brings them together? Oh, wouldn't that be a kick in the fucking nuts!

I'm still confused. Is Sara right? Am I really dead?

I'm grappling with how I feel about all this, as the thought dawns in panicked waves that I don't know how my parents will feel about all this. I'm lying in the bathroom with a cling film–wrapped baggy and a needle spilling out of a worn Transformers pencil case that I've never seen before, and a block of Afghan hash and rolling papers in my camel bone box.

What will my folks think when they see the drug paraphernalia? I bet they won't even know what it is. I don't think my mum has even had an alcoholic drink in her life. I remember when I got stoned for the first time. I nearly brushed the enamel off my teeth in the morning. I washed my hair and the bedsheets and spoke to her in monosyllables, thinking that if she ever found out, she would KILL me.

I mean, after the Edinburgh Episode, they effectively tried to ruin my life.

Will my dad be furious, as usual? Will my mum despair of me, as usual?

Will they want to kill me, and have I beaten them to it?

Funny, it's just occurred to me that it hasn't occurred to me if they'll even be sad about me dying.

I'm not even my *own* first thought.

I just never felt that important.

12.20 p.m.

After a sigh and a moment of closing her eyes, Sara calls Mamma Mia next, who is over here in Muscat from Dubai, "babysitting" us while the parents are away. As much as we love our aunt, we protested that we didn't need babysitting. At almost twenty-three and nineteen, we are clearly old enough to take care of ourselves. We have a maid who cooks and cleans (I guess that contradicts the idea of us looking after *ourselves*), we can both drive, and *conveniently* every one of my dad's million Family members lives a nosey ten minutes away. And Bibi and Grandad live thirty minutes away. Grandad didn't want to live in the centre of town, surrounded by people who would 'gossip every time he farted'.

Anyway, we said we didn't need our aunt to make the four-hour drive here to keep an eye on us. We were fine on our own.

And then I remember that I've somehow managed to kill myself.

So, yeah, maybe not quite fine.

Shit, Mamma Mia won't take this well. I told her once that I heard of someone who had got hold of heroin; she warned me that she'd kill me if I ever tried it. Irony upon irony... I promised her I wouldn't touch it, and out of respect for that promise, I never did again. I thought.

Is Death the karma you get for breaking a solemn vow to an aunt? Damn, that's extreme.

Sara asks Mamma Mia to hurry, before anyone else gets here, in case there's anything they should hide. She seems, however, to be having trouble communicating with Mamma Mia, who is obviously not okay on the other end of the call. Sara has to repeat the news of my death a few times.

Yes, I'm pretty sure.

Silence.

What do you mean, what do I mean?

Silence

Well, she's cold and has no pulse.

Silence.

I don't know what happened.

Silence.

I found her on the floor in the bathroom with drugs.

Silence.

Well, I know what drugs LOOK like.

Silence.

Please don't cry, Mamma Mia, just get here.

Silence.

I love you too, MaMi.

Why is Sara so flipping calm? She must be in shock. Yes, that's it, she's shocked into emotional paralysis. She was never one for big displays, always the measured voice of reason, but this isn't exactly your average trigger.

I want to hold her. That would help! I wish I could just hold her!

Please just give me a little more time, so I can hold my baby sister.

Sara comes back into the bathroom and slowly lowers herself to the ground and sits opposite me, not taking her eyes off me and fiddling with the edge of the bathmat.

I'm watching Sara watching me. I look at her pretty oval face, the colour of warm caramel sauce, and eyes of spiced gingerbread with flecks of honey. She's in her pyjamas, little shorts with pink love hearts on them and a tank top with a teddy bear holding a heart saying 'I love you'. I have the same pair.

Her curls of chocolate and cinnamon are pineappled on top of her head, and after a night's sleep, several curls have escaped to frame her face. She looks perfect.

We're wearing the same necklace, a little yellow gold 'Allah' written in Arabic on a short chain. They were a present from our parents when Sara turned ten and I turned fourteen. She felt so grown-up with her very own gold jewellery. Even though I'm older, it was my first piece of jewellery too.

We often got the same things. I think it's a creepy habit—or perhaps a lazy shopping ploy—to dress sisters the same. Mama and her little sister, Mamma Mia, used to get the same clothes all the time. My mum clearly thought it was cute, whereas the younger Mamma Mia hated it and wanted her own identity. Deep down, I actually loved having the same things as Sara; the logic being if I could emulate her in style, then maybe my spirit would follow.

I don't see any fear in Sara's face, but she's not touching me anymore. I wish she would.

I wouldn't be able to feel her, but I still wish she would.

She picks up my phone. My password is her birthday.

She looks for phone call records or messages for clues as to what happened last night, but all she finds is an update on my Facebook status at around 1 a.m.

I see you can't resist it,

My mind, deliciously twisted.

What was that about? I used to do that all the time when I was stoned: get caught up in a very deep introspective moment, a philosophy that solved the world's greatest problems, but being too lazy (stoned) to record the whole theory in full, I would write a note-to-self, secure in the knowledge that this briefest, most enigmatic of codes would trigger a reminder of the entire ideology when I was sober.

Things like, *Allergic to Gravity* or *At what age does a Happy Meal become sad?* or *Can I pass the test of time?*

Of course, I could never remember what I was thinking, and the wisdom disappeared like curling smoke, along with my high.

Who couldn't resist my deliciously twisted mind? And does that person know what happened last night?

Sara's humming quietly, so quietly I can barely hear what it is. But I know. "A Whole New World" from *Aladdin*. We used to sing it together in front of the mirror, singing into hairbrushes and deodorant bottles. We didn't even know what we were singing about; we couldn't even imagine the Whole New World that was waiting for us. I always let her be Princess Jasmine, because I would have given her anything in the world.

She hasn't shed a tear yet.

Everything is so tranquil in the bathroom that I actually feel calm. Looking at Sara's beautiful, serene face, I'm not scared. There's something about this bizarre, peaceful death tableau, however ephemeral, that seems more desirable than the alternative: being alive and dealing with people, and parents, and my issues, and my future.

And studies and guilt.

And Life.

We sit together for almost ten pure minutes, listening to her tuneless humming.

God, I love her.

But she can't bloody sing. She's butchering *Aladdin*, for fucks' sake.

Side note:

Is it for fucks sake?

For fuck sake?

Or is it possessive? I guess the sake belongs to the fuck...?

Although this particular question was probably not on the curriculum, I know I should have focused more in school and not attempted to teach myself everything there is to know in the final three years, when I realised the only hope of escaping Oman would be by going to university.

Uncle Mo would quote *The Simpsons* when he teased me: 'Me, fail English? That's unpossible!'

Or say in a Swahili accent, 'I speak England very best!'

Rude.

But honestly, he was right; at fifteen, I was practically unable to spell and completely uninterested in studying (wait... uninterested or disinterested?).

Well, I'm not saying I have figured it ALL out, and I'm still certainly no mathlete, but I was determined to escape my narrow life, which looked narrower and darker with every indistinguishable passing day, and the only escape seemed to be an education. So, I read a thousand books and had a Word of the Day every day. I developed an insatiable appetite for learning, and trying to understand history, politics, philosophy, psychology. Things I just didn't care about before.

My grandad was a wealth of knowledge of international history and politics. Uncle Mo had travelled to more countries than anyone I've met and was a natural raconteur (Word of the Day). Mamma Mia loved literature and called herself a cunning linguist (her words, not mine). I forced them all to sit with me and I devoured their knowledge. My mum's family was thrilled at my sudden interest in self-improvement and stopped teasing me long enough to teach me what they knew.

I learned about the countries of the world, their capitals, their flags, and at least ten interesting facts about each of them. I watched *Planet Earth* and developed a creepily inappropriate crush on David Attenborough's voice. I stopped hanging out with my cousins. Female cousins who were only interested in starving themselves to attain and maintain their enviable figures, poking fun at each other, and waiting in horny puddles for a spouse. And male cousins who liked to smoke up and get fucked up.

My English teacher noticed the difference immediately and embraced me like a prodigal daughter return   ome after an almost unforgiveable betrayal.

Mrs Higgins (yes! Like *Pygmalion*) had been one of the first teachers to come to Oman to help teach English, when the country was in its infancy and there were only a handful of expats' children to be taught. I don't think she lost her passion for a single moment in those thirty years. Legend has it that she also hadn't cut her hair in that time, and the mystery was coiled in a greying blonde bun at the back of her head—never to be revealed, she winked.

She gave me books from her personal library and entertained and encouraged my hypotheses when we discussed them after school, and she eventually proudly helped with the application forms for university.

She cried when I fled at the first acceptance letter to study Business in Scotland. When I went to say goodbye, she unfurled her bun and showed me, and only me, her wavy hair that got thinner as it flowed down her back, until it disappeared into tendrils by the backs of her knees.

I realise now that I will never learn anything new again. If I'm dead, that's it for me, for life. No new words, no new countries, no new history to watch repeat itself. No one to ever fall in love with.

Either that, or I will suddenly learn Everything. The answers to all the Big Burning Questions.

Is there Life after Death?

Are Heaven and Hell real?

God.

Satan.

Angels. Jinn.

Rewards. Punishment.

And ignorance once again seems so appealing...

•

Mamma Mia is my mum's little sister, but they are not alike at all. Not in nature, not in lifestyle, not in looks. They were born nine years apart. My mum was the planned and celebrated first pregnancy of my grandparents, whereas Mamma Mia was a surprise last addition.

When my Mama was born, she was handed to the exhausted and ecstatic new parents. They counted her perfect ten fingers, her adorable ten toes, but when she opened her eyes and they saw that they were green, her parents wept with joy. For Bibi, especially, the green eyes were almost a victory. We all want what we don't have. White women tan and dark women use skin-lightening creams. To have green eyes was so unusual that people from far and wide would talk about her daughter, and although this was almost a huge feather in Bibi's cap, and a source of great personal pride, Bibi would have to pray over her new daughter to ward off the evil eyes that would no doubt follow her wherever she went—especially in Oman!

The arrival of this little girl was such a blessing to the over-joyed proud pair that they named her after Jesus's mother, Mar-yam. And because Bibi has the OCD of a clinically organised nurse, and a homesick heart, she named her other children with names beginning with M.

Mohammed and Mina.

Mama was a beloved only child for a little while before Uncle Mo came along, but she didn't resent the new presence; she doted on and took care of her little brother and they were great allies.

Then came the wild and wilful surprise little sister, six years after Uncle Mo. The squealing, screaming, singing Mamma Mia made a dramatic entrance and disrupted everyone's peace with hugs, tears, and constant questions. When Bibi was pregnant with this latest addition, she craved fresh chillies, which she ate whole, sweating and cursing, so it's no surprise really that the vocal new baby had the fiery, stubborn, know-it-all nature of her ancestors.

Mamma Mia is not as beautiful as my mum; instead of my mum's raw-emerald eyes, hers are more like rain puddles, but when I was little, I always wished I had a doll that looked exactly like her with her butterscotch skin, long wavy hair, and little upturned nose. She has high round cheeks stuffed full of smiles and speckled with freckles and tiny skin tags that she calls her 'bits and bobs'. Her tiny twinkly eyes somehow match her huge mouth that she can fit her fist into—one of her famous party tricks!

She's a cross between a big sister and a mother, and she thought calling her Aunty was a little solemn and ceremonial; we have plenty of big-bottomed, stern Aunties. However, calling her by just her first name would have been a shocking display of disrespect.

(I was stunned the first time I heard a white person calling their elders by their first name. I stood aside waiting for the slap!)

We were so close, when we lived back in England, that we called her Mama too. Her name is Mina, but when I was little, I could only say Mia. So, she became Mamma Mia and the name stuck. She loves her nickname, especially when you camp it up and say it like some big drama.

MAMMA MIA!!

She is a raving thespian (her words, not mine).

I would say that I am Mamma Mia's favourite, and to be favoured by her was simultaneously special and scary. She is not afraid to give an abundance of affection, knowing that the well would always replenish itself, but Tough Love was very much a part of Love for her. She has high standards for herself and those she loves.

She is tactile with those close to her and mistrustful of those not. She is hilarious and earnest in equal measure, and always a little overdramatic.

She would have been the woman refusing to move on the bus, the little girl insisting on going to school despite threats to shoot her in the head. She would have been the battered wife who killed her husband, got put in jail, and made everyone her prison bitch. She is fierce and tells everyone exactly what she thinks, which is not always wise or popular as a woman in this society. But she manages to do it all with such a cheeky charm that before you know it, you're agreeing with her and she has won the argument.

I am her biggest fan and she is my greatest ally.

She was only thirteen when I was born, and she was more excited than my own mum about the little bruised and swollen new edition to the family. She treated me like her own baby, like her project, like her prodigy. She changed my nappy gleefully, watched me sleep, sang me silly made-up songs about how we would sit in the garden, under trees with lots of kittens to play with.

Come and sit with me,
Under the shady tree,
In our garden.

We will have three pussycats,
They're all furry and fat
In our garden.
Summer in the garden
Kittens in the garden
In our garden

Probably not going to win any Grammys.

Later on, she taught me how to read, spell, and write, so I was ahead of all the other kids in school. She would come and stay at our house in South London as often as she was allowed, and we'd sit at the dining table, covered in yesterday's newspapers, and have art project days. We blobbed dollops of paint onto paper and then folded them in half to make butterfly paintings. Or made collages with cut-up pictures from old magazines. Or Christmas decorations from pieces of coloured paper and Pritt Stick.

At night, she would put her arm around me, propped up with extra pillows, and read bedtime stories with all the appropriate voices of the growling animals, the mellifluous (Word of the Day) princesses, and the scratchy-throated witches. As I got older, she would pause in the middle of the story to comment on the choices the story's protagonist was facing and ask whether I would do things differently and how things could have turned out if I had. We would stay up late and whisper under the covers, so we wouldn't wake up the very young Sara, and giggle until my mum or dad would shout up the stairs at us to be quiet and go to sleep.

We were happy.

When I was almost seven years old, Baba announced that we would be moving from England to Oman; his brother had offered him a job that he, and therefore by extension his young family, could not refuse.

What an upheaval that was, for my mum and for us, to move to a country that we girls had never even been to, that Baba was now traitorously calling Home. For Mama to leave her family, quit her job, and for us to leave our schools and our friends. But Baba had made up his mind, and they do not come more stubborn than Baba.

Even worse, I was to be sent there alone, ahead of my parents and Sara, so I could start the school year on time in this new, strange, desert country.

Grandad and Bibi were so sad to see us all leave, but Mamma Mia was devastated.

Suddenly, I acted like I hated her. I can't remember why. She said that I wouldn't speak to her between the announcement of the move and me being shipped off to Oman. When asked, I would use the excuse, 'coz she's mean'. I didn't want her spending the weekends with us anymore. I shut her out completely and didn't even say a proper goodbye to her, even though she stood at Heathrow with the rest of the family, bawling her eyes out as I was led off by the unaccompanied minors' airline staff.

I was later told that she fell to the floor, sobbing and calling out to me, begging me not to leave her.

I didn't even turn and wave.

I know now, of course, that it was my crude and immature defence mechanism, the only way I could deal with missing her. Acknowledging how difficult this separation was would mean being a witness to my own heart shattering into dust.

I felt like I was being dragged away from both of my mothers.

12.39 p.m.

Mamma Mia has just burst into the bathroom, interrupting the peace with almost comedic hand wringing, face clutching, wailing, and expletives. 'Oh God, oh God! Please, please, fuck, fuck, fuck. Sara! Summer, Summmmmeeeeeerrrr! No, noooo!'

I try, fruitlessly, to stifle a giggle. Honestly, the histrionics are worthy of a Bollywood movie, or the overly dramatic soap operas on Egyptian TV that we always watched together in Ramadhan.

Mamma Mia catches her own risible hysteria and starts laughing and apologising between giggles.

It's so bizarre.

'I'm sorry, baby! It's not funny, Sara. I'm so sorry, I really don't know why the fuck I'm laughing! If Summer saw me, she would laugh at me and say, Oh, the drama! That's what she would say! Wouldn't she?'

She grabs Sara, stops babbling, looks in my little sister's eyes, searching, and then holds her close to her, carefully looking over Sara's shoulder at the scene beyond. She scopes everything quickly. Scanning the baggy, the needle and the spoon, the papers and the hash and the broken ash on the floor by my hand. I see her face drawing conclusions, shifting from sceptical to incredulous to actually terrifyingly pissed off... There is nothing scarier than an angry Aunty of Colour, if you don't know.

Then she looks at my body and bursts out crying again in Sara's hair. Sara has to ease the entire weight of her slumped body to the ground slowly where Mamma Mia, my favourite aunt and second mum, crawls over to me and puts her head in my lap and sobs like a baby, begging me not to leave her again.

•

After my family moved to Oman, I would see Mamma Mia often enough for holidays. She'd visit occasionally during her school holidays and she would try and make it for some of Ramadhan, when we would stay up talking into the night, snacking on spicy potato balls and ice cream (not together). We bonded while everyone else slept, laughing till the last glass of water before dawn prayers, until she cornered me one day in Muscat when I was fifteen and told me that I was wasting my life, my brain, and the good genes inherited from her side of the family. My bad grades were proving nothing to anyone, and I was only hurting myself with my sullen ineptitude. I was only ruining my own life, not my mother's or my father's. They had their lives already; my shitty grades wouldn't change their lives, only my own. I was swallowing poison and expecting someone else to die.

Honestly, I had given up on most things until that intervention. I was emotionally withdrawn and didn't see the point of much. Not even photography, which had always been my passion.

No one understood me, not my cousins, my parents, even my sister. I guess I never really gave them a chance.

I felt like life in Oman was a dead end, where you lived with your parents until you got married to a man that you would end up hating.

My parents weren't happy together and they weren't happy with me.

I didn't want to become another vainglorious, vacuous kid who snuck out of their parents' house to steal a snog and a grope in the back seat of a car in the desert hills behind Al Khuwair. I didn't want to get married young, have kids, gossip, and live a fatuous existence.

I felt that I was better than that, that I was more interesting than them. I felt I was destined to amount to something, and yet I could sense that somehow, I was never going to. It was so frustrating.

Mamma Mia showed me that the only escape from that life was to get out of Oman and into uni. However, she gave me the harsh wake-up call that with my abysmal grades, I wasn't getting into any university.

And that's when I decided to live.

To be something.

To leave the life of limited returns behind me.

Time to live and let die.

I rebelled against my own rebellion. I picked up a camera again and I started inhaling books.

When she visited that same year, Mamma Mia found out that I smoked weed with my cousins. She didn't freak out. Quite the opposite! She set aside evenings that we could spend together and smoke. As irresponsible as that may initially seem, her rationale was that I was going to smoke weed anyway, I may as well do it with her to watch over me. She said I was completely abusing the herb. I was using it to numb myself, so I wouldn't hear my parents fight, so I could get through the next week of school, so I wouldn't have to think about the impossible choices hurtling toward me—marriage or living with my parents forever.

She would sit me down to listen to songs by Pink Floyd that would take me into far-off psychedelic reveries, or Rage Against the Machine that would fire us up about The System—The System that hadn't changed since it first fired her up in the '90s. She would force me to listen to lyrics and truly understand an artist, a movement, a time in history, a whole range of emotions that I was yet to experience. Nothing was ever "just a song".

She would set books for me to read and we would discuss them at length, until we completely forgot what we were saying and went to the fridge for munchies.

She said she was sure that I had the same old spiritual soul that she did. I just had to peel off all the layers of apathy that had settled on me like desert sand.

Sometimes, we would just chill and watch *Anchorman* or *The Party* and laugh till we cried. She peed herself once and made me promise not to tell anyone.

Of course, I told everyone at the next family dinner...

Or we would watch documentaries about the pervasive evils in this world and how we had to change things. We would talk religion, for surely as Muslim women we had the most to talk about, the greatest obligation to educate ourselves and arm ourselves against patriarchal ignorance.

She was a feminist bordering on something else, something sadder or angrier, with more motive than simple equality.

'Men's fragile ego!' she would scoff. 'I mean, women? Women are amazing. We can grow humans inside our bodies. We can endure unendurable pain. We are so strong and so delicate in ways they cannot fathom that it scares them. So men took the one strength that they had over us.

'Brute strength.

'And they turned it against us. Forcing us into alleyways, into trafficking, into marriages. Raping us, holding us down and taking us at will. And then blaming *us* for it, so we would now associate this aggression with our own guilt. Calling us sluts and temptresses, distractors from their faith. They covered us up, and they hurt and attacked us when we dared come out from under our shrouds.

'They told us to cover ourselves up, and convinced us to tell *each other* to cover up, to close our legs, sit properly, laugh quietly, anything so that *they* could never be blamed when they lusted over us! Imagine the fucking audacity, the brilliance actually! They convinced us to accuse each other of being witches or whores, and to look down on those who own their sexuality, or blame each other for dressing a certain way, or having too much to drink.

'They said we shouldn't be educated, coz imagine if we actually read what's in the Quran and realise what they are doing? Imagine that?!

'We are all, men AND women, supposed to lower our gaze and guard our modesty, so how did women end up head to toe in black, walking around like a murder of crows, and yet the men end up wearing the pure white of the religion?

'If we're all supposed to be modest in dress and thought, why is the onus all on us? (onus is a funny word—sounds like anus).'

We would giggle.

See, she is very silly.

'Images are powerful', she said, picking up her dropped thread. 'The colours black and white make us feel guilty and them feel pure. The hidden faces make us feel that we are shameful and should be hidden. They need to take responsibility for their own lusts.

'Women tempt them. Gay men lust over them! Poor straight men, it's never their fault.

'Oh, and God forbid we show resistance, question their condescension, or generally get emotional! Well, then they demean and ridicule us, calling us crazy or unstable! Ha, as if anger isn't an emotion. Or lust. Or greed! As if starting wars and creating poverty for profit isn't crazy and unstable.'

She said she didn't want revenge, she didn't want equality. She wanted liberation!

She spoke with such hurt and conviction.

See, she is really earnest!

Mamma Mia loved my photography and always encouraged me to expand my mind, my vocabulary, and my limitless horizons.

She expected so much from me.

Mamma Mia said that men were mostly a sick and depraved species. She didn't have a husband or a boyfriend, so considering that Grandad and Uncle Mo were the closest men in her life, her opinion really surprised me.

But she told me darkly that she'd seen their licentiousness first-hand too many times. She didn't want to elaborate, but I insisted. What had happened to her?

She gave me one of 'many examples': a married man that she trusted. He was at their house while her parents were out, and he held her and tried to kiss her. She resisted, struggling to escape his grip.

She pleaded with him not to, reminded him that he was married.

He pleaded back, 'But you're so hot. My wife just lies there like a spatchcock chicken!'

This really stuck with me, coz I had never heard that word before or since. Spatchcock.

Spatchcock.

Objectively a funny word. Does it count as a Word of the Day?

I had to look it up. The spatchcock chicken is an interesting description of a sex position, lying there flattened, legs open.

Mamma Mia was so shocked at his comment, she actually laughed. She has a real problem with inappropriate laughter. It saved her, coz he also started laughing, thinking they were now bonding and she was easing into the idea of his lust and was about to allow this to happen.

As he laughed, he loosened his grip and she twisted away from him and ran to the wife's room.

'No way! Did you tell the wife?' I breathlessly asked Mamma Mia.

She looked me in the eyes and said regretfully, 'I couldn't. It would have ruined her life. It would have ruined a lot of lives.'

Mamma Mia was only thirteen.

12.52 p.m.

Mamma Mia and Sara kneel by me. Mamma Mia's tears are spent. For now.

They look at each other and start to clear up the drugs. They work silently, avoiding looking at me. I'm not sure they're really thinking this through. Surely the police or the morgue or the Family will want to know how a young and basically fit (okay, slightly out of shape) twenty-two-year-old winds up dead on a bathroom rug.

Sara picks up the small camel bone box I bought in the market in Muttrah souq, where I keep my rolling papers. She places the baggy, the needle, and the spoon into it. She stuffs some toilet paper in there too, so they don't rattle around. She takes some red lipstick, unwraps a tampon, and paints the top of it. She is working like a machine, single-mindedly, with no expression. I know it looks like madness, but I know exactly what she's thinking right now. She knows a man would immediately close a box when the first thing they saw was an apparently blood-soaked tampon.

While Mamma Mia is distracted, sweeping up the ash by my fingers, Sara slips the hash into her pocket.

'Haha, she won't care, Sara! You should share it with her!' I feel like I'm saying it out loud.

Sara looks up sharply.

Did she fucking hear me?

'Sara! SARA!! Raraaaaa!!! Can you hear me RaraaaaaaAAAAA!'
She looks down again.

I guess not.

Sara picks up the old Transformers pencil case and looks at it, turning it around in her hands. She's never seen it before and it is incongruous in our pink, perfumed, lacy, girly bathroom. It's not hers, and it's definitely not mine. I mean, we hated the *Transformer* movies with passionate disdain. Well, she did. I just used to fall asleep. Too much action. My eyeballs couldn't keep up.

She places the tattered pencil case and the camel bone box in the plastic bag that lines the bathroom dustbin. It's filled with makeup-smeared cotton wool and several wet balls of curly hair. She then takes it to the dustbin outside the back of the house in the dusty heat. As she exits our bedroom I hear Lucy, our maid, complain that 'Miss Summer is sleeping again all day' and that she is late to clean our bedroom and bathroom, and it will make her late to do all her chores, and then to make lunch and go for her rest. Sara asks Lucy not to clean our room today.

'Madam told me every day,' she protests.

'Today is different, Lucy,' is Sara's answer. Calm as you fucking like.

Is my sister a robot after all? I always teased Sara about being the perfect child. Even her bloody hair behaves! How did she get the bouncy, defined curls and I got the frizzy, crispy-dry ringlets?!

•

My baby sister came along four years after me, almost to the day, with two miscarriages between us.

I always felt like I came along too quickly for my parents.

They got married after a very brief courtship in London and honeymooned in Oman. It was my mum's first time in Muscat, and they stayed at her new sister-in-law Aunty Baby's mansion. It was all so foreign and grand to her: the chandeliers, the large cars, the hired help, the shoulder-padded Dynasty-style dresses. Her in-laws were an intimidating flock of colourful birds, moving as one, tantalising to look at, sharp beaks ready.

She was a terrified, young, virgin bride, and my dad, thirteen years her senior and apparently quite the philandering ladies' man in his youth, took three frustrating and torturous days to finally get it in without her crying out in pain or fear.

They got pregnant right there, on their honeymoon, two days after my mum lost her virginity at the age of twenty-one.

Mama was pretty clueless about life, and as a couple they hadn't had the chance to really fall in love, before she was dealing with a difficult pregnancy. I always thought that the stress of having me might have been the start of their problems.

The fact that I was apparently not the easiest of babies surely added to the stress. While in the womb, I apparently made her very sick; she had to be rushed to hospital for bleeding twice, and she barfed on the same work colleague three times. During labour, they realised that I was breech and in absolutely no hurry to turn myself right-side up, so they prepared her for an emergency C section, which was all for naught as I decided to push myself out, ass first, ripping her from one hole to the other (sorry, Mama) while entangling my tiny neck in the umbilical cord and stopping my own breathing for a few terrifying seconds, guaranteeing myself a lifetime of respiratory issues.

Nailed it.

For Sara, they were better prepared, it was more carefully planned, and, perhaps because of the heartache of two four-month miscarriages in between, more appreciated? Her birth felt like so much more of a blessing than mine. The pregnancy was easy, joyful even for Mama, and Sara practically slipped out after forty minutes of labour.

Plus, her beautiful face made everyone happy, no one more than me.

We actually looked similar. We'd been mistaken for one another many times (one short-sighted Aunt said to me, 'Oh I thought you were Sara! You look the same, except you're on the plumpish side.')

Bitch.

Yes, Sara was definitely the more refined version of me. She was like my mum, who had the beauty of the islands from Bibi's side, and my grandad's straight nose.

I had the islands on my face too. And my dad had doubled down on the mixed island vibe, and that's why I had a nose with no discernible bridge and no idea how to properly condition my hair.

Even though Sara was everything I wasn't—hard-working, dutiful, sober, wanted—I couldn't resent her because she was genuinely kind and naïve, and I was fiercely protective of her. I wanted to make sure no one hurt her. I would have ruined a man's existence if he had touched her inappropriately or broken her heart. I would have jumped on the landmine of life to make sure it didn't blow up in her face.

We shared birthday parties, gifts, a bedroom by choice, and all her secrets. And almost none of mine. She looked up to me and I couldn't explain to her why she shouldn't.

It's such a huge responsibility to have a young girl look up to you. It felt to me as big a responsibility as being a parent. Or a pop star. Especially in this society, where women walk such a merciless tightrope, where the decisions you make define your reputation and the mistakes can define your future.

Where humility can be construed as subservience, and having an opinion can be reviled as witchcraft.

Sara looked up to me. Who am I kidding. She dressed like me, liked the movies I liked, wanted to take up photography coz I did, disliked going to Family functions, even though she loved everyone and it was always annoyingly reciprocated. I tried not to abuse my pedestal. I tried to guide her well and be an appropriately cynical role model. She had her own mind and opinions but wouldn't use them, because she wanted to use mine. I tried so hard not to be miserable and pessimistic, because I loved her sunny disposition and didn't want to ruin it. I wouldn't have been able to bear it if I'd heard her being sardonic, because it wasn't in her nature. She made me a better person, just by virtue of me wanting her to be a better person.

She kept me sane, happy, and still a believer in good.

She wanted to hang out with me and the older cousins when we got high, but I refused to expose her to it. I didn't want her to be a loser like them.

Oh yeah, a loser like me...

She worked hard at school, and I'm embarrassed to say that my apathy and ineptitude at school, and the resulting parental frustration, overshadowed her exemplary grades. Her achievements should have humiliated my tepid efforts, but I was fiercely proud of her.

Someone at uni once said that the Squeaky Wheel gets the oil.

Well, I was squeaky and they kept trying to fucking oil me.

And the Perfectly Capable Wheel kept trundling along, unrewarded for doing exactly what it's supposed to do.

And yes, I'm going to keep running (rolling) with this wheel analogy. My parents and teachers had no idea what oil I needed. Because they weren't looking for the signs and they weren't listening.

I mean, I wasn't just born detached, sad, and lazy. I was so happy in England, growing up with Bibi, Grandad, Mamma Mia, and Uncle Mo nearby. I didn't want to be deracinated (Word of the Motherfuckin' Day!) to Oman, and I certainly didn't want to be sent there months ahead of my little family unit, as an unaccompanied minor. But I had to go, coz the school term was starting, and they still had to pack up our life in bloody Bromley and see out their work contracts. And I had to stay with Baba's sister and her husband in Muscat.

I wasn't always like this.

I was actually a sweet, loving seven-year-old who adored constant hugs from her family.

I was smart, already picking up Swahili from Bibi and Arabic from Grandad.

I am QUITE sure I was hilarious. I certainly didn't shy away from being the centre of attention and the joker in the family.

I had a pure, magical imagination.

And I was obedient, the kind of obedient girl, who, when told to keep quiet, keeps quiet.

That all changed in the space of one summer.

1.04 p.m.

A mobile is ringing.

Mamma Mia is taking the fag butt from between my stiff fingers.

Ah, British English! What on earth would an American make of that sentence?

She doesn't release my fingers as the phone continues to ring. She is frozen in place. She doesn't want to let go, because otherwise she will have to start dealing with reality. She doesn't want to deal with whoever is on the other end of the phone. She doesn't want to know what they want.

How will she say the words? What words could she possibly use? She's never had to say those words before.

Sara comes in wide-eyed. She crouches, puts her hand on Mamma Mia's knee. They nod at each other and Mamma Mia answers.

It's Bibi and Grandad. They inform us (yes, us. I'm listening too) that they have told my parents. My parents are flying out on the next flight.

This is the most unnatural order of things. My grandparents telling their daughter that her daughter is dead. That's not the way life should flow.

This is all moving so fast. There is no turning back now that Mamma Mia is here, now that my parents have been informed and my grandparents are on the way. Their involvement has solidified this day in fact. There are no surprise plot twists, or practical jokes, or a sudden inhale as I regain consciousness. If it were just me in the bathroom, maybe God could have decided to let me off this one with a warning.

Now it is real.

My grandparents are in the car, five minutes away. Mamma Mia begs them not to start calling everyone else and the police until they have spoken. They agree unquestioningly. This tragedy needs to be private before the circus arrives. Within this sea of this enormous Family, our little family unit has always felt like a tiny intimate island, and my grandparents want to see me before sharing me with everyone else. The same way they shared all of our milestones.

•

Mama's parents, Bibi and Grandad, moved here to Oman a few years ago.

Bibi has been a nurse all her life, a midwife, ER nurse, lecturer, and had more recently worked closely with hospitals in Oman training their nurses, newly recruited and flown into the Middle East from India and the Philippines.

Grandad was a professor of comparative Abrahamic religions at London University for many years.

They are perhaps the coolest grandparents ever, with their combined knowledge, bottomless capacity for love, and ridiculous sense of humour. We teased them good-naturedly, and although they were always strict with discipline, they were always available for advice and hugs, especially hugs, both having had childhoods devoid of physical affection.

We saw them almost every weekend when we lived in London. They were such a part of the fabric of that city for me that I never thought they would leave. But Bibi wanted to be with her "people", who had been exiled from their home and granted nationality by Oman in the '70s and '80s. Almost everyone she knew and loved, the ones who were still alive anyway, were now in Oman, converging from Libya, Kenya, Egypt, England, and America. Some school friends, cousins, aunts, and neighbours from her homeland.

Bibi's "people" come from the magical-sounding island of Zanzibar.

Grandad's "people" are old school British. Really British. He speaks with a posh accent, even though he travelled around a lot with his parents as a child, living in Rhodesia and Ceylon (did I mention *Colonial* Old School British?) and ending up in Cairo, which is where he left his heart when he was shipped off to boarding school. Until he found it again in Bibi.

He likes spanking her bum when she walks into the room, and saying embarrassing things like how kinky she looks when she removes her hijab! And she never passes by him without kissing or stroking his elbow (she's MUCH shorter than him). These old lovebirds are my absolute ideal of love, the embodiment of opposites attracting and being inseparable.

This is going to hurt.

1.10 p.m.

Of all the horrible things about death that I may now have to face, witnessing my family's pain will undoubtedly be the worst. I know my heart has stopped, but it feels like it is breaking.

Here they are: my grandparents, literally and genetically the foundation of everything I am.

Mamma Mia and Sara stop them in the bedroom and they all fall into each other.

I've never seen my grandad look so old. Caucasians don't really age well anyway (let's be honest), but he looks *really* bad... So pale that the beginnings of the liver spots on his temples are showing through. His eyes are red rimmed, and he holds on to Bibi, the support roles always changing between these two ageing sweethearts.

They are silently wiping tears from each other's faces.

'I'm here, guys, I'm right HERE!' I feel like I'm shouting at them, trying to make them hear me. Waving nonexistent arms so they can see me, or feel me.

'It's okay,' says Grandad. 'She's right here, I can feel it.'

What? WHAT?!

It's true! When people say that they can feel a deceased loved one, they actually can! All those mediums and clairvoyants, maybe they *can* communicate with the dead, maybe it's not all bullshit. Maybe the dead are around us, perhaps not forever, but sometimes. How can I tell my family that I'm here? How can I reach out to them? Will I always be around them or is my time limited?

I wish I was physically part of this circle of love. A love that is so powerful it could almost bring me back to life. The love that raised me. That centred me like a faith, rocked me as a baby, nurtured me as a child, and talked me off pubescent ledges. And, of course, took the piss out of me when I was sulky or got too "emo".

Mamma Mia would sing The Smiths songs when I was particularly lugubrious (Word of the Day) and full of teenage angst and they would all laugh, never allowing me to take myself too seriously. They would grab me in bear hugs that I resisted initially and then warmed into, having no choice but to release my tantrum.

(Mamma Mia never realised, but the joke was on her, coz I'd never even heard of The Smiths...)

Sometimes knowing that they loved me so much made me feel really sad. Would they love me if they really knew me? Sometimes those hugs would make me cry myself to sleep at night. Sometimes I cried myself to sleep for everything else. My family were always good natured with their teasing, but they didn't understand that I wasn't just suffering from teenage tantrums. I felt genuinely broken.

I can see them all in front of me. Not clearly, though. It's as if there's a veil between us, like I need to blink something away from my corneas. Like a witness looking at a criminal line-up through a one-way mirror at the police station.

Or like Harry Potter looking through his invisibility cloak.

The bedroom feels small with all the weighted emotion, and words crashing into sobs, and arms reaching for shoulders, and tears blurring features.

I watch the way they look at each other, touch each other, and hold each other. I'm envious and grateful. And petrified.

•

Mama, Uncle Mo, and Mamma Mia were always close to their parents. They are a hilarious and intellectual family, who are as happy talking politics as playing cards. Uncle Mo was an unapologetic cheat; he would stand up to go to the loo and cards would flutter out of his trouser pockets.

They were as happy analysing a movie as fighting over Monopoly. I witnessed the very competitive Mamma Mia reduced to tears and flipping over the board once, made worse when everyone giggled as she stormed out.

Mama told me that when they were younger Grandad would read to them. Back in the olden days in England, there were only three TV channels.

Three!

They would have evenings of listening to their dad read to them, gathered in the living room in their small house in North London. *Robinson Crusoe*, *The Count of Monte Cristo*, and the whole C.S. Lewis *Narnia* series that Mamma Mia ended up reading to us as we were growing up.

(Three channels!)

They would tease Bibi for the traces of Swahili accent when she scolded them. When I farted once in front of her, she threatened to 'put a cock in my arse'.

She meant cork.

She still didn't get the joke after ten minutes of us rolling on the floor, crying with laughter.

'Yes, that's what I said! COCK!'

Or if she scolded any of us to 'focus', it always sounded like she was telling us to 'fuck us'. Which would guarantee, for another hilarious ten minutes, that there would be no focusing on anything.

They would tease grandad for having *mzungu* (white man) rhythm, made worse since he had given them all his surname: White!

Mzungu White! Brilliant. There was no one more White.

People always looked at us incredulously when we said things to each other that were un-P.C., borderline hashtag casually racist, laughing at his rhythm and their surname, or Bibi's accent. We just didn't do Political Correctness in our house, coz we thought it was bullshit. If we were taught anything, it was the power of words, and also how to remove that power. If you didn't want something to offend you, take away the power of the offender's words.

We were also taught about *nia*, which means intention. Words with intention have meaning and power. Otherwise, they are letters strung together.

Plus, between us all, we were black, white, brown, and yellow. So we were brought up, in theory, not to feel superior, inferior, or different to anyone.

The funny thing about being an intellectual family is that none of Grandad and Bibi's kids got conventional jobs, which did cause the odd clash, with Bibi being a traditionalist and Grandad being Old School. For Bibi, as for most Africans, the only "real jobs" were doctor or lawyer, and Grandad expected his children to educate themselves, get onto a career ladder, and work up from there. They both expected their children to get married and have children themselves.

I think that Mama, Mamma Mia, and Uncle Mo are great offspring—funny, considerate, present. But I know that their parents despaired of them.

They would have many questions:

Why wasn't Mamma Mia married? It was frowned upon to be single and living alone as a Muslim girl in the Middle East. 'Cats aren't children!' was a phrase Mamma Mia often heard. Plus, she was more interested in her career.

Why couldn't my mum have more patience with her husband? She should sometimes 'hold her tongue and let him be the head of the household.' 'White women have opinions!' was Mama's reply, challenging her own Mother White, who was a real ballbreaker.

Why didn't Mo invest in some property, instead of travelling constantly? 'This is no career! Why are you lecturing other people how to have a better life? What about you?'

I guess with every generation, we stray further from what our ancestors used to be. And isn't that just nature? It's not necessarily the evils of the internet or Western influence. Or Elvis and rock 'n' roll. Or the dangers of educating women.

Change is gradual; it just feels radical when it's your own offspring changing things.

My great-great-grandmother was the first Zanzibari woman to leave Zanzibar and travel to Uganda all alone for university. I'm sure that was absolutely scandalous at the time.

My grandmother married a white man—shocking behaviour!

And her own children were being unconventional and controversial.

And my generation would do the same.

It's not necessarily that we are losing our culture, it's just the natural evolution of society. I mean, firstly we're living longer than we were two thousand years ago, so if I don't want to get married as soon as I hit puberty, then it's because I'm going to live beyond thirty.

Well, at least I expected to...

They couldn't understand their children's unconventional paths, especially with the education they had been given. Bibi had had her job since she was a teenager. Grandad had moved up the academic ranks to become a professor and a well-respected lecturer and author. Why couldn't their kids get on a career path, on the property ladder? Get a real job?

'You can be anything you want to be!' To which the child in question would answer, 'And I am.'

Uncle Mo's "real job"? He's a world traveller, adventurer, public speaker and life coach.

Mamma Mia is an artist and writer.

And my mum? Got married young, then eventually got an online masters and opened up her own recruitment company.

Overachievers? Underachievers? Scared of a real job, or too interesting to be contained by one? I don't know, but I always wanted to be like them and not work at one of the Omani Ministries, like all the local girls that were able / allowed / needed to work.

I wanted to be a photographer. Or maybe a writer! Or a traveller. I spent so many years in an emotional coma that I didn't really zone in on anything particular. But I didn't want to work in an office and be told by a bored boss with too much power how many days holiday the government says I'm allowed to have. I didn't want to answer to someone who didn't deserve my loyalty. I didn't want to fulfil quotas, have pay cheques or a pension, or a mortgage, or do anything conventional.

I wanted to be like my mum. Well, apart from the loveless marriage. She was her own kind of messed up, but I would have preferred to be messed up than run of the mill. I wanted to fly under the radar of convention, but I also wanted to soar so high above it, you'd have to squint into the sun to find me.

1.23 p.m.

The way they're holding each other is breaking me apart.

Sara is comforting everyone. She is often the glue in our family, the peacekeeper. This might sound like a weird thing to say, because I don't want my sister to feel pain, but why isn't she absolutely GUTTED? In pieces. On the floor, broken, being held together by them.

As they dry their tears and compose themselves, Mamma Mia says to her parents, 'There's something you should know before you go in to see her.'

Oh shit! I'm about to be in some big trouble, once everyone knows that I had drugs scattered like memories around my dead body. I mean, they can't physically punish me, but I reckon they can put in a word with God. Ooh, the curses I'm about to receive.

But Bibi ignores her and walks toward the bathroom alone.

Grandad calls out to her, 'Don't step over her body!'

'Why not? Not that I want to, but why?' she asks.

'I don't know. It's disrespectful, or against the rules, or bad luck.' (How much worse can this luck get?) 'I can't remember. Please don't step over her body!' His voice breaks.

Bibi comes back to stand by him, agrees not to step over my body, squeezes his hand, and walks into the bathroom.

Mamma Mia follows to control the situation, to see if she can put out any fires before they start.

Or because she can't resist the pain.

She holds on to Bibi, for comfort or support (I hope she doesn't start the hysterics again).

They hug tightly and swap 'I love yous' before Bibi turns to see her firstborn granddaughter on the floor with most of her flesh on show.

(Ugh, cellulite...)

Come on, Bibi, what's the deal? I'm just really sick and stiff, and not breathing and a bit blue at the edges. I'll be okay though, right?

She squats down next to me, holds my wrist for a few seconds. Her lip trembles, she drops off her haunches, and slumps to the floor.

So that's it then. I have been pronounced dead by the attending nurse.

I hear her heartbeat falter.

No, actually I *felt* it falter.

'I love you, Bibi. I'm so sorry', I whisper to her.

'I love *you*, SumSum.' She kisses my cold forehead.

(What the actual... She heard me, I'm pretty sure she heard me.)

'BIBI! BEEEEEBS!!'

I'm trying to twitch the body I don't control anymore. Trying to push it like Patrick Swayze in *Ghost*.

Nothing.

I try to hold her or nudge her somehow. FUCK!

Grandad can feel me. I'm sure Sara heard me earlier, and I felt Bibi and she heard me. I know this!

Okay, THINK! What can you remember about Death?

You are a soul. You have a body, temporarily. And you will continue to be a soul.

So that's what I am now...

Okay, what else?

The Angel of Death takes your soul out of your body when you die. It usually hurts. Unless you are super pious. Well, it hurt me, so there's my answer.

I think that the soul hangs around the body for a while and then goes to the grave with the body. I'm sure that's why, at funerals, the mourners speak to the deceased, and always read the Quran, and mention God's name.

And mourners have to repeat The Answers to The Questions you are asked in the grave, to remind the deceased what to say.

What are The Questions? I can't remember!

It's okay, people will be here soon, and they will remind me. Genius.

Can I move things, like a poltergeist? And speak back to people? There must be some way to communicate.

I know that your good and bad deeds are counted and recorded throughout your life by angels on either side of you, and now that I am dead, there's nothing I can do to adjust the tally.

So...

Have I been good? And what *is* good?

Bibi comes out of the bathroom.

She mumbles some medical jargon about cyanosis, hypercapnia, and submucus something.

Everyone looks at her funny, waiting for her to say it in English.

'Her lips and fingernails are bluish grey. Her airways have always been narrow, but they were permanently narrowed after the Edinburgh Episode.'

Mamma Mia chokes on unexpected laughter. Apart from Sara, they actually all allow themselves a little smile.

Oh, oh, oh.

It's still fucking hilarious, is it? It was a huge joke in our family, and I was teased mercilessly about it. I was such an idiot and they wouldn't let me forget it...

They stop the mirth and Bibi adds, 'Summer stopped breathing. Asthma attack. Sara, does she still smoke?'

(Correction, Bibi: 'DID she still smoke?')

Sara and Mamma Mia look at each other, trying to figure out if they should tell my grandparents about the drugs.

Oh, God! We might be able to get away with this. My biggest allies can control the entire narrative. If it just looks like an asthma attack gone wrong, no one will ever know. Bibi is a nurse. She can tell the coroners that there's nothing to see here! I don't have to get into trouble! I can keep my slightly tarnished reputation as the Family weirdo intact. And not as a drug-addled disappointment to our Family, Culture, and Religion.

More importantly in this society, we can keep everyone from dragging my mum and dad's names through the dirt. We can prevent everyone looking at them with disdain or condescending pity, with holier-than-thou judgement. The hope is to avoid the hypocrites burying me one minute and then turning their back on my grave and my memory the next. So that they won't be reading the Quran with one hand and gossiping about me behind the other.

Okay, Mamma Mia, Sara. Do the right thing! Keep my secret. Let's take this one to my grave!

'Bibi, we have to tell you something.'

Oh poop.

Bibi must have seen a million things at the hospital over the years.

She told me about tending to young children with stab wounds, limbs hanging off bodies, rape victims, drug overdoses.

I remember she told me about a sick old man who was admitted and who was so filthy, they had to clean him from head to toe before treatment. She described what he had under his foreskin as 'cottage cheese'.

Yeah, that stuck with me.

Nothing can shock her.

However, she refuses to hear about the heroin and insists that my body shows signs of a sudden onset fatal asthma attack. There are no track marks on my arms, and they all nod in agreement when she reminds them that I don't like needles. And even if it is true about finding a needle near my body, asthma is the story that they will tell everyone. It's not anyone's business and we should keep it that way...

Oh, thank God! Thank you, Bibi!

Grandad isn't listening. He's sitting on my bed, which is still made—sheets pulled hospital-tight, duvet smooth, pillows plump, just the way Lucy was taught to make them.

I guess I didn't sleep in my bed last night.

Grandad is looking down at his shaking hands, catching silent teardrops. Poor Grandad. He lost his twin sister a few years ago, mere months before they moved to Oman. That's when I first noticed that he had aged.

His sister, Wanda, had returned to their childhood home of Cairo as soon as she completed her degrees in England. There she married a kind Egyptian man and instead of children, chose to have many cats. 'Like the Pharaohs', she joked to me.

We visited her in her bohemian-style, book-cluttered apartment near the Nile, when I was around eleven. She took us to see the Pyramids and made us take photos while pretending to kiss the beautiful Sphynx, 'the world's biggest pussycat'. That's unfortunately all I remember of her.

And the reason that's all I remember is because in our photo album, there are pictures of me and Nana Wanda holding two of her cats in front of a bookcase, and another photo of her carrying a smiling Sara in front of the Sphynx and me trying to kiss the air near its head.

I watched a documentary once about memory. They asked a bunch of eyewitnesses about their memories of 9/11. One lady described her ordeal, watching the second plane crashing into the tower from her desk. Turns out her desk was on the blind side of her building and what she described were the scenes she had seen repeated on TV.

Memories become skewed, mixed up with other people's accounts, confused with images on TV, exaggerated, played up, played down. Confabulated (Word of the Day).

Grandad said the worst thing about losing his sister was knowing that he could no longer make any more memories with her. She, herself, would just be a memory, not a person he could call up on the phone.

And the memories he DID have of her would soon change and warp into anecdotes. They would become like pictures, just snapshots of a human being that used to breathe and laugh and love. It killed him that he would have to go on living on this earth without her, and all she would ever be from now on is a memory, distorted with every reminiscence and fading like a photograph in the sun.

He said that there were two versions of him: the Walter before her death, and the Walter after her death. And she would never meet the latter. Because the latter was *created* by her death.

Grandad never really recovered from losing her. He regretted not travelling to see her enough, even though they were inseparable as children with their special twin's gift of ESP and their secret language of Arabic when they were living back in England. When Wanda died, Bibi managed to convince him to move to Oman. She wanted to grow old with the few family members and friends she had left from her days in Zanzibar. And Grandad agreed that that was best.

I can see him now, sitting on the end of my bed, realising that I too will eventually dissolve into just a series of photograph-assisted tales and will freeze in time as his eternally twenty-two-year-old SumSum.

1.33 p.m.

Bibi walks to the edge of the bed, sits next to her shaking and silently weeping husband, and puts her arm around him and kisses his shoulder. He looks down at the beloved wife who gave him an amazing life and a beautiful family, and his eyes overflow with untold sadness.

I suppose every death that someone goes through reminds them of the others they've been through.

I lost a cat once.

God, I loved that cat. We rescued her from under our car when she was a kitten, scrawny and mewling loudly. We searched fruitlessly for her mother or siblings, and Sara and I swore up and down to Mama and Baba that we would take care of her and clean up after her, so we were eventually allowed to keep her. Sara was eating a banana at the time we found her, so we named her Chiquita. The kitten put on weight. She slept with me and Sara every night, and as not very responsible cat owners, we didn't realise that we had to spay her and she got knocked up by some neighbourhood lothario (I always picture Top Cat, leaning against a telephone pole, sweet-talking my cute little pussycat).

Chiquita died in childbirth, taking all her unborn kittens with her. She looked like herself when we found her, lying stretched out on the kitchen floor—she looked like Chiquita. But when I moved her, I was horrified at how stiff she was. Petrified. No floppy limbs and curling tail. Just a fur-covered statue. And she was cold.

Everything that was Chiquita about Chiquita was no more.

I cried for about a week at the injustice. How unfair it was. I remember sobbing that I didn't want to miss her. I wanted to keep her. I didn't want to only have memories of how playful she was, and how she'd purr into my neck and curl up on my homework. I wanted HER. And I was very petulant about it.

Actually, I was angry. Fucking furious.

Perhaps that's what grief is: anger that you will have to live without someone / something. Sadness that you will only be left with memories and frustration at the injustice.

I wonder if anyone will be angry with me. Or angry about me.

Anyway, after Chiquita died, my asthma got better, so no more cats for us. I really have to dose up, take pills and inhalers if I ever pay even the shortest visit to Mamma Mia in Dubai. She has two rescue street cats and I'm clearly allergic. She says she'll 'never give up the pussies'.

·

Bibi fled her home during the revolution of 1964 and never spoke of what happened or how many of her family members were murdered. She was tight lipped about that, but loquacious and wistful about her childhood, the same stories set on repeat so that we only had a romantic vision of her playing with her siblings in the narrow streets of Stone Town and mischievous schoolgirl anecdotes. Stories of beloved aunts who lived a bus ride away, through tree-shaded avenues that snaked through monkey jungles and fragrant clove farms and led all the way to the powder-white beach. Stories of the breeze that blew in from the Indian Ocean onto those east-facing beaches and the dhows that would fill their sails with it.

We could never follow the many names on the complicated family tree. There were tales of her diminutive grandmother who was from South Africa; she was half Malay and half Dutch. She would then tell stories of the Comoros side of the family and which branch of the family still lives on those islands, and how the wealthy carpet and diamond merchants from her grandad's side came to Zanzibar with the trade winds from Yemen and Somalia. When she said that we had the same long fingers as some distant aunt or the eyes of a favourite cousin, we pretended that we recognised those people and their names and relationship to us, because it made her happy to talk about them and compare us to them, keeping them alive in our features.

I always visualise my ancestors as cardboard cut-outs, or silhouettes. I could never flesh them out. I couldn't imagine them having real emotions, of which I have thousands every day. They are just storybook characters, who did one job, or ruled here, or died there, who were known for their beautiful singing voice, or for being a great horse rider. They are defined and remembered by the single most important thing they did, not for any secret thoughts of escape, or any bi-curiosity, or boredom, or mischief.

It felt tragic to me that a whole life could be dismissed in one sentence, summed up in one casual comment.

(Will I always be remembered as the girl who died in the toilet?)

Grandad told us Bibi's story one day in confidence: how she had been forced to flee her homeland with her cousin, leaving her entire family, siblings, parents, friends behind to their fate. Just so happens that Bibi's cousin was the last queen of Zanzibar, whom Bibi was visiting that day at the palace. The guards had rushed into the House of Wonders, having waited till the last possible moment to desperately shove the women and children onto ships and smuggle them from Zanzibar to Mombasa, and from Mombasa to Portsmouth, England, where they all hid until the British government unequivocally told the Revolutionary Government of the newly formed Tanzania that they would not send them back there to a fate of imprisonment or worse.

Bibi eventually moved from her cousin's house in Portsmouth to London, still a teenager, and moved into Halls of Residence at University College London Hospital, studying to become a Registered Nurse.

Bibi loathed London.

Gone was the open horizon of the island, brushed gently by clouds and swells, palm trees exploding like fireworks against copper sunsets and nights so deep you could make out spiralling galaxies. They were replaced by a gruelling, claustrophobic sky pierced by the slick turrets of a dystopian penitentiary.

The rain didn't come down like the triumphant, tropical Hallelujah chorus of Zanzibar downpours, but rather like the drizzle earworm of an annoying jingle. The exhaustion in everyone's eyes, gait, and attitude started to wear her down.

She ran one day to the River Thames. The island girl in her just wanted to be near water, but the brown sludge lurching forward made her weep with disappointment.

She didn't understand why it was still night-time when she woke up at seven o'clock in the morning, and also still night-time when she emerged from the hospital at five p.m. She was completely unable to comprehend the idea of putting coins into machines to get electricity in her tiny, arctic room. And she couldn't fathom the notion of sharing a toilet in her building with questionably hygienic women to whom she was unrelated.

London was a strange, dark animal to her and so she threw herself into becoming the top in her class so that she wouldn't have to look up from her books at the grey buildings and the greyer sky.

She and Grandad met at the UCL Student's Union on "Africa Night". He was studying Islamic Studies at the School of African Studies. The only white man on that particular course, he was a six-foot-four-inch lanky Englishman with a Foreign Service dad and an obsession with his childhood home, culture, and religion of Egypt.

'He was a gentle man', Bibi would say. And the unusual emphasis was not because of her Swahili intonation. Grandad has always been a gentle man.

And a gentleman.

Grandad—Walter—had the Old World manners of a diplomat, the empathy of someone who had grown up among people of a different culture, the tenderness of someone brought up with an adored twin sister, and the silly sense of humour of a twelve-year old schoolboy.

He says that he fell in love with my barely five-foot-tall grandmother at first sight. 'She always stood out. Something in her regal gait.'

That was the official story, although he preferred to tell the story of how they really met on a rainy night. Even without an umbrella, her feet were still dry.

'Coz of her big boobs!' he'd explain, giggling.

He giggled *every* time he told the story...

Grandad was Bibi's comfort and joy in a dark and cold new life. He absolutely doted on his 'African Arab Princess'. He had finally made her smile, a lot, and he asked her almost immediately to be his wife.

She knew her parents wouldn't approve of him, this skinny white boy, but she also didn't know where her parents were, or if they were even alive, all desperate attempts to get news of them having been frustrated and foiled. So, she said a prayer to Allah for her beloved parents and married him in an Islamic bookshop on the Edgware Road.

He converted to Islam without her having to ask and became a true scholar of comparative Abrahamic religions.

I always admired converts as opposed to those of us born to a religion. We who are born into it almost take for granted the faith that we learn at the same time as reading and writing. We also confuse our regional traditions with religion, like arranged marriages or female genital mutilation, neither of which have anything to do with Islam.

He was non-judgemental and unfettered by traditions or culture. He learned it the way it was supposed to be, and I tried to learn my religion from him. When he spoke of Islam, people listened, even people with closed ears and hearts, so beautiful and reverent were his words. There was no spitting vitriol about the death of infidels; only of God's Mercy and acceptance. He extolled the similarities of all religions, not the differences.

His Arabic was faultless, and although he tried to learn Swahili, always jovially referred to himself as 'the mzungu' (white man).

Bibi LOVED Margaret Thatcher. She understood nothing of her politics, which drove Grandad mental. She didn't care. She loved living in a country with a woman at the helm.

She also *loved* Christmas and always celebrated it with their kids. To Grandad it wasn't a big deal, and after he converted, he couldn't really care less. It was Bibi. She loved taking the kids on the Tube to Oxford Street to watch the lighting of the Christmas Lights. It was the one time that London lit up, festooned with fairy lights, sparkling in shop windows and twinkling in the neighbours' houses on the walk home from the hospital. It would give her a spring in her step, despite the cold.

They had the prettiest tree in their living room, with plenty of modest toys scattered around it. Bibi was filled with glee and was definitely the biggest kid of them all.

I don't think she really believed that was Prophet Jesus's actual birthday.

It just made her feel better.

Later in life, when I Googled pictures of Zanzibar, I immediately understood why the colour turquoise would always make Bibi happy. The colours on the island were so vibrant; it must have felt like all Technicolor life had been washed down the drains of the streets of London, and the austere drabness must have felt all-consumingly depressing. The other nurses on her ward— young Irish girls in impenetrable cliques and Jamaican girls with opinions as thick as their accents—would comment bitchily about Bibi turning up on a heart-breaking, wet North London night, her eyes bleary for the graveyard shift, in a hibiscus-red coat or a scarf the colour of palm leaves after the rain.

They couldn't understand that the only things keeping her heart on her beloved island were the colours she wore.

1.35 p.m.

My grandparents sit at the edge of my bed, touch foreheads and breathe each other in, and then with a big sigh, Bibi takes her phone out and quietly makes a phone call to the head physician at the Royal Hospital, which is a few minutes away. He is a kind and erudite gentleman, and they have been friends and colleagues since she moved to Oman and made herself indispensable to him; they have a great deal of respect for each other.

For all her conviction that my death was sudden onset fatal asthma, she is asking her friend and colleague to please send an ambulance and call the police. She is asking him to please be there to examine her grandchild's body personally, and to tell the police exactly what the cause of death is: sudden onset fatal asthma.

My grandmother is not exactly breaking the rules here, but she is using her connections at the hospital just in case there is some truth in the needle theory. Rather than have an investigation, she is using her Jedi mind trick to influence him into taking her word for it.

He is beside himself trying to console Bibi with her cracking voice interrupted by sobs. He offers the phrase *Inna liLlahi wa inna Ilayhi rajioon* (Surely we come from God, and to Him we must return).

A reminder of what we are.

As Muslims, we invoke God's name in whatever we do; if we plan to do something, we know it will only happen *insha'Allah* (if God wills). If something unfortunate could happen, we ask God to forbid it. If something good has happened, we thank Him. If something bad has happened, we still thank Him; after all, He could have been saving us from something worse. If something above average happens, we glorify Him. He is the first and last word in everything we do.

The head physician will do whatever it takes to help Bibi, and he doesn't press her further for details, promises her that he will do as she asks.

Fuck me, we're going to get away with it.

Omanis call this vitamin W. The W stands for *wasta*, which loosely translated is "connections" or "nepotism". It's still the Wild West out here, and people are given jobs, awarded contracts, and let off parking fines because of vitamin W. And now potentially even a drug cover-up.

No family could withstand this scandal. No family wants the police sniffing around like drug hounds, tearing the house apart, interrogating Sara about who my friends were and who I might have got drugs from and did she have any? No, she doesn't have any? Well, then she wouldn't have a problem with them searching her room and her person? They would find the bit of hash that she snatched from the bathroom floor. Then she'd go to jail. For life.

Then they would ask my nurse grandmother about some of the opiates they find in her medicine cabinet in case of an emergency, and for the excruciating back pain from which Grandad suffers. And she would go to jail. For life.

And they would ask my aunt what she gets up to in Dubai. And they would find the two Valium tablets she brought with her for her anxiety. And she would go to jail. For life.

It'll be a miracle if they still mourn me after this is all over.

Having dealt with the hospital, Bibi next sends a single text message to my father's oldest sister, Khadija, more commonly known as Aunty Baby, considered by all as the Matriarch of the Family. Once Aunty Baby knows, everyone will know.

•

It's such a silly name, Aunty Baby. Her three older brothers called her Baby when she was born, for lack of a better nickname. It stuck. Like Aunty Dolly and Aunty Sweetie stuck. They knew a few English terms of endearment back in Zanzibar, and they were all quite hilariously and charmingly misused.

Aunty Baby was truly the juxtaposition of terrifying aunt-witch and all-encompassing love bug. No one crossed her, for as diminutive as she was in stature, she was wicked in tongue and could cut you down with a withering stare.

Her many members of staff were all terrified of her, but she sent them to their home countries once a year laden with suitcases full of gifts for their families.

She knew everyone's name, which was no small feat in the Family, and what they were up to in life. 'How is university? How's the pregnancy, you're due in March, right? How is little Lulu and Laith?' She knew it all. People came to her for advice, for money, for a holiday.

She had married young, to an obscenely rich man who died in a car accident, having given her no babies at all, leaving her instead with an enormous house and untold wealth.

He also left her to discover that he died in the car with his secret second wife, which came as a shock to all.

We always gathered at her glorious mansion every Eid, dressed up in new clothes, fresh from the salon, greeting elders so we could collect Eid money from them all, and playing with cousins in the gardens. Aunty Baby would feed one and all, with long tables laden with biryani, salads of fresh tomatoes and red onions, leg of lamb curries, sambusas stuffed with spicy minced chicken, and rows and rows of crème caramel, cheesecakes, and chocolate gateaux.

Included in the Eid festivities were her newly found stepchildren and their families. They were her beloved husband's children and therefore, they were family. With her enormous heart, she treated them as her own, God bless her.

That's one amazing thing about the Family: From their days in Zanzibar all the way to their days as broke students in Brighton, and now here in Oman, whatever size the house, there would always be room for everyone. That was their mantra.

Contrary to popular belief about Muslims, the women of this Family were the strong ones. Like all African women. Even if a man was the head of the family, you'd better believe a woman's hand was up inside his neck, telling him which way to look. They ran things, in the home, in the office, in the family, and being Muslims to them meant that they were obliged to educate themselves. We had girls travelling abroad to study medicine, languages, law, all the way from my great-great-grandmother's generation.

We were not fooled by traditions of women being inferior or forbidden from study. Or the culture of arranged marriage or honour killings. It's all a nonsense, and our women were having none of it. These gorgeous warriors ranged from tiny Asian frames to 80 percent cocoa Amazons. Waves to afros, flat asses to junk-filled trunks. They were soft-hearted yet hardened like diamonds, having endured years of pressure, emerging devastatingly dazzling and brilliant, but impenetrable and unyielding.

1.41 p.m.

Satisfied that the message of my demise has gone through to Aunty Baby, Bibi suggests that they all pray while they wait for the ambulance to arrive. They avoid washing for prayers in my bathroom, since I'm still in there. They don't really want to look at me, or step over my outstretched legs after Grandad's warning.

After ablution, they unfurl the prayer mats to face Mecca and stand shoulder to shoulder in my bedroom and pray for my soul.

My Soul.

Something hits me. Hard.

If I overdosed, even accidentally, does it mean that I committed suicide? Which of course, is expressly forbidden. It means you have been arrogant enough to have taken Life into your own hands and made the decision without waiting for what was Written.

If that is what I have done, my family may be wasting their time...

Praying always played a big part in our lives. I know that I'm not an exemplary Muslim, but prayer? You don't mess with prayer. Isn't going astray part of the reason you pray? A big reason to pray is to ask for forgiveness, for guidance, for mercy and understanding. It's not just perfect people who pray. In fact, show me a perfect person, I'll show you a liar. Whether it's cheating in business, lying to your spouse ('No, your butt does *not* look big!'), not sharing your wealth with others, or just plain sneaking a bacon sandwich, everyone has something to atone for.

(Although, weirdly enough, despite the drugs, the fornication, and the lying, swine is where most Muslims I know draw the line...)

So, yeah, I always prayed hard. I missed the odd prayer. To be honest, I missed most of the five obligatory prayers when I was living in Edinburgh. But I prayed to God when I woke up, and I spoke to Him when I went to sleep. I prayed in thanks, I prayed for my family, and I prayed for forgiveness for who I was.

For knowing too much ugliness, far too young.

In Ramadhan, we would even pray all the extra prayers. My grandad would lead us all perfectly with his beautiful melodic Arabic after our break-fast meal. We would fidget behind him, our bellies full of heavy rice, fried fishcakes, and coconut curries, trying to perform all the moves with stomachs of lead, and groaning coz every year the prayers got longer and longer, with him adding a few more supplications and invocations in there. We made a game of timing him and teasing him afterwards. The prayers went from nineteen minutes originally to thirty-seven minutes at last count.

My last count.

We also used to giggle. Yes, that story probably won't put us in the best light on Judgement Day, but it's that awful thing where you giggle at the most tasteless, improper moments, you know? Inappropriate laughter is a real problem for us.

Grandad would go from a standing position to bending over, and occasionally would let out an unsolicited fart. Just aimed right at our heads. We always said he had the mouth of an African, loving the island food of cassava, curries, and chapatis, but the stomach of an Englishman, taking the delicious spices from the plate and turning them into something evil and foul in his stomach.

He would have to end his prayer and go to the bathroom and wash again, leaving us all desperately trying not to break our prayer by laughing out loud. And it was hard. The noise of his fart echoing around the room, and the rancid smell lingering around our faces, still bent over near where his arse used to be. I could feel Sara's shoulders shaking next to mine or feel my mum exhaling through her nose in a high-pitched shake. Mamma Mia would crack up and style it out into a cough. Bibi would then clear her throat, signalling that we should all behave ourselves, and we would all start cracking up again.

I'm actually laughing now, watching them pray, as the memories flood back! Oh, I have a lot to be afraid of, but the memory is too funny!

I don't know what the hell is happening, but Sara's shoulders start shaking, Mamma Mia's eyes open in shock, and she chokes on an unexpected chortle. Sara snorts, which is one of the cutest things about her. And they have a giggle for around ten seconds before Mamma Mia sobs and Sara touches her arm to comfort her.

Okay, it's happening again. Sometimes I laugh and they laugh. Sometimes I'm almost sure they can hear me, but I can't control what they hear. If I can just figure it out, so I can tell them that I love them before it's too late.

Yeah, I suppose it already IS too late...

2.16 p.m.

They are sitting on the floor at the end of the prayer, each saying *duas*, supplications, their palms upturned to the sky as if hoping to catch answers or comfort falling from Heaven. They are each in their own world, praying for their own things.

I mean, that's the other thing about grief: Are they sad for you, or sad for themselves?

Are they mourning my thwarted potential and that I will never fulfil my Destiny? That I won't love and procreate or have a shining career, or travel and suck the marrow out of life, like I thought I was meant to. Experience and taste everything, and then maybe write about it, or take photos of it...

And what the fuck is Destiny anyway? Just the inescapable hurtling down a predetermined train track toward an inevitable fate? Everything decreed and set in stone already.

We have Free Will. We are Homo sapiens, and we were given brains, souls, consciences, and Free Will to choose our own paths, to choose right or wrong. We can choose to help others in need, or greedily collect more than we could ever spend. And we are judged on those decisions.

But I also know that everything is Written.

If it's Written, what free will is there?

It is that we can choose whichever path we want, but God already knows what path that is going to be.

Bloody hell! That's made sense for the first time ever!

He knows what we're going to choose. We are free to choose it, but He already knows what our choice will be, because He is omnipotent and He knows US. Simple!

But that means it was Written that I would die here in the bloody toilet. That was my Destiny! Not to be the next great photographer. Not to fall in love! Not even to have sex EVEN BLOODY ONCE?

Are they crying coz the toilet was my Destiny, or are they crying coz they will have to miss me? That my parents have to bury me and not the other way round? Are they crying coz their lives will be changed forever?

I'm asking genuinely; I'm not trying to be a smartass about it. Truly, I want to know why people mourn. For themselves, or for the deceased. I only ever lost Chiquita the cat, so I just don't know this pain that they're going through. I've never lost anyone.

I guess that's not true anymore. I am literally losing everything and everyone I have ever known.

My loss is the greatest loss of them all.

The doorbell rings.

Sara runs downstairs with Bibi following close behind her. The ambulance is here with the head physician and his cousin, a police officer.

Vitamin W.

They come upstairs. Quietly, respectfully, they greet everyone in my bedroom and give condolences, with *Inna liLlahi wa inna Ilayhi rajioon* (Surely we come from God, and to Him we must return).

It is a sobering phrase. However you feel, for whomever you are mourning (yourself or the deceased), this reminds us that we are all just in a queue, working, laughing, texting, sinning. Just in that queue, completely unaware of our position in that queue. We might be next in line. We might be two billion, seven hundred and nine million, four hundred and twenty-six thousand, eight hundred and ninety-fifth (2,709,426,895[th]) in that queue.

Whether you believe in God or not, while you're busy doing something else, suddenly it's your turn.

The physician and police officer step into the bathroom, but on seeing my state of undress, the policeman waits outside. Normally he would be looking for clues of suicide, of an overdose or anything suspicious, but this is why the physician brought his policeman cousin.

The physician steps over my legs, and Bibi looks around at Grandad and tries not to giggle. More inappropriate laughter.

He bends and needlessly takes my pulse. He examines my fingertips, my lips, my tongue, my throat. He exits the bathroom, looks at Bibi, at the police officer, and says, 'It is clear that she died from sudden onset fatal asthma, my dear friend. My sincerest condolences. She had asthma, and she already had one serious attack that resulted in hospitalisation, correct?'

Bibi answers in the affirmative.

'This is a very unfortunate repeat occurrence. As you know, it can happen. Such a young girl. We are so sorry, my dear friend. We will take her immediately to the hospital and return her within a few hours, so you can prepare her for burial.'

Just like that.

He calls two men from the ambulance downstairs while he quietly speaks to his cousin, the policeman, in Arabic. They enter the bathroom with the stretcher and cloths and begin.

Oh shit, now all hell is breaking loose.

Somehow my lifeless, blue-tinged body, lying on the floor with lolling head and one ample thigh dressed in really not-hot hot-pant pyjama bottoms, has been a comfort to everyone. Because as the two ambulance men come to take it away, the wailing starts. It's as if THIS is the end. Not the actual death, but the removal of my body. Grandad is a mess. I've never really seen him cry and it's killing me—bad choice of words. Sorry. Bibi is trying to be strong, but she is sobbing into her hands.

Mamma Mia is quite hysterical. I feel so terrible for her. She said she would never have children and that she preferred pussies, and so I will be the closest she will ever come to that feeling. And the fact that she didn't give birth to me means nothing. She promised that if anything happened to Mama, she would automatically be our real mother. And when she died, we would inherit everything she had (I love her little red sports car!). And when she was old, we would have to wash her bum (sorry, Sara, you're on your own). Poor Mamma Mia. Her body is wracked with sobs and I feel like the world's most selfish arsehole.

Her grief is clearly defined. It's for her and it's for me.

Sara is... Actually I can't really see what she's doing, as she's now out of sight. They all are.

I am following my body. I'm no longer in the room with them. I'm going down the stairs.

I'm travelling with my body.

2.35 p.m.

Bibi walks down after me and sees me placed in the back of the ambulance. Sara runs after her and asks if she can go with me.

Yes! Please let her come. I don't want to go alone, please don't send me alone!

But they tell Bibi that it may take some time, depending on the backlog. They will try and expedite the process, but it is no place for a girl to be.

They look down at Sara's clothes. She's on the street wearing⁻ a *kanga* (our version of a sarong) around her waist and her teddy bear pyjama top over a sports bra that she wears to sleep.

She looks defiantly at them, challenging them to comment on her state of dress. Ha! I trained my sister well.

But Bibi holds her and says, 'I need you here to help me, Sara. Please stay. There are things to sort out in the house. People will arrive soon, and your Mama isn't here. And your Mamma Mina is a mess. Can you help me, please?'

Torn, my baby sis follows Bibi into the house, looking back at the ambulance as it drives away.

There are no windows, except the two on the back doors that are blacked out, so I sit very still next to my body, almost expecting it to move and praying hard that it won't. I already feel a complete detachment from it.

The two men sit in the front cab. There's nothing they can do to help me back here, in this sterile metal meat wagon, so they talk amiably between themselves in Arabic. I don't understand exactly what they're saying, but it's something utterly mundane, like their kids' school, or an issue with an in-law. Their lives continue obliviously as before, even with a dead body in their vehicle. But in my small family unit, *everything* has changed.

•

Baba has a huge family in Oman; *everyone* is a relative, and if you see a Zanzibari-looking Omani (we don't look like Omanis and we don't look like Tanzanians—welcome to our limbo) in the mall, you'd better greet them with a hand kiss and an '*Asalaam Alaikum*' or risk being told off as soon as you get home, because that "relative" had called your dad to say that you didn't remember her and / or have no manners. A life of duty. And a family of snitches!

So Baba's sister, Aunty Baby, having been notified of my demise by Bibi, would have sent the message out on our very efficient grapevine to all her siblings, and they would have sent a group text to immediate family, cousins, who would then tell their spouses and kids and they in turn would tell more distant relatives and those abroad. Which is the way it works when someone dies.

I complain a lot about the Family, but that is one amazing network.

My dynamic with them is very much a love/hate relationship. They shaped me and gave me a solid foundation, my beliefs and humour, and conversely also nurtured parts of me that I wish I could cut out like a septic boil.

Some examples:

They were a joyful bunch, and I loved the way they always laughed and found amusement in simple things, but I simultaneously hated the way they laughed at the lowest common denominator jokes or teased you for having physical traits that you had little control over, like big boobs or a stutter (that really annoyed me).

BUT I loved the way they would gather together and support one another (and totally redeem themselves).

If they heard some misfortune had befallen you, they would inundate you with calls and descend upon your house or hospital room (very considerate).

BUT they had no regard for your peace or privacy and had no idea when to leave you to sleep (annoying!).

You will never be ill at home or in the hospital with no visitors (sweet).

You will have a constant stream of well-wishers when you give birth, bearing gifts, offering support (lovely), and unsolicited advice (mostly annoying).

They will grab your newborn and make it dance like a marionette, to what can only be described as Swahili beatboxing (know your boundaries) and then hold said newborn while you enjoy the ever-elusive new-mother nap (so appreciated).

They always ask after your health and well-being (so nice) and ask more questions, and probe and pry and judge (fuck off!).

They have a uniquely entertaining way of talking: loud, expressive, and musical. If something is far away, they say it is faaaaaaaaaaaaaaar away, as if distance is measured in "a's" rather than in kilometres (hilarious, yet often too shrill).

We don't even have old people's homes in Oman. A family member will always return the love and care to the older generation. And when it comes to death, no one is left to mourn or bury a loved one alone. Or arrange for food or even figure out where people are going to sit. Suddenly people appear at your house with carpets and cushions, which then line the entire marble or tiled house, so people can sit on the floor. There are suddenly numerous Qurans passed around, so that there is a constant murmur of hushed reading, invoking God's name.

People arrive with their maids to help in the kitchen. They arrive with dates, thermoses of coffee and, later on, enormous vats of biriyani, plastic plates, plastic cutlery, and multiple boxes of little water bottles (an environmental nightmare). And as quickly as they arrive and are dished up, they are cleared up, so that the person mourning has nothing to concentrate on but their grief.

There is always someone to help with paperwork, and a network of ladies that sew the shroud together. Sheets of plain white cloths, sewn with white thread, in which to wrap the body for burial. And someone preparing the cotton wool infused with incense, so they can be placed in all your orifices, (yup, ALL) for when your body begins to decompose in the grave.

It's a raucous, supportive, Swahili assembly line that somehow works like smooth, efficient Swiss clockwork, without anyone being told what to do. Everyone pulls through and I have never been as grateful for them as I am today.

•

I would always enjoy seeing certain characters at gatherings, like my cool, controversial older cousin, Laila, nicknamed Lolly, ostensibly because she's been licked so many times. I was genuinely obsessed with her. She was almost beautiful, with slightly bulging eyes and a huge gap in her front teeth, but she threw her head back when she laughed out loud, and I always wanted to know what was so funny. If they were honest with themselves, EVERYONE wanted to be in on her joke, but they denied themselves Lolly's glow, choosing instead to judge her. Who doesn't want to throw their head back when they laugh? What other way is there to live? But because they couldn't laugh out loud (either because they were miserable or because they were expected to be quiet and discreet) they bitterly envied her.

Lolly's husband ran off to Australia (far enough to make chasing him awkward), and she raised her daughter with the help of her mum. Now, she was no longer young, and she had no virginity or reputation to preserve for a future husband, so she said a mental Fuck it! and went clubbing with her male cousins and matched them drink for drink, and fag for fag, and while the men's reputations were unscathed, she was a cautionary tale to young girls everywhere.

She gave exactly...

(hold on, just calculating...

add the four,

carry the one)...

...

ZERO fucks.

She would strut into family functions in sleeveless dresses that were cut above the knee, and leave ripples of scandal behind her. Whispers of how 'her mother must be so ashamed.' Or how 'a daughter like her is a curse.' Or that she'd 'never find another husband'.

She didn't care. She greeted all these women—twisted with their own bitterness—by kissing their hands and offering them a greeting of peace, so that *they* were now the ugly ones, gossiping about a perfectly polite woman.

As she passed me in the corridor, she'd wink and say, 'Don't let the fuckers get you down'. It was like being acknowledged backstage by a rock star!

She wasn't exactly my role model: Being a single mum stuck in this town sounded like Hell (I shouldn't joke), but I *did* want to be brazen, independent, and challenge every one of these hypocrites and their clichéd expectations. She was honest about who she was. I aspired to that. Would I ever have been honest about who I was? How could I when I didn't even know?

Some of the same women who were looking down at Lolly from their high horses, couldn't see their daughters from such a height, daughters who would sneak off to snog boys (one of my cousins had taken to having anal, to keep her virginity intact. YES, ANAL... TO REMAIN A VIRGIN. Let that sink in!)

Some of these uncles, who secretly wanted to drink and laugh in Lolly's circles, had sons who were caught up in the new heroin tornado.

In the Family it seemed that everyone was too busy scrutinising the hot scandals in other people's lives to notice that their own houses were on fire.

3.12 p.m.

At the hospital, they have taken me out of the ambulance and into a clinical room full of chrome slabs, human-size drawers, and medical equipment.

It's an episode of *CSI*. Without the beautiful people.

They must do this every day, multiple times, because they do it respectfully but without any care at all for me. I want to tell them that I am a human with feelings and a story to tell, and that I am scared.

But I am just another corpse, and they are just doing their job.

They leave me there and walk out to finish the paperwork. They don't check my fingertips or tongue. They don't check my blood or cut me open with deep incisions through the chest. The physician has announced my cause of death and that's that. I am nothing more than a carcass with a tag hanging off my freshly varnished-in-dark-red big toe. My toe is dark blue against the thick string.

I'm trying to look at my body objectively. What would I have thought of me, if I had met me? What observations would I make?

That my big toe is long, but not as long as my second toe. Weird.

Big boobs, big hair. I used to have a big smile too, when I used it. People would say that I was much prettier when I smiled, which would guarantee them an immediate scowl. I think I had a friendly face; sad but friendly. Maybe I would have been nice to me, a supportive cheerleader "let me fix your crown" type of friend, encouraging me not to constantly be so self-deprecating.

I recently lost a lot of weight from a pretty bad bout of depression, but it's hard for me not to see myself as still chubby. But objectively, I think the puppy fat has gone and if I were a stranger, I might even have said I had a nice figure.

Not in time to be attractive to anyone, though.

Nailed it.

No, wait! Someone found me attractive. Last night, someone flirted with me.

That makes no sense at all. It's so hazy and so crazy, it must have been some handsome stranger in a dream.

Speaking of strangers, I don't know if there are other bodies in this room. There must be, in those big drawers. And if there are, there must be other souls like me hanging around their corpses.

I try to say hello.

Silence.

Maybe there aren't any bodies. In Islam, as in Judaism, we bury our dead immediately, so there won't be any two-week tenants here. A Christian friend in England had to wait for a whole month before they buried her grandma, who died of old age. I found that so odd and sad, because her family had to mourn her actual death and then had to grieve all over again at the funeral, just as they were starting to accept her absence.

Here, the bodies would have arrived, been registered, *perhaps* an autopsy in a case of crime or suspicious death, of which there are so few in this safest of cities, and sent home immediately. With us, it's twenty-four hours of intense pain and then the rocky road to recovery.

I say hello again.

Maybe I can communicate with other souls. Maybe they can tell me how I can communicate with my family.

Maybe the souls are scared, wondering what happened to them, or what happens to them next. Maybe, like me, they just woke up dead! Or they're relieved to be released from a long and painful illness. They're having regrets. They're angry, or bargaining, or accepting. They're wondering if they've been good enough. What *is* good enough?

'Hello?' I pray really hard that no one replies.

They're waiting, like I am, to go back home and see their families one last time. If indeed they have families. Maybe I'm the lucky one with so many people waiting for me.

'Hello?'

I'm alone.

•

I've always felt like a loner. Even (or especially) in this huge Family.

As I said, my dad's family is an immense presence in Muscat. Our beloved Sultan granted the Zanzibaris citizenship because, I believe, quite frankly he needed us. His vision was to modernise Oman, build roads, open schools, educate girls, and allow sunglasses (all things banned by his father). He brought in expats and experts. And he brought in the wealth of education, progressiveness, and experience that was the exiled Zanzibari Omanis. We were the nationalised expats, the local experts. We are originally Omani, except that was centuries ago, and now we were mostly mixed with a bunch of other things, Zanzibar being a coastal trading post. Most of our people, after being kicked out of Zanzibar, had been in the UK, Egypt, or America, working, getting experience and degrees. The Sultan gave us all a new homeland and passports, in a country barely in its teens that none of us even knew.

Some of our forefathers were from Oman, but some were from Somalia, Yemen, South Africa, even Holland and Ireland! It's ironic to think that our people were brutally murdered during the Zanzibar Revolution, for being "from Oman", a country they had never even been to.

Baba and his siblings were well known in Zanzibar's Stone Town for being rough. There were so many of them, almost a village's worth, and they had had to fight over everything growing up, to assert dominance over each other. Fight to be heard, fight for affection, fight for the best part of the chicken at dinner. (Which was, bizarrely enough, the neck. The scrawny, stringy, curved bone with hardly any meat. My dad has a scar on his forehead from trying to steal the neck at dinnertime once.)

They were known as the cool kids and the bullies at their school in Zanzibar. They had their own stretch of talcum-white beach where they played football and did somersaults off short walls, and no other kids dared trespass on their turf. They played rough, they spoke rough, and they were always being reprimanded at school but could never be expelled because of their father's high status at the hospital and his patronage of the school.

Their father, my Babu, whom I never got to meet, was a brilliant surgeon and had changed the face of healthcare on the island. Well respected, revered, almost feared, he ran the hospital and his home with precision and little cheer.

Babu's first wife was literally his childhood sweetheart, as they were married at sixteen and fourteen respectively. He adored her in that innocent First Love way, but she died giving birth to their tenth child. He mourned her as his one true love, and those ten children were sent down the road to be brought up by their aunt. Which, incidentally, is totally standard.

He didn't check in on those first ten children often, reminders that they were of his lost love. Babu was alone. He became miserable and cantankerous and threw himself into his work, focusing on rising in the medical ranks.

At the height of his career, as Medical Director of Mnazi Moja Hospital in Stone Town, Babu was presented with a beautiful, light-skinned seventeen-year-old as a wife. She idolised him, looked up to the powerful man. She called him Doctor even in private, and swore that one day the Doctor would love her as much as he loved his dead wife. If the dead wife had given him ten children, then so would she.

Babu obligingly proceeded to implant ten children in her. Almost one per year. But he was strict, unloving, and unforgiving with her and her children. I don't know if Babu hit her, but he sure kept her barefoot, pregnant, and unhappy.

Women have to spend forty days at home after childbirth, not leaving the home for fear of infection and to give mothers time to heal and bond with their child. On the forty-first day after she had given birth to her tenth (my Aunt Zaina), the once beautiful child-bride, now worn and bitter at thirty-two years of age, snuck out of the house and was never heard of again.

She left all ten children, including the suckling baby behind, to bring themselves and each other up. That's why they were unruly, unyielding, and fiercely protective of each other. Their love for each other was truly something to behold.

They were mercilessly rough, almost mean-spirited with each other, but they would bury bodies for one another and, forsaking all others, never ask questions.

They vaguely knew their half siblings (Babu's first ten children) when they all met and mingled on Eid holidays in Zanzibar, but they weren't close to their older siblings until they were all reunited in Oman in the '80s. Suddenly they clung to each other. Their family had doubled and those twenty siblings and their *countless* offspring united to create an entire community of about a hundred imposing characters. And this family dominated above all others, just from its sheer size. One Family to rule them all.

Just the way they wanted.

Babu didn't have much of a hand in shaping any of his offspring, but he did instil certain things in them. They were to stick together and support each other, against all odds and against anyone else. They were brought up not to admit that they were wrong. His children were the authority and should always behave as such. They were to always speak with conviction and the confidence that what they were saying was right. Even though they often weren't.

This is my father in a nutshell.

When Baba and his siblings in turn had kids, my first cousins were all raised exactly the same. They went through the Family initiation of being teased savagely as young children, until they learned not to cry or show emotion. Their parents and uncles would find their weak spot, (acned skin, big nose, a lisp) and rip the piss out of them until they learned how to fight back and learned to never let anyone use those things against them. No one would ever insult or hurt them, because they had heard every insult since they were three years old. And they had been given years to prepare comebacks, unlike the rest of us who only come up with a zinger hours after the fact.

They were also brought up to believe that if someone hit you, you hit them back.

You hit them back five times over and shut that shit down.

They were taught to have the confidence of *knowing* that what they said was right, and to never allow anyone to try to prove them wrong. It was an intimidating arrogance far up the Dunning Kruger scale, and it was effective.

On the other side of the spectrum, my mum and her siblings, Uncle Mo and Mamma Mia, were brought up in England, far away, physically and psychologically, from this upbringing-by-fire. They had been warned a hundred times *not* to think they were better than anyone else. They were taught modesty and humility. They deferred to others' knowledge and listened.

Since Mama's family weren't represented at all in Oman (she left her whole family in London when Baba dragged her to this new country) she had no allies here. She was alone in a strange land, dropped into her new family full of strangers.

For a long time, Mama faltered, trying to find her footing and then her balance, like a baby Bambi. She was welcomed heartily by a barrage of overly hospitable siblings-in-law, and told where to send her kids to school, which tailor was best, and where to get her waxing done, and then who she should talk to and what she should wear. And who she should like and who she should judge and how she should scold her children and that she should defer to her husband.

Even the "friends" she took from the smorgasbord of characters in the Family soon proved themselves to be petty and backstabbing, collecting secrets to add to their arsenal of information, should they need it later for gossip or blackmail.

She tried to find quality girlfriends among them but found that she was only flavour of the month in their clique sporadically, and then unceremoniously ignored by them all. She wanted so much to be liked, so she repeatedly forgave them their fickleness, and she would join the gang of mean girls again. It took her a couple of years to figure out her place in this stupid high school soap opera, and then she removed herself from it and watched them create their hyena circle around unsuspecting new additions to the Family.

This bizarre idea of friendship was so far removed from the loving, loyal sisterhood she had in London. Everything here was so different to her upbringing, her beliefs and scruples. Her moral compass pointed to a loyalty these people couldn't find.

So, alone, she had to work overtime to assert her values in us, against this overwhelming force of Baba's siblings and their crushing presence in her life.

Back in Zanzibar, as kids, Baba's siblings used to torture and kill ants under the glare of a piece of curved glass. They did the same thing to Mama when she moved to Oman, and my mother's spirit slowly died under their scrutiny.

3.15 p.m.

As I lie here in this earthly hospital limbo, waiting for my body to be dealt with, I feel like my life is flashing before my eyes. No, not flashing—that happens quickly. This feels like a slow airport conveyor belt, where the luggage is not in chronological order but all there to be picked apart, analysed, considered as part of your whole. And the baggage before my eyes right now is my parents.

It's weird to think of Mama and Baba in these different ways. To think of them as children themselves, loved, ignored, desperate, happy. To think of their upbringings, years ago and miles away. To think of them as young adults, flailing to understand life and how to navigate it. As products of their upbringing or of their environment. As a result of how fucked up or otherwise *their* parents were. We just expect our parents to know everything, until the dreadful day when you realise that they don't have all the answers. When you realise that they are just a sum of all the parts that potentially fucked them up, and (if you're lucky) their attempts to correct them.

I often think of nature and nurture, mostly because I often think about why I am the way I am.

I'm lying here in the morgue, body cold and soul afraid, and I wonder if nature or nurture brought me here, or sheer bad luck.

The waves of panic start again as my solitude hits me. I'm yearning for my parents the way grown men cry out for their mothers as they lie in agony on the battlefield. I'm pining for them. I wish they were here. I wish we had left things in a better state before they ran off to England. I wish I had treated them as fallible human beings, rather than expecting them to instinctively know how to deal with secrets I hadn't told them, and a depression they couldn't understand.

What would I even say to them, if they were here and I could make amends? How could I even explain what happened to me, when even I don't know?

Are they on their way back yet? How did they take the news?

Of all the days they were absent in my life, why this one?

At the risk of sounding ridiculous, I want my mummy.

•

Mama and Baba.

From the stories I have heard, mostly from Mamma Mia, I can deduce that my mum and dad's relationship was born from a double misunderstanding. They each had an idea of what their marriage would look like, and they didn't consult each other on that image.

Maybe they did talk about that image, but the other party wasn't listening, too involved in their own fantasy. Perhaps most couples do the same.

My Baba was objectively gorgeous in his youth. He lived in Spain in his twenties and into his thirties. He spoke perfect Spanish and could dance like he was born wearing Cuban heels. He had twirled a slew of sexy, raven-haired señoritas into his bed in his time, and he would travel with a different one every year, visiting one of his many siblings in London, Muscat, and New York.

I have no idea what dodgy dealings he did in Spain, but every time he passed through London and descended in a cloud of aftershave on a gathering of his old Zanzibar crew, he would hand out £5 notes to all the kids, like a pimp Pied Piper. He wore immaculate three-piece bell-bottomed suits and made all the women blush with his charming, off-colour compliments and tongue-in-cheek jokes. His favourite was, when being offered a cup of coffee and asked how he likes it, he would wink and say,

'I like my coffee the way I like my women. Hot, strong, and sweet with plenty of *maziwa*.' (In Swahili, maziwa doubles as "milk and "tits".)

This would sometimes be accompanied by a Connery-Bond style slap on the bottom and always by a coquettish giggle. He would then turn to the men, giving them Harlem sliding high-fives while regaling them with tales of his Mediterranean antics.

Ah, make chauvinism great again!

Of course, this was all before everyone moved to Oman and became a little too conservative and a lot less hedonic. This was a time when being a good Muslim meant being a good neighbour and not doing the Big Ten—you know, the stealing / lying / killing / coveting etc. of the Commandments, rather than what being a good Muslim had come to mean for them nowadays: covering every speck of hair and growing long beards and not touching anyone in greeting.

Baba was the true definition of the life and soul of any party. He was joyful and included everyone in the joy.

When my mum was younger, she had a crush on the charismatic playboy, who would coax the teen with the train-track braces onto the dance floor while she squirmed with feigned reticence but was actually gagging for his attention.

She was thirteen years younger than him, so he only treated her as one of the many kids he pulled onto the dance floor, until he noticed that she'd become a young woman from one year to the next. Suddenly he was the one blushing when she greeted him with the familiar innocence of a child but with her beautiful face and (now) straight-toothed smile, her woman's curves and the sudden confidence that comes from leaving home for university. He talked to Mama for a while, ignoring poor Carmen, or Monica, or Esme, leaving the unsuspecting Spaniard to be surrounded by a host of single hopefuls and some married fools.

He was hypnotised by Mama's green eyes, intoxicated by her youth, mesmerised by the promised potential. He listened to her talk of her education but conveniently didn't hear anything when she spoke of her ambitions.

The next year he only had eyes for my mum. And the following year, the year of Mama's graduation, he came to London without a girlfriend.

He visited Bibi and Grandad at their home, driving up in a swanky hire car, with gifts for all and £5 notes for Mamma Mia and an unimpressed Uncle Mo. He was 'in the vicinity' and came ostensibly to pay respects, but watching Mama cook and serve dinner (what an irresistible combination!), he made up his mind and asked for her hand in marriage, right there in the kitchen.

Grandad was flabbergasted. He was not going to get in her way, but she had just bloody graduated. She should live first!

I think Bibi was a bit happier. When she got married, she was also young, she was also a virgin, and she had always been blissfully happy with her decision. Also, she loved the fact that the suitor at the door was a Zanzibari and would bring her daughter closer to her roots. Despite her own choice, Bibi didn't want her daughter to marry an Englishman, further diluting her disappearing ancestry.

What the beautiful, fiery señoritas lacked was culture, Baba had mused to himself. No, they weren't devoid of culture; it just wasn't *his* culture.

I may cynically add that what attracted him to these sirens was their wild and exciting ways, but what he ultimately wanted to marry was a virgin.

He never thought it would happen to him, but just like maternal instinct manifests itself later for some women, Baba's need to settle down and procreate took him by surprise when it suddenly kicked in. He was utterly bewitched by my mother and saw her by his side in the movie in his mind, the ideal accessory. She was the perfect woman to bear his children and with whom he could build his home. He couldn't wait to worship this woman-child and give her everything she needed. She would bear him a boy and a girl, and she would stay home to raise them, and he would shower her with love and gifts. And they would be a happy young family unit, surrounded by his Family in Oman.

He was marrying his idea of a picture-perfect wife: virgin, mother, young, beautiful, silent.

And that was the first of the double misunderstandings.

Mama couldn't have been more different to Baba.

It is a truth universally acknowledged, that a quiet child is a child that is ripping up the only copy of your birth certificate or pooping in your Jimmy Choos. But not my mum! My Mama,

Maryam, had a sweet, romantic spirit, and she could happily spend all day alone, daydreaming. They used to leave her for hours, humming to herself, lost down the magical tube of a kaleidoscope or watching her music box ballerina go round and round to melancholy music and no applause.

She mostly imagined herself traversing the globe, changing careers without the requisite years of training and agonising reflection over a life-altering decision—just a new outfit and the desire to go from air hostess to glamourous opera-singing diva.

She would only leave her room to come downstairs when called for dinner. (She would also come downstairs the *first* time she was called, unlike me.)

My mum wasn't just a romantic; the hot air balloon of her daydreams was tethered by the inherited pragmatic nature of her parents, and she knew the right thing to do was to get a degree. She knew that she should have some letters at the end of her name (yes, letters would look so fancy!), and that university, with all the colourful characters and the distance from home, would prepare her for her exciting Life!

Notice, the plans were all very amorphous, because, unfortunately, being a jack of all trades, she wasn't really sure what she wanted to study or what career she was aiming for. In her head, however, the daydream was very clear: She wanted to wear chic suits, carry a briefcase into the Business Class cabin of the plane, and fly to Paris for a very important (but absolutely vague) business meeting. She would sit at the head of the conference table and dazzle everyone with her presentation on something ambiguous but fascinating.

Her main fantasy was travel. For business, for pleasure, alone, with friends, with the love of her life.

She wanted to travel and see the cherry blossoms floating down on traditionally dressed geisha in Tokyo. She couldn't wait to watch a basketball game courtside, with a (halal) hot dog in hand, in the States. And she hoped one day to hear the mournful rasp of Andalusian singers accompany flamenco dancers by an open fire.

And then Baba came along, flitting between countries with a string of stunning women, handing out money, laughing and strutting, staying a short enough time to create a mystery and a long enough time to leave an indelible impression. What a charismatic man, what a seductive life!

When he proposed to her, she was still calling him Uncle (related or not, anyone older than you is Uncle or Aunty OR you get a smack!) She even mistakenly slipped and called him Uncle a couple of times after they were married, mortifyingly once when they were mid-coitus. (Thanks, Mamma Mia, for that piece of information that I can never un-hear.)

Baba, on the other hand, called Mama his Little Bird. It was a term of endearment, of course. But deeper than that, he *wanted* her to be fragile. He wanted to provide, to protect, to be her hero and saviour. That idea suited his purpose but not the reality, and when he realised she could stand on her own two strong legs, he took them out from under her, moved her to Oman where she became completely dependent on him, on *his* family, on *his* money and knowledge, and on him puking up little bits of food so she could eat. You know, bird analogy (ANAL-ogy).

When he proposed back in London, she was absolutely thrilled.

She had had a million daydreams about him as a teenager, of being the lucky girl he twirled from one city to the next. But *she* wouldn't just be his lover, to be replaced the very next year. She would be his *wife*! His life-long travel partner, and now her fantasies of kissing someone on a bridge over the Seine, and swimming naked in the warm, moonlit waters of the Indian Ocean were about to be realised.

He was perfect, she thought to herself: well-travelled, older, experienced, and rich! She had no idea what he did for a job (maybe she wasn't listening), and she had no idea what she wanted to do as a career, but he could be her benefactor and give her the luxury of time to decide (maybe while in a chalet in the Alps or dining on pasta in Rome).

She wanted kids too, after many years of seeing all there was to see, long after she'd turned thirty and established herself in her career. Then they would have a boy and a girl, who would give them both years of joy.

And to top off this most romantic of pairings, my dad and all his brothers had been named after prophets.

Baba's name was Yousef.

Arabic for Joseph.

Mary and Joseph.

Oh, it was going to be a glorious, glamourous life!

And there was the second part of the double misunderstanding.

She wanted a patron who would twirl her around the world and support her while she figured out her high-flying career.

He wanted a young, innocent wife to bear his children and stay home to be the perfect hostess to his family's gatherings.

They didn't stand a chance.

•

When Mamma Mia told me stories of their childhood in London, she referred to her sister in two ways.

Before she was married and after she was married.

The Virgin Mary

and

Mother Mary.

When Bibi chose the names Maryam, Mohammed, and Mina, all her children named after close family members, Bibi and Grandad as a couple had agreed on the names.

I heard that our names, Summer and Sara, were a hugely contentious issue for Mama and Baba. He wanted some traditional names, like Khadija or Fatima. But Mama being half English, and because they lived in England at the time of our births, insisted on names that could cross over. I mean Fatima would immediately be shortened to Fati, and given the size of my thighs and belly, would have been absolutely mortifying.

6.07 p.m.

Thank God, the morgue guys are back. It was too quiet and too eerie in here. They are going about their business, ticking something off on a clipboard, looking at me as a corpse and not as me. The business of death, so cold and detached.

They compare my name on the sheet of paper to the label on my toe, but they don't comment on the unusual choice of my name and the trouble it might have caused. Baba wanted it to be Samar, but Mama insisted on spelling it like the season.

They note cause of death but don't say that I look too healthy to be an asthmatic.

They indifferently take off my tag and don't notice the pains-taking care Sara had taken painting my toes. Or wonder why she didn't paint my fingernails too, which are a hot mess.

They don't wonder about the circumstances that landed me here on this slab. They have no curiosity or sympathy. They don't worry if my parents will be okay.

They lift my body but don't comment on the weight that I've recently lost. They carelessly strap me into a hospital hearse, not worrying that my arm is at a strange angle underneath me.

They casually cover my face without commenting that I was young and probably had a bright future ahead and this was such a waste of youth and life.

I just want a remorseful shake of the head, an empathetic tut, an ounce of compassion.

They hand my papers over to the driver and never think of me again.

The ride back from the hospital to my home is only seven minutes long. It's on a long, lonely valley road that takes you from one part of town to the next, but on a secret back path between the imposing, arid hills of Muscat. Here, everything is one colour: the sand, the mountains, and the haze circling around the sun that makes you feel that you are in an old cartoon, parched within an inch of your life, vultures buzzing around your dehydrated body.

•

When I was young, they called it Death Valley Road. It was a short cut, but a lethal one.

With no streetlights and only one lane going in each direction, in the '80s and '90s young boys in their souped-up Honda Civics would take the blind twists, precariously overtaking each other for shits and giggles.

And death.

Maybe that's why they put the hospital there. Or why they finally put up streetlights and speed cameras.

On this eerily quiet and ominous road, between these craggy hills, you'd be excused for thinking that you were miles away from civilisation.

In a way, I like that about Muscat. You'd turn a corner and see nothing but sand, and then look behind you and find a Zara in a sparkling new mall. A dusty lot with unmarked graves would be right next to a glorious mansion. A cramped cold store for the "sale of food stuffs" would be next to a chandelier emporium. And just five minutes from anywhere you could look up and see a million stars.

Muscat deliberately avoided copying its sister city, Dubai. Sultan Qaboos refused to have skyscrapers or modernise his country to the extent that it could have been a city anywhere in the world. Our ancient, sixteen-floor Sheraton Hotel has the claim to fame of being the tallest building in Oman, and nothing else comes close.

The only chain stores are in the malls—Marks and Spencer, Forever 21. The other shops around town are family-owned restaurants selling Swahili food. Or a *dhobi*, an Indian man in a tiny storefront, ironing bedsheets, surrounded by towering bundles of clothes wrapped in kangas. Or an enterprising local lady who has opened a women-only salon (spelled saloon), where an Arab lady could get *any* kind of epilation for *any* part of her body that might need it.

The houses are all white, flat-roofed, two-story cubes. In the centre of town, they sit huddled in cramped quarters, like an old lady's crooked teeth. In the suburbs they have a larger buffer around them, a few metres, but the houses are all similar. Pillars, arches, and very small gardens. The Omanis prefer to use their plot of land for the house and not for the garden. Even ours is just a narrow flower bed around the perimeter of our land, where bougainvillea grows high and wild, bursting with colour and thorns.

Our main highways are clean and wide, lined with perfectly equidistant palm trees and strips of grass, watered constantly by irrigation and migrant workers. Our roundabouts are ornate, with themes, like the Book Roundabout near the University, or the Mosaic Mural Roundabout near the airport that depicts the ancient Omani crafts of boatmaking and fishing in pictures to delight the arriving tourist. There are enormous incense burners and even a roundabout with fake palm trees. All part of the '80s Beautification of Oman Project.

They needn't have tried so hard. Oman is breathtaking.

The red, stretching Wahiba sands; the green, cascading mountain terraces of Jebel Akhdar; the hidden wonders of the endless blue coastline, from the whale shark waters of the Musandam tip to Salalah in the south, with its melodramatic monsoon season and misty waterfalls.

And when the rains arrive, heavily beating down on our desert city for one day a year, the water comes rumbling down the hills, bringing pebbles and rivers of dirty water with it, settling in the valleys with no drainage system to flow into. It washes away cars, floods everything in its path, and the city grinds to a halt. You have to stay home and wait for the earth to guzzle it up before you can venture out again.

I loved looking out of the car window while my dad drove. That used to be my favourite thing as a child, because it usually meant we were driving up to North London to see Bibi and Grandad. Mama and I used to try and spot yellow cars and count them all before we reached her childhood home in Edgware, where Mamma Mia would be waiting in the front garden for me, practically hopping with excitement. We counted twelve yellow cars once, which is surely some kind of record. We must have double counted a few of them, while passing local fried chicken cafes, hair salons for afro hair, off licenses, council flats, then posh estate agents and wine bars, parks, parks, and more parks.

•

Now this dusty valley road comes to a set of traffic lights. When we first moved to Muscat, there was hardly any traffic; now it seems everyone is always stuck in some kind of jam. There's early morning school rush hour, rush hour for government workers getting to work, rush hour for the private sector, and then the same at going home time.

The sky is wide and dark blue and orange. I didn't think those colours matched, but they look beautiful together.

I would sigh if I could.

The ambulance gets through the next green light. It passes our pathetic excuse for a local mall, which has no interesting shops apart from a good place for waffles and frozen yoghurt, where we would have birthday breakfasts and get all the staff to sing along. It has a shop selling men's sandals, and another selling cheap watches and suitcases, and of course, the ever present *abaya* shop.

We turn left, past the tailor my mum uses for special occasion dresses, and drive past several identical houses. Ours is set back a little from the main road, and the ambulance drives past it.

'You passed it!' I shout.

Woah! Déjà vu moment! 'You passed it!' That feels familiar. Like I said it last night. 'YouPassedIt! YouPastid!' To whom, and why?

No time to ponder that as the ambulance slams the brakes and my body slides a little on the bench. He turns to check on me, and slowly reverses the vehicle to the front gate of my house.

6.41 p.m.

It feels like the opposite of Narnia. Like I've been away for ten minutes, but the rest of the world and all the people in it have aged seven years.

Cars are parked outside our house as if they were thrown in the air and were left whichever way they landed. Textbook Omani parking.

I spot a yellow car.

Mama, I spotted a yellow car!

There are hundreds of shoes at our front door. Someone stole my shoes once at a funeral. I loved those shoes, white slip-ons with a flowered pattern punched through the leather at the toes. I wanted to make much more of a scene about this inexcusable theft than I did, but I wisely took into consideration that someone had just lost more than their favourite shoes. After that I always hid my shoes behind a flowerpot.

The house is heaving with people and humming with gossip and Quran.

Bibi greets the ambulance staff then leads them as they carry my body via the side path that leads to the back of the house, rather than walk through the crowds with it. God, this feels so weird.

They go through the kitchen and to the second staff quarters, which is usually used for storage, stacks of ornate trays and thermoses of varying sizes, and around twenty assorted ice cream containers and biscuit tins, none of which, annoyingly, contain ice cream or biscuits. And bags of rice, big enough to feed a village.

A red-eyed Lucy has already cleared out the bathroom and placed a bucket, cloths, kangas, soaps, sponges, and a plastic table.

Oh fuck. That's right...

They're going to have to wash my body.

Mamma Mia, who has started to sob again, and a composed Sara enter the room.

My body is going to be washed by the women closest to me.

I guess I should count myself lucky, really. I didn't die in Scotland; I died here at home. Some people don't have relatives around and have to be washed by strangers who don't care about you.

I have Bibi.

She is literally the person that everyone turns to here to help with this part of death's ritual. She is used to cadavers (fuck, I'm a cadaver), and she is so gentle, discreet, and meticulous. She has done this hundreds of times, having helped so many people in London and here.

She will be clinical about this, but she's going to have to get Mamma Mia through it.

She talks them through it first, so they don't freak out.

Oh bollocks, how mortifying.

I'm between waxes.

•

Lucy is our maid, and she's been in our family for years. She's from the Philippines, her English is accented but perfect, and her Swahili cooking is below average. She is a Catholic and goes to church at the weekend, and she has learned to be as fastidious at cleaning as Mama's OCD demands.

When we were younger, Lucy used to take us out of the house for walks when she heard my parents starting to shout. I used to find the big mole by her nose a little disconcerting, but I loved her hugs, so I would close my eyes.

She knows several phrases in Swahili, and I forced her to teach me Tagalog swear words. It's because of her that I say weird things like 'up the roof', instead of 'up on the roof', or mortifyingly mispronounce 'bowl' so it actually sounds like 'bowel'. She has a degree in English Literature, which makes me feel inadequate, guilty, and entitled in equal measure.

I often ask to see pictures of her children, because it makes her happy to show me and tell me their stories. I feel like I know them both and I celebrate their successes with her, toasting their graduations with apple juice and sending them video birthday greetings.

I will never meet them, even though I know their mother better than they do. Lucy has had to accept that her own mother has raised her children. In turn, she raised two little girls in Muscat. This heartbreaking reality is all too familiar to many migrant workers in the Middle East. I often wonder if it wouldn't just be better to be poor and happy, surrounded by your family. By the grace of God, a birth lottery, and geography, that could have been us having to make those decisions.

Lucy and I also clash almost every day, because she has to clean the bathrooms by a certain time, and I like to sleep in.

Lucy will miss me as much as any one of my relatives, but it won't occur to anyone to give condolences to the maid.

Things I know how to say in Swahili:

Close the door!
Be quiet!
I will beat you!
Turn the volume down!
Bring me... (water / remote / something to beat you with)
Cat
Chicken
Donkey
You have a face like a donkey
You are as lazy as a donkey
Boobs, Balls, Arse
Your mother's fanny!
Do your hair!
Are you hungry?
Are you full?
Let's go!
Your nose looks like poop! (It really is quite funny in Swahili)
You have no brains
You have no manners
I love you

7.27 p.m.

I think the worst thing about this process is the pressing of my bowels (pronounced 'bowels') to get whatever is in there, out. There is no dignity left. My waste is being emptied into a bucket, my little sister is holding me up, Mamma Mia is looking away and gagging, and my legs are hairy.

No. Dignity.

No doubt.

Sara manages to unclasp the necklace around my neck as she holds me up and puts it around her own neck where it joins its identical twin.

My torso is covered, but I can see my limbs and my skin, blue and turning darker. And it's freaking me out a little. That was me, for almost twenty-three years. That's how I identified myself, how others recognised me. People characterise you by your physical attributes: the girl with the long hair, the man with the broad shoulders, the crooked nose, the hairy back, the winning smile.

And you're nothing more than a collection of bones and muscles held together by skin that starts to rot as soon as your heart stops sending blood to it. And yet we value IT above our own souls.

I fleetingly pity humanity for its tragic superficiality.

I have never been more impressed with Bibi. She covers me with kangas, such colourful, joyful sheets, with sayings on them. This particular set says *Fitna ni sumu baridi* (loosely translated as 'Shit-stirring is worse than cold poison').

She wears gloves and washes me underneath the sheets, so no part of my body is exposed.

Which I am grateful for.

People think I didn't care about my size, because that was the vibe I gave off. I wanted to separate myself from my physical appearance. I wanted to denounce it, even though everyone values beauty so highly. My mum would suggest diets, or new exercise fads. In this town where everyone is obsessed with looks, she couldn't understand why I just didn't care, but I hated the way we were judged by our bodies.

The truth is that I would self-consciously pull down baggy tops over my genetically big boobs, to try and cover the extra tyre around my middle, and I would try and lift my legs off the sofa, to minimise the "spread" when I was in company. I wasn't huge; I just had these awkward extra few kilos in embarrassing places. I didn't want to be looked at, or admired for my young woman's body, or judged, or whistled at, or compared to my slender cousins. I didn't want anyone to look at me, period.

Wait. Someone whistled at me last night and I loved it, which doesn't sound like me at all. That's gross! Is there anyone from whom a wolf whistle is acceptable, let alone something I would enjoy?

I try in vain to remember as Bibi continues to wash me gently with sponges, saying little prayers to cleanse me, an ablution for the grave.

They wash my curls, struggling to run their rubber-gloved fingers through my tangles.

They finish the first wash and then cleanse me as if purifying my body for prayers. They aren't crying now. They work silently, apart from the invocations, which they say together, sounding like a three-part harmony Gregorian choir.

Bibi discreetly checks between my toes and the inside of my elbows for any tell-tale signs of junkies. Nothing. She wants to question Sara about the needle, ask if she's *sure* there were drugs, confirm the information, but she doesn't want to upset Sara. She doesn't want to upset herself. It was an Asthma Attack. Done.

They put pads of cotton wool in my creases, elbows, armpits, fingers, toes, and a huge one, like a supersize night-time sanitary pad that goes the whole length of my (unwaxed) crack. In case of any leaking, explains Bibi.

Cringe.

The cotton smells so good. It's been infused with *bukhoor*, from the sap of Omani frankincense trees, steeped in expensive perfumed oils.

The smell evokes hectic Eid mornings, getting ready in our new clothes, hair freshly blow-dried, someone always shouting for us to hurry up, and our often subsequent tears. We were occasionally even allowed to wear kohl around our eyes, as long as we didn't refer to it as makeup. Local children would ring the doorbell at ever-decreasing intervals to receive Eid money; we would have a pile of 100 baiza notes to hand out to them, and then the visiting of the relatives would begin.

And always bukhoor burning. We would gingerly step over the clay pot of red-hot coals, so the smoke would billow up inside our dresses, and then fan our hair over it, so we smelled good all day as we swished our silky hair around.

Back in the tiny room, they slip a simple white tunic over my head and pull it down past my bum. They then wrap pure white sheets around me and secure them tightly.

My closest female relatives never got to dress me for my wedding day, never got to zip me up, button me down, twirl me around. No taffeta, no organza, no lace or satin. Just simple cotton.

Bibi kisses my cheek gently before pulling the final simple white cotton veil over my face.

I'm restricted, cocooned, waiting to metamorphose into the next stage. Not the next stage of Life. What, then? The next stage of Matter.

I'm just a carcass, and now I'm getting ready to be interned. Buried under sand and gravel. Already decaying. No more me.

Yeah, I'm panicking.

Bibi sits her tiny frame down on a stool in the corner, her face sweaty from exertion. She puts her face in her hands and weeps.

8.20 p.m.

Some male cousins come to the maid's room to pick up my body. They lift me up onto their shoulders to carry me up the stairs as people move out of the way. Bibi, Mamma Mia, and Sara walk beside me, as they would have at my traditional wedding (we don't have one man "giving" you to another man). They hold on to each other's arms, shocked into silence by what they just performed.

They take me to the guest room, lay me down as carefully as they can, then adjust my position so that I am facing *Qibla*, the same way we face to pray, toward Mecca. I am supine, wrapped tightly in white.

Tighty whitey.

I got away with never having to do this to anyone. To have to wash my sister's or mother's or aunt's corpse. It's Mamma Mia's first time washing a body too, and from the look on her face, she will never be the same again.

I've been to several funerals here in Oman, but I've never been in the room with the body. That room is reserved for close relatives. It must be the saddest place in the world. Like the air is different in this room. All joy seized at the door by Death, standing vigil like a scythe-carrying bouncer.

Even people who aren't crying still look slammed by grief as they walk in to give respects. Tears are like yawns: contagious. Seeing people that *you* love, crying for the people that *they* love. You walk in to greet people, but then you just start crying. Crying over memories of your own losses. Crying in empathy for the close family. Crying out of fear of your own mortality. Or fear of losing someone un-loseable.

For most, it's a direct grief. They are somehow directly affected by my death.

At funerals, I have only ever cried in empathy. I remember my cousin wailing the loss of her father, who died in a car crash. I *felt* her pain. I saw it in her eyes, in the wringing of her hands, in the beating of her chest, and eventually in her zombie dehydrated exhaustion. Seeing that made me sob by her side. It wasn't about losing my uncle, necessarily (although it did make me fear losing my dad and reminded me to try and be nicer to him). But it was mostly seeing her so bereft. I was so sad for *her*.

And now I see the same empathy. I also see many people genuinely devastated.

I always felt alone and detached here, but I wasn't an island. Maybe a peninsula. I was a part of this Family, a blacker sheep than most, perhaps, but we were connected and I was loved. I realise that I have memories with so many of them.

I feel like I was more morose and miserable than I needed to be. Why couldn't I have appreciated them at the time? Why do humans always realise things too bloody late?

I touched these people's lives and they shaped me. As large as this Family is, most people are mourning me. I had no idea.

I don't think it's something that Westerners understand. I didn't understand it until today. You are not alone. You are a part of something much bigger than yourself. Resist as you may, this enormous village is a multi-tentacled creature, and will influence and permeate everything you are and do. And they will talk shit about you, and they will help you celebrate your milestones.

They will laugh at you, and ultimately, they will help bury you.

It makes me think about natural disasters, or terrorist attacks. Think about three hundred people dying at one time in one place. If there are fifty people who will be directly affected by EVERY SINGLE person, whether they're close family, lovers, friends, work colleagues, that means fifty x three hundred, which, you know, is a lot.

Fifteen thousand.
   (I'm not good at maths, okay? It took me a moment!)
   Fifteen thousand people mourning at once. So many hearts broken, so many lives irreparably, irrevocably changed. The exponential grief caused by a car bomb, a landslide, an earthquake. Ripples of grief that feel like a tsunami.

Remember the wedding in Iraq, I think? Or was it Afghanistan? Where everyone died? The wedding was bombed. God, I think there was one in Iraq AND in Afghanistan. The US bombed weddings and didn't apologise. And I was so desensitised to it, I didn't even really pay attention.
   But can you imagine? Imagine losing your whole fucking family. Imagine being the one with the flu and staying home that day. Imagine being abroad at school, unable to attend your cousin's wedding, and then the next day not having one single fucking relative left??
   I wish I had paid more attention. I wish I had spoken out more. When a single celebrity perishes, Facebook is inundated with tributes. Or if fifteen people in America or France die, the news covers it from every angle.

What about those eighty-seven people in Iraq? Are they less?
What are we humans like?

9.02 p.m.

Among the tears and the tributes, people are whispering.

Whispering prayers for me.

Oh, but I can also hear other whispers.

Our funerals are also social gatherings. Sometimes you don't get to see a relative for a while. Funerals, weddings, Eid—these are all times for a good natter and a catch up. Sometimes you care very deeply for the deceased, sometimes you're there to support those who care very deeply, and sometimes it's just duty.

When it's the latter (and I confess sheepishly to being guilty of this several times), you find a corner where people aren't reading the Quran, and you have an inappropriate giggle. You catch up on married life, or chatter about someone else's married life. You reminisce about how fun it was to live outside Oman, or you plan your next smoking session.

Today, I can hear people talking about drugs.

They are saying that I died of a drug overdose.

Seriously, this grapevine is something else. How the hell do they know drugs were even involved? The police, the coroner, the head physician. None of *them* even know...?

And then it dawns on me.

My dad...

Someone, maybe Mamma Mia or Bibi, told my mum and dad, and he told one of his siblings, which means all of his siblings, which means everyone in Oman, which means I haven't spared anyone any heartache.

•

The deal is, I smoked a lot of hash when I was a teenager.

A lot.

We live in a country where *who* you hang out with dictates your reputation, and as a direct result, your marriage prospects. A woman's social life is therefore mostly restricted to family. This often backfires into lots of second cousin weddings.

I was always allowed to hang out with my cousins; they were "safe". No one could gossip about me hanging out at my uncles' or aunts' houses, and Baba was more than happy that I had a relationship with his Family and therefore *encouraged* me to hang with them.

And that's how I ended up hanging out with Adel.

My hilarious burnout cousin, Adel, had a supremely cool basement-style apartment in his parents' house, which had its own entrance, a TV, and a fridge. It had an old brown sofa that had been retired from their living room upstairs, with thread-bare upholstery and cushions that exhaled when you slumped into them. The basement also had low lighting, a wicked sound system, and a door that locked the main house out. You know, all the essentials. You could even park on the side of the house, which meant my nosy aunt couldn't tell at what godless time I left her house at the weekend.

Most importantly, he always had a hash-stash and we would smoke up, talk shit, listen to music, tell increasingly disgusting jokes, zone out, watch crap movies—good wholesome stoner stuff. Sometimes other cousins would be there, also allowed out at the weekend to hang at their uncle's house. A few of us liked to get high. We were the black sheep, the Family misfits, with dreams beyond our small city, secrets we were running from, and restless spirits.

Sometimes we were joined by Adel's school friends.

School friends like Fido Dido, so named for his spiked-up hair, like the 7Up character.

I loved Fido Dido (not the 7Up character). He was already nineteen, and I was an impressionable fifteen-year-old, looking for an object for my blossoming lust. He was tall and lean, with that hard, almost scrawny torso, no-body-fat, six-pack, smooth brown skin, with those muscle lines that run from either side of his stomach and disappear into his jeans, a trickle of hair also leading down there, Marlboro Lights–smoking, eyes-droop-a-little-when-stoned, bottom lip biting, sexy mutha-fucking… Ugh! Fido Dido.

He lived for music. He DJ'd at our pathetic attempts at a weekend nightclub and would choose new artists for us to listen to. We would get stoned, lean our heads back, and get lost in EDM beats, and I would tingle, aware of how close his arm was to mine, while our bodies leaned toward each other on the sagging sofa. I had my special spot on that sofa, in the crack between two cushions with my legs tucked up close to me. And he always sat on the cushion on my right. I would sneak glances at him while we watched movies. He had a wicked sense of humour and we all teased each other in that basement, for taste in clothes, grades, each other's parents.

We would talk about a higher calling than our restricted life in Muscat: a different, faraway place where music and art reigned. Where people's consciousness was opened by drugs and you weren't judged for being different but judged instead for conforming.

Conformity! Ha, conformity was a swear word in our basement.

We were the small pebbles that would break the Wheel of Society, that evil, eternal Wheel that lurched on, turned by the hand of The Man, keeping bureaucracy and institutions rolling in its endless cycle.

The Wheel that ground down individuals and their audacious individuality into a pulp; the pulp that would eventually end up oiling the Wheel, in a mean, ironic twist of fate.

We, on the other hand, were the pebbles that would get caught in the gears and grind everything to a halt!

We were the rebels that would shake up the status quo!

We would change this narrow-minded world!

We would start the revolution!

We would save the planet!

We would...

...roll another joint.

Fido and I got on really well, but after a while I started yearning for his attention and hoping he would pick on me, to talk to or to tease. And I would get nervous before I went to Adel's in case he was there, and then disappointed if he didn't turn up, or stuttering slightly when he talked to me.

I have loved him for almost eight years. Yes, I understand that that is weird. You either get on it, or you get over it. I did neither.

I was smitten and I placed all my eggs in the basket of my huge teenage crush, so you can imagine how crushed I was when he came over to Adel's one day, crumbled some heated hash and tobacco into a rolling paper, rolled it up, used his tongue to seal the joint, and said, 'Guess what?'

We made some stupid joke guesses about his finally admitting to loving cock, or realising that he actually was a shit DJ, when he said, 'I'm in love, and I'm going to propose!'

My heart stopped (well, obvs not literally).

I was completely blindsided. Blindsighted? Blind side or sight? Your sight could be blind. But the surprise could come from the side of you that's blind.

Fuck, either way, I guess I had just assumed that one day I'd be brave enough to tell him how I felt, and he would say that of course he knew, he was just waiting for me to be ready. And we would end up together, laughing at each other and listening to music, getting high, travelling, creating a beautiful and unusual life. I thought we were a perfect match. In a place where you were supposed to assimilate, we were two misfits who fit together perfectly.

Instead, he had chosen a distant relative visiting from Mombasa. She caught his eye at a wedding, with her round arse and shy, seductive glances, and the two mothers arranged a meeting. And with a chaperone nearby, she fluttered her eyelashes and said all the right things. About education: She had just enough to be interesting and not enough to be threatening. About religion: She was a good Muslim girl and yet was open to his music and lifestyle. About kids: She would be a hands-on mother and would raise them well. He was intoxicated by the combination, and they married when they both turned twenty-one.

I was disgusted, disappointed, disillusioned. I should have known that it was all talk. No one is really brave enough to break the Wheel. No Omani man would actually want to be with someone like me. I was okay to smoke up with, but no one would want to marry a girl who's just one of the guys... Stupid me. They want to smoke, but God forbid they marry a girl who does. But then they would hide their smoking from their "good" wives. It made no sense.

I was furious at myself and totally heartbroken.

I asked Bibi about it once, changing all names to protect the guilty, of course.

She said most men want a simple life when they come home. A simple girl, who doesn't talk too much, or ask too many questions, or challenge them. Men want to be smiled at and fed and agreed with.

I objected that surely men want a friend, an equal, with whom they could laugh and spar mentally, challenge each other intellectually?

Bibi laughed at me, shaking her head.

'But what about you, Bibi? You're not a shy, quiet lady! You always give as good as you get!'

'Ah, but my dear granddaughter, I married a mzungu!'

9.39 p.m.

So many of my cousins are here in my parents' house, as they have been hundreds of times before.

Some are my age and we got on like siblings, and some I found a little vacuous.

Some older, sterner, more like aunts and uncles, who cared for us and scolded us.

And some younger, who we in turn cared for and scolded. Or ignored.

We range from our fifties to newborns.

Some are totally Westernised, speaking only English, going to work in business suits. Some speak only Arabic and wouldn't dream of taking off their abaya in front of men. Some speak Swahili as their first language and keep the island alive in their homes.

Some girls want to make a difference by becoming doctors, and some want to make a difference by becoming mothers. Many want to do both.

Some were genuine friends. I don't resent their raucous laughter between hugs and tears and incredulity. I love that they're sharing stories and laughing at me! Yes, they're mostly laughing at me, the way I liked to use big words, the way my moods would swing. They're taking the piss out of me, with great affection. I'm actually laughing with them. I feel like they know that, somehow.

My favourite ones are apparently flying in from the States today. I hope. I hope Tish and Tania get here before they bury me. They can't see me, but I can see them, and I need that.

•

The way our parents' generation ridiculed us really took its toll on us kids—me and my cousins. They thought it was a way to make us tough, invincible, leaders in this world. But they forgot that this wasn't Zanzibar in the '60s. It was the '00s with the internet and Oprah. A time of sharing your feelings and talking about your childhood. A time to give everyone a chance, not just the bullies.

We were just kids wanting to be loved, and some of us were more sensitive than others.

They passed on this bizarre, tough-love tradition of teasing, the tradition of reminding us that we weren't special, that we were all flawed and ridiculous. Reminding us of our place and that we were not to strive for anything.

But some of us couldn't believe that this was it. And often, we were the ones who turned to drugs.

We were judged harshly by whether we were beautiful, clever, talented or not, and yet reminded that even if we *were* beautiful, clever, talented, we were nothing special.

We were ripped to shreds when we were young, so that we would never talk back, never rebel, never question their authority, their rules. And we wouldn't stray too far from our parents, from our culture, from our home.

They could beat us or touch us with impunity, knowing that we would never talk back or report them. If we had been allowed to express opinions, to question them or even sound the alarm, maybe there would be fewer casualties among us.

But something interesting started happening recently. Some of us were daring to be different, to be individuals, to dissent! To choose art as a career (not just lawyer / doctor), to be vegetarian and defend the choice (Africans who don't eat meat?!), to laugh at adults when they made fun of us, to dress differently and express ourselves, to be openly effeminate. To rebel.

(Not talk back—we weren't suicidal!)

For a long time, only white beauty was valued, so our mothers wanted us to have straight hair and stay out of the sun. Suddenly, my generation started to embrace our Afro Arab looks. Some of us had big, round, juicy butts, and the dresses at the all-female weddings would accentuate them, girls proudly dropping Beyonce's or Jennifer Lopez's name if an aunt tried to ridicule them. Boys were growing their afros out, to the despair of their fathers. There were piercings popping up all over the show, more piercings than were visible to the eye. Girls were embracing their natural curls and not allowing themselves to be forced into the salon's chair to blow-dry them straight for Eid. We would come back from holidays proudly glowing with deliciously accentuated melanin.

The cousin who was as camp as a row of pink taffeta tents was turning this "shame" into his livelihood. The rich ladies in town would exclusively wear dresses designed by him in his atelier.

And one older cousin left her husband and opened a shelter for abused women. This was such a maverick, gangster thing to do, the inference being that she left her husband because of his abuse and intended to help others in the same seemingly inescapable situation. She never denounced him or admitted anything, because we don't expose men for their depravity and corruption, lest it reflect badly on *us* somehow, but her actions were an audacious and damning testimony.

I am proud of them all.

These black sheep, me included, we are the only reason our family tree doesn't rot from the inside from inertia. We make sure that stagnation doesn't take root. We are the ones who challenge rules and traditions. We make sure that the tree blossoms with every new season and generation, with our bold ideas and our rebellious ways. A tree wants to remain constant, though, and a Black Sheep's path will always be fraught with criticism, judgement, and even rejection. But we are vital to the continuation of our species, by making new branches thrive and fresh flowers bloom.

•

Our parents were wonderful, but ridiculous. 'Because I said so' being a genuine answer to a question. Or 'I'll give you a reason to cry' when you're blatantly already crying.

The hypocrisy was also strong in their generation. They scolded us that we should dress modestly and follow Quranic teachings, when we had *all* seen the '60s and '70s photos of them in Brighton clubs wearing miniskirts and holding suspicious looking cocktail glasses. They had their arms around each other. They had afros, and wore faded flared jeans, and tight t-shirts. They looked like a jovial gang, the kind you'd want to hang out with. They were refugees ripped from their homeland, so they were trying on a new culture for size, and it looked *good* on them.

They seemed to get on with life, never pining too much for the islands, considering the horrific way they were ousted. They were free and they were going to enjoy their freedom. Even when they congregated once more in Oman, a family displaced but not disheartened, they got together for *tarab* musical evenings—a blend of East African and Arabic music with sometimes risqué call and response lyrics, judging by the whooping and hollering. And we were amazed by home videos of their dance moves in the '80s.

This was before the rhythms of Quran recitations took over the sounds of the oud and the synth, and the kangas that were wrapped around their undulating hips were washed, ironed, and wrapped around their heads. Suddenly the weddings they used to celebrate together as a Family, they now celebrated in two separate venues, divided by gender.

I'm not sure who among my aunts and uncles started the wave of religious zeal, waged a war on dancing, a crusade on physical contact, and the absolute excommunication of the miniskirt. With advancing age, they became more conservative, perhaps knowing they now lived in a Muslim country and having respect for its dress code, or maybe understanding that death was looming ever nearer and wanting to be closer to God. But how did they go from trying on their new English swinging '60s culture to this unreasonable, unbending piety and judgement?

They tried on those mantles, but they demand that we cannot, and they punish us for experimenting in exactly the same way that they did. Surely they remember what it's like to be immature, inquisitive, and impulsive!

When pressed on their hypocrisy, they always said, 'We know better now', to which I would reply, 'Can I also please learn at my own pace?'

They would say that they don't want us to make the same mistakes that they made, and that they were trying to guide us on the Right Path.

It would confuse and infuriate me, because I was born in the West. I wasn't taught this Old Country culture because, in a way, they'd left a lot of it behind on the island to die in the revolution with relatives, friends, and neighbours.

They didn't teach us our language. They didn't teach us a true identity. Yet, when they suddenly picked up their old traditions and customs, they expected us to simply accept and follow suit.

Things you can get beaten for:

Talking back to an elder.
Crying while being beaten.
Crying without getting beaten.
Not crying while being beaten.
Asking not to be beaten.
Putting padding down your pants before a beating.
Crying while getting your hair braided.
Not saying thank you to your elder, after the pain of getting your hair braided.
Talking back to an elder.
Not greeting an elder.
Not saying goodbye to an elder.
Not standing when an elder walks in.
Sitting when elders are standing.
Talking when an elder is talking.
Not talking when an elder talks to you.
Talking back to an elder.
Fonya'ing or kissing your teeth.
Complaining about having to play with strangers' children who aren't your age.
Singing at the table.
Not finishing your food.

Complaining about your food.

Saying you don't eat meat.

Talking back to your elder (specifically, 'Well, you should send the food to Ethiopia, then').

Comparing your house to your friend's house.

Saying that your mum's burgers aren't as good as McDonald's.

Making noise inside.

Not going out to play.

Making noise outside.

Staying up late.

Crying coz you're tired.

9.42 p.m.

Two aunts are arguing in the corridor with Lolly about my possessions. One aunt is saying she should take all my clothes out of my cupboard immediately and she will send them to our poor relatives in Zanzibar. She says this should all be done before my mum gets here from London, so that Mama doesn't have to deal with the heartache of looking at all the clothes I will never wear again.

In a sense my aunts are being doubly considerate—to my mum and to our relatives—but once again they are being quite opinionated and stubborn about getting their way. However, Lolly stands in their path, and as politely as possible, tells them it isn't their business to remove things without consulting an immediate family member first.

'Mtchewwwww (teeth kissing), what do you think we are, if not immediate family?' dismisses one aunt.

Lolly is still polite (how does she do it?) when she agrees with them, but insists that my mum should make that decision herself.

The same aunt scoffs and says, 'Ha, anyway, her clothes are probably not right to send to Zanzibar. They are probably all mzungu clothes, short skirts and whatnot that she was wearing abroad.'

The second aunt agrees, clearly amused. 'After all, she was probably playing about there in Edinburgh, not studying properly! Why else did she come back?'

'Ah, who knows what any of these kids get up to over there?'

'*Wallahi*, it's better to keep them right here with us, where we can watch them.'

•

Right there in my uncle's basement was where Fido Dido introduced us to heroin.

While Fido's round-bottomed fiancée from Mombasa was
preparing for her wedding by being taught by her *somo* (a close
aunt) how to please her husband sexually, he was teaching us
how to smoke heroin up from a piece of tin foil with a cut-up
McDonald's straw. The day he got it out, this little baggy of brown
powder, we were all intrigued, but I was nervous. I didn't think
I should poke my head any further down the rabbit hole. I was
already praying furiously for forgiveness for other things. Did
I really need something else to atone for?

Adel convinced me that he was going to be there for me and
would protect me.

And I only had to try it once to say that I had done it,

and Fido Dido had already tried it

and knew what he was doing

and it was a safe environment

and when would I ever get this chance again

and didn't I always say that I wanted to experience all life
had to offer

and suck the marrow out of life

and...

I agreed.

That shit hit me hard. I puked the first time. It wasn't pretty.
I crawled to the toilet and the retching made me so dizzy I saw
stars. Beautiful stars that kept moving away from me, constantly
eluding me, like the meaning of life.

Then as I sat on the bathroom floor, it happened.

I felt a Euphoric Nothing. Which sounds like an oxymoron, like an Empty Bliss.

An Ecstatic Void.

It was what I had tried to find in the anaesthesia of hash.

The lines between the tiles on the floor stretched up onto the walls and onto the ceiling and into infinity. I saw their journey, but I didn't focus on it, and although I travelled on the journey with those lines, I didn't care about them.

This was the feeling I had been searching for. If you want to numb The Pain, then there is no alternative. You put your head back and close your eyes and let life pass, let time tick by in a shrouded paralysis, soaring far above any of your dramas, so far above that you can't remember them, see them, or care about them. Surrounded by clouds, untouchable and fuzzy.

Sinking so low, cushioned by the warmth of the earth as it wraps itself around you, where pain can't find you.

The spiritual exhale felt like a mini eternity.

Despite puking that first time, I did it again a few times, with some of the others, as often as Fido had a stash. We looked forward to those times, urgently asking him when he was going to get his hands on more. When we got the text messages, we would gather, excited, at Adel's house. We were hooked.

They would play music or talk to each other, but I had my own way of getting high. I shut everyone else out. Like my own version of meditation.

I would roll my head back and fill my eyes with the blank canvas of the ceiling that would throb and swell before my unfocused eyes.

Music would play, and I would see the notes on the ceiling, and suddenly I WAS the notes, swirling around the canvas like a dancer or a piece of chiffon in the breeze. But without any of the effort.

I wanted to be music notes. Or a dancer. Or a piece of fucking material.

Anything but me.

This foray into my hard-core *Trainspotting* lifestyle only went on for a few months. I had become more listless, more aggravated and, according to my parents, more churlish (not their word).

This was the year when Mamma Mia came to Oman for Ramadhan as usual, and we stayed up most of the night, watching *Sex and the City* reruns. She noticed that I was more spaced out and detached than usual. I admitted to her that I smoked weed, but not about the heroin. No way!

And that's when she turned off Carrie Bradshaw. Yup, turned Carrie OFF.

And that's when I knew I was about to get a serious talking-to.

And that's when she told me I was wasting my life. She said I could smoke weed, but at least wait till Ramadhan was over. Have some respect!

And that's when I realised that I could escape this Life, by creating a Life. A Life that I *wanted*. A life where I was smart, where I could choose my future. I could pursue photography, educate myself, not be average, not settle for a small life. Not settle for a man who, despite all his protests to the contrary, chose conformity.

I realised that there was no merit in mediocrity. I was only punishing myself with my apathy. I mean, why *wouldn't* I want to be extraordinary? In the Family, anyone who strove to do something remarkable was teased and ridiculed for daring to think that they were better than everyone else. I didn't think I was better. But I didn't want to be the same.

I was so far behind in building that Life. I had to start now!

And because it wouldn't be easy to build it, I stopped visiting Adel's basement, only smoked with Mamma Mia when she visited, and never touched heroin again.

Until yesterday, I guess?

.

Now I think of Fido, I think I remember seeing him yesterday.

His image is coming into focus, in fuzzy flashes.

Yes. He was there. We hung out together.

And he had heroin, and he gave it to me... I think. But everything else is blurry...

There was something else.

Something *really* cool, but also really NOT cool.

Yes...

Fuck. Fido Dido kissed me.

9.45 p.m.

Fuck, Fido kissed me.

It's interesting being a fly on this wall. Watching mourners surreptitiously check Facebook or make a show of reciting the Quran too loudly. Those who thrive on being flustered and others who are quietly helpful and want no recognition for it. Those who are gathering to talk about me, desperate to drag me back into the world of the living for just a little longer. And those who I don't even recognise.

There were tongues. Hot breath and tongues!

And then there's Sara. She hates the fuss, the tears, crocodile and otherwise. She's almost disdainful of the wails and chest beatings. She's resentful of having to comfort others, when she was the one who walked in on her big sister's lifeless body. She hates them right now, and because she knows that she can't show it, she is hiding out in our bathroom, sitting on the rug under the extractor fan and wondering what the hell I was thinking. I wish I could help her.

•

There were few places to hide from the Family growing up. They were at our school, at all the functions, weddings, Eid, in our home at all hours. Even on our holidays.

I have to admit though, we were very lucky to have some epic summer holidays.

We weren't rich, but Baba's sister, Aunty Baby was. And she insisted that we be among the several chosen families to keep her company on her annual cruise. We did the Caribbean and Mediterranean twice each, and the Baltic once.

Another of Baba's siblings lived in the States, so we stayed with them a couple of times too, with my favourite cousins Natasha (Tish) and Tania, who were a year older than me and Sara respectively. They came on one of the Caribbean cruises with us one year. Their parents stayed in Texas to work, so essentially my dad was in charge of his nieces. Standard practice.

We had an absolute ball that year! The adults had their own agenda, going to salsa classes (Baba was the star pupil), taking in the shows, making the most of the buffets, and going on silly, overcrowded excursions on every island and buying overpriced souvenirs.

Tish and I sat by the pool, her in a string bikini, me in a T-shirt over my one-piece, checking out all the talent. Teenage boys, almost too old for family holidays, sullenly lounging and reading. Young European buddies, taking a summer break Stateside, wearing tiny banana hammocks. The Entertainment staff, young, fit dancers from the show, walking around being helpful. We rated them all, from one to ten. From shag to throw overboard. From terrible kisser to great in bed.

At this point, of course, I had never really been kissed, which Tish swore would change this summer. I was sweet sixteen, and that was long enough to wait! She was only a year older than me, but her experience and confidence made me feel like the backward country cousin.

I didn't think I could go through with it, so while I was procrastinating about choosing an appropriate candidate, she set her sights on a gorgeous, strong-jawed German, Norbert, who was on holiday with his friend, Norbert.

I shit you not.

They were more than happy to keep us company and swim with us (it was safe to flirt around the pool because the adults wouldn't wear swimsuits and get in the water with a bunch of strangers).

Norbert 1 was completely smitten with Tish: her brown skin, boobs so pert they were practically earrings, her confident laugh, and the way she kept touching his oiled-up body. Irresistible. He was up for a holiday romance with this fun girl with the charming American accent.

Norbert 2 was sweet. Certainly not the Adonis that Norbert 1 was, but he was easygoing and chatty, and so interested in the history of Oman and Zanzibar that I had to do some Google research overnight, to get a more accurate handle on it and speak with more impressive authority the following day.

We met up every day and swam, walked around the small city on water, chatting. I wasn't romantically interested in him, and I don't think he was in me either.

One day, the folks got off on one of the islands, as usual, and we stayed on board. Tish and Norbert 1 went off on their own, so Norbert 2 and I hung out.

I don't know if he did it just to be a good wingman, taking one for the team, keeping me distracted while Norbert 1 made out with Tish, but he snuck me into the theatre, abandoned during the daytime, and held my hand as he leaned me against a wall, moved in close to my face, and gently touched his lips to mine. I could taste swimming pool and spearmint gum, and warm masculine Germanness (not a word). His breath was so hot, and I could feel his breath more than his lips. I didn't move away. Well, the wall was behind me. Instead, I parted my lips slightly, hoping that my breath was also, at the very worst, swimming pool and mint.

That was my first kiss.

He breathed, 'Ach, Summer,' into my mouth with his funny and suddenly very sexy accent and I just about flooded my basement. I didn't even realise that my basement *could* flood like that!

Then the way that he touched my face, before introducing a little tongue.

'A Little Tongue, meet Summer.'

'Summer, meet A Little Tongue.'

'Hellooooooo, Little Tongue.'

I might have overenthusiastically put my fingers in his damp hair and begged for a Little More Tongue.

It was a magical four minutes, with both of us barely coming up for air. I triumphantly thought that I actually got the longer straw with Norbert 2. I actually genuinely liked him!

Of course, this beautiful moment was short-lived.

The problem was a member of the Family. This particular member had also stayed on the ship and had seen me and Norbert 2 sneak into the theatre.

So, while I was in the shower that evening, getting ready for dinner, smiling to myself and touching my lips, reliving my amazing first kiss, my father was getting briefed by the Snitch. Of course, the Snitch had no idea what I was doing in the theatre. I could have been testing the acoustics, or I could have been giving a blowjob. My father had no idea either.

I want to believe that my father would have dismissed it. I was generally a well-behaved daughter; moody, yes, a little contrary, perhaps, but hardly recalcitrant. I was not a wild girl or a boy chaser. I didn't even want to wear makeup, and he knew that. I want to believe so badly that Baba wanted to ignore it. But he had the judging eyes of his Family on him now, and they were waiting for him to set an example in discipline.

My poor dad. He had his wild days back in his youth, and now he was expected to fall in line on everyone else's road to pious fervour, and march at the same pace. And he had a lot of catching up to do. This was his opportunity to show them that he was now in step. It was Abraham's chance to show that he could sacrifice Isaac for the greater good.

So, from the classic Hypocrite's Playbook of "Do as I say, not as I did", he called me to Aunty Baby's luxury cabin and, in front of his siblings, took off his belt and beat me.

I never really forgave him for that. And he knew it.

But he was brought up to never admit culpability, so instead of bridging the gap with me, he doubled down.

While my mum would tell me to condition my wild and crunchy curls, my dad started telling me to cover them. One of his siblings had said that it was the pious thing to do, and that all of *his* four daughters, all devout girls bound for Heaven themselves, were doing so.

(One of them was taking it up the shitter.)

My dad and I struggled from that day on the cruise, until yesterday.

A year or so after the Cruise Crisis, I was sent to fetch something for Baba from their dressing room.

I wonder if other kids sometimes feel like a courier service for their parents. It's like they feed you and change your nappies for the first few years and can't wait for you to become old enough to return the favour in fetching and carrying.

Mama's side of the wardrobe was like a rainbow explosion with a few black abayas at the end of the rail. Baba's side was all regulation white *dishdashas,* gleaming so white they looked almost blue. I often wondered how he avoided getting sand or sweat or food on them. I never saw a single stain on his perfectly washed and ironed *thobes.* As I was rifling through their drawers, I came across two little camel bone boxes, similar to the one in which I keep my hash stash. Each one had a label with Baba's neat handwriting: 'Summer' and 'Sara'.

I opened mine to find my baby teeth, cleaned and polished smooth, tiny little pearls lying on a cotton wool bed. He'd kept them this whole time. The Tooth Fairy had been really generous at the time, I remember, and, when I discovered that other girls didn't get as much in return for their teeth, I believed Baba when he explained that my teeth were special.

This tiny box saddened me. I wanted to hug him and talk to him and be close to him. But I guess Baba passed on his stubborn genes to me, and I couldn't soften my heart enough to say anything, to start that conversation, in case it took a turn that I was unable to navigate. In case he turned it on me and what kind of a disobedient, disappointing daughter I was and,

and,

and...

Sometimes I would remember this box and try and understand Baba and feel so much affection for him. I would try and have empathy for his tender, loving side, and the reasons he couldn't show it more.

Sometimes I would think of it and know that he loved the idea of his cute daughters, not so much the reality of his growing women. And that is why he only treasured the baby parts of us and put them away in a sentimental little box.

Baba was a big fan of Muhammad Ali when he was younger. He loved his arrogance, his showboating, his skill. Something about the way he pronounced himself the prettiest and the best, amused and resonated with my father. He also loved that a famous man at the top of his game had converted to Islam. And he loved his stance in refusing to fight in Vietnam in a war that had nothing to do with him, despite costing him his title. Muhammad Ali was unapologetic. Like Baba. During one of my protests about having to cover my hair, Baba told me a story about his hero.

Muhammad Ali's daughter had come in dressed quite scantily, and he said to her that Allah had put everything that was precious away from eyes. All valuable things were hidden under layers: diamonds deep in the ground, pearls in protective shells at the bottom of the sea, gold in mines under layers of dirt. Ali told his daughter that her body was more precious than diamonds, pearls, or gold. And it should also be covered.

I was very quiet.

I was actually embarrassed because it made total sense to me for the first time. My body was precious. And it wasn't for just anyone to see. Someone had to earn it, work hard to uncover my treasure.

Why were the adults in our family unable to teach like that? Why was it always a lecture, or Do as I say, or Because I said so? A gentle parable, an empathetic cautionary tale; they would have made the difference between us hearing defensively and *really* listening.

And I was also embarrassed because for a moment, listening to that tale, I wished that Muhammad Ali was my father.

Baba really struggled with the idea of me leaving for Scotland. He put his foot down. His daughter was not going to leave him and the Family, her culture, and his house! His show of power came up against resistance from all three of his women, so he changed tactics and tried to get me to go to Sultan Qaboos University, with a bribe of a cute little car.

Mama took my side in a loud but short-lived argument, and it was settled.

Was it a control thing?

Was it because he would miss me?

Was it coz he knew the potential mischief I could get up to over there—the same things he got up to?

Was it d) All of the above?

He became quieter and more withdrawn as my leaving date approached. We avoided each other. I avoided him because I didn't want a lecture before I left. I like to think he avoided me because the Cruise Crisis hurt him as much as the belt hurt me.

The day came for me to fly via Dubai to Edinburgh, and my suitcases had caused untold drama. Lucy, Sara, and I sat on the cases to try and close them. We distributed everything between cases, carry-ons, handbags, and the clothes I was wearing down to an exact science. I was going to get away without having to pay excess luggage, so when he silently handed me a package, I almost cried with irritation.

He said, 'Be careful, my daughter', which had me really nervous opening it.

Inside was my very own Leica Rangefinder.

It was such an expensive piece of equipment! My dream camera! How did he know? How did he find one? How could he afford it? For ME!

I threw my arms around him without thinking, and almost let go immediately, but he held on to me and leaned his head gently onto mine.

The truth is I felt really stiff and a bit awkward inside the embrace, but I let him hold me because I think he needed to.

Maybe it was his version of an apology. And my version of accepting it.

10.04 p.m.

People are milling in and out of the spare room, touching my body, saying farewell to me. Some of them are starting to leave our house to go home and rest. Taking their maids and their thermoses. Taking their opinions and their grief.

I am ignoring them to focus on the conveyor belt of memories.

And while on the memory of kissing Norbert...

Fido!

I'm getting flashes of us kissing last night.

It was amazing. It was really only the second snog of my life, and a snog from Fido was what I have wanted for eight years. But I'm confused because he's married, and although I know that clearly doesn't stop people from kissing, it still sits badly with me.

And another thing: It was sexy and exciting, but it was uncomfortable.

Not personally awkward, but *physically* uncomfortable.

Fuck. What was he thinking?

What was I thinking?

I was at Adel's last night. Yes! I remember that.

I'd gone to my cousin's house for a smoke.

Fido was there. We were drinking. Why were we drinking? Fuck, I don't drink anymore! Bad experiences...

Maybe because I was so nervous to be in his presence? I hadn't seen him for ages, and I must have wanted some Dutch courage. What happened last night?!

I actually admitted to Sara, long after the fact, my brief foray into the world of heroin.

We shared a bedroom, so she was there when I pretended to be sick for a week while my body was getting used to the idea of never doing it again. She remembered that week well. She had been so worried about my fever as she lay in her bed next to mine, listening to me curse.

We chose to share a bedroom, even when we were both grown. The truth was, it was me who insisted. I needed her near me. I could tolerate being alone in my head, but not alone when I slept. At night, before I could doze off, the voices started and I had to drown them out. I used to listen to music and wake up tangled in my headphones, or read books and fall asleep with them on my chest, or beg her to tell me stories till I dropped off. Mostly, I would cry, as silently as possible.

Sara was the only person who soothed the voices.

I think Sara was happy with our arrangement; we could stay holed up in our space talking for hours. If you asked me for a sample conversation, however, I would be stuck. I think we squandered a trillion words between us, idly wondering about boys, casually imagining what we would do with a billion dollars, playing word games between Swahili and English—we loved word games, puns and homonyms, portmanteaux like MediterrArabian; nothing of any consequence whatsoever. Trying on clothes, designing dream houses, applying face masks and nail varnish, doing sit-ups and laughing at each other's farts.

I think she liked our arrangement, because often I would wake up and she would be curled up in my bed, her ringlets tickling my face. I loved her more than sunshine on those mornings.

I tried to describe heroin to her, without glamourising it or letting her know how fantastic it really was to feel complete escape and liberty, but rather how I had puked and how addictive it is. I told her about doing pills in Scotland, and how amazing it was the first time and how horrible it had been the second and final time. I wanted to be as honest as I could, so she wouldn't want to try any of it.

She has seen me puke. She's picked my wasted body up from Adel's. She's seen my eyes glazed and witnessed my mornings, suffering through comedowns.

My death will either scare her off drugs forever, or drive her to them.

10.26 p.m.

In a breathless moment between serving coffee, receiving condolences, and showing people the direction of Mecca for prayers, Mamma Mia squeezes past the cousins who have gathered on our beds, and finds Sara hiding in the bathroom.

She locks the door behind her and looks her in the eyes.

'Honey, are you okay? It's okay not to be okay, you know', she says. Oh no, she's about to cry again. Sara is still as composed as a perfect symphony and she tells Mamma Mia that she is sad, but she is fine.

'I think that maybe you're in shock, Babyface.'

Mamma Mia always had nicknames for us. From Honey and Baby, to Sugar Plum Bums and a very exaggerated Dahhhhhling.

My favourite was Pussycat.

'MaMi', Sara began. When she was younger, she couldn't even say Mamma Mia, so she used the contraction MaMi, which I thought was adorable. I was jealous I didn't invent it myself.

'MaMi, Summer was my entire life. I will never be the same again, I know that. Everything from now on will be like one long winter. I know that's corny, but that's how cold it feels in my heart.'

Mamma Mia is crying and waiting for the tears from Sara.

She'll wait a while.

'The truth is, MaMi, as much as she was the clown in the family, Summer was unhappy. She was almost consumed by her sadness, and I will only admit this to you, but I'm actually glad that she's free from it. She used to be so funny and happy, remember? You two would stay awake all night in London with your giggling. But here in Oman, something started torturing her, and it seemed that it was exhausting being her, like she was putting on a show all day, you know? She used to cry herself to sleep at night, did you know that?'

Mamma Mia clearly did not know that, and it makes her sob.

'It was like, at night the show was over and she could finally be herself, and whoever that was, was in a lot of pain. I used to climb into bed with her after she'd finally dropped off to sleep and spoon her from behind. It broke my heart to hear her cry like that, and since she wouldn't tell me what was wrong, the only thing I could do was hold her. She never cried when I held her.

'I don't know what happened to her to make her so depressed. I wish she felt she could have told me. If we ever got too close to the topic, she'd act the clown again and the mask would be firmly back in place. Do you know, MaMi? Do you know what happened to her?'

'I don't know. She mentioned something once, but...' Mamma Mia pauses. 'I just don't know, Sara. Why did this happen? Why?'

'I don't know,' muses Sara, 'but if we truly believe that God knows best, then we have to believe that He took Summer for the best. We don't have His knowledge or wisdom, so we just need to have faith. Maybe Summer's fate going forward would have been worse than death. Or maybe she would have struggled or been miserable all her life, and God loves her too much to want that for her. And so do I. Everything happens for a reason. "Perhaps you hate a thing and it is good for you, and perhaps you love a thing and it is bad for you", 'she quotes the Quran. 'God knows, and we don't.'

Mamma Mia looks at her in surprise and admiration. 'Even in grief you are gracious and good,' she says and kisses her on the forehead.

'Ha! Summer would have enjoyed that alliteration! I am sad, of course, MaMi. She's left a hole in my life. A Summer-size hole. The hole that Summer left. The whole summer is gone. Ha, sorry. She would have enjoyed that word play.' She smiles sadly. 'Oh MaMi, I've been thinking all day since I found her, that I don't know who I am without her. Have I lost my meaning now that I've lost her?'

Mamma Mia can't answer. She just holds her stoic little niece and cries.

10.51 p.m.

I can't believe that I'm saying this, but we are genuinely having a nice time. Sara has joined my cousins in our bedroom, and they are sitting cross-legged, four to a bed, reminiscing. One cousin has a flask of coffee Patron tequila and is passing it around to the girls who are into that, getting them giggly and sentimental.

They hold Sara close. There are the odd tears (not from Sara, obvs), lots of holding hands and arm rubs, but sometimes they are tears of laughter and back slaps as we remember ridiculous tales of Muscat life.

Nadia and Sara are regaling the others about the size of my balls. I just refused to be hassled by people.

Young boys that drive dangerously too close to your car, trying to get your attention going 100 km down the highway, holding up signs with their telephone numbers on them.

I would pretend to be writing a number down, and as they looked eagerly into our car, I would slowly lift my middle finger up to the window—very unladylike and, in fact, punishable by law. But so is tailgating women.

I once gestured to one car to follow us. They couldn't believe their luck! They followed us all the way to the Intercontinental Hotel, where I drove up the ramp to the two-lane valet and stopped next to a tour bus. Their car was right behind mine, and suddenly a taxi pulled up behind them. When I was satisfied that they were completely blocked in, I got out of the car, Sara's little face pressed up against the back window, terrified of what I was about to do.

I banged on their window, screaming at them, demanding to know why they were following three single women on the road. Who had raised them, what did they want from us, and why were they endangering our lives?! Security came over to help. Tourists on the bus looked over curiously, taking pictures. The boys were mortified and looked away from me, as if ignoring me would make me disappear—a tactic they assumed would work as it has for centuries.

My cousins giggled hard. 'No way!' and 'Yes, that's so Summer!'

'Oh, the drama!'

'Haha yes! Summer's favourite saying: Oh, the drama!'

Another story was about me picking up a piece of paper with a phone number that had been thrown at my feet when I was at the mall with my mum. I picked it up, feigning ignorance, and called to Mama, 'Mama! These young gentlemen have dropped this note for you! Would you like me to get them back here to speak to you? Yoo hoo! Boys! Did you want my mother to have this note?' The boys had disappeared.

My cousins guffawed. They found everything a little funnier than it actually was. Like a desperate laughter, almost hysterical.

'Summer just didn't care! We could all learn from her fierceness. We should all wish to be so brave.'

I am shocked and touched to hear this. I spent so long being pissed off and sarcastic and being TOLD that I was miserable and petulant, that I never once considered that it had turned me into anything but a royal pain in everyone's ass. I didn't realise that I had become a passionate, un-fuck-with-able force. I protected my little sister like a savage, and I had learned how to start sticking up for myself.

'Hahaha, with her big words, she knew how to be sarcastic to any uncle and shut them up without being openly rude!'

'Not even big words! She always used to say to Aunty Khola, I hope your day is as nice as you are! While smiling! The smile threw Aunty right off!'

Hahaha yeah, I remember that one! Aunty Khola was a bitch.

'Remember when Malik was making fun of me? God, I was near tears, and she stood up for me. I'll never forget, she said, You want a battle of wits, but you came embarrassingly unarmed.'

'Haha! She said once, You want a battle of wits, but you only brought your brain!'

'Or, I'd agree with you, but then we'd both be wrong!'

'She loved saying to Uncle B, See you next Tuesday, even though we weren't going to! He never got it!'

'I don't get it,' says Iman.

Everyone laughs at her until Sara kindly explains. 'C U Next Tuesday? C. U. N. T.?'

It still takes Iman a few seconds.

'That bitch used to tell me that my intellect was *literally* unmatched,' says Iman.

We all piss ourselves, coz we all agree.

'How about her weird, cryptic Facebook statuses?' Lots of chortles of agreement.

'She wrote one today, about her twisted mind. Did anyone see it?' A pause. 'Guys, do you think she was okay?'

'I don't know. Some things she wrote were really macabre, like she was already preparing for death.'

'One world to another, another world to one.'

'How about, I have to feel alive, even if it kills me?'

They are all silent for a moment. They swallow uncomfortably.

Iman attempts to lighten the mood. 'Do you remember the birds you had? What did Summer name them?'

Sara replies, 'Yes! Uncle Mo bought them for us. Summer named them Shut-Up and Mind-Your-Own-Business.'

'Yes, that's right! My mum's face when she asked Summer the names, it was like she'd been slapped!'

They talk over each other, relieved at the diversion, and resume their track of reminiscing and cackling.

An aunt pops her head into the room and scolds us for laughing so loudly.

'Have some respect! This is a funeral, not a wedding!' and then promptly leaves.

They look around, chastised, and then crack up laughing even louder.

I'm so glad they are enjoying my memories. I'm glad that I made them laugh while I was alive, and I'm really glad that I am making them laugh now.

This is a good legacy. The best.

I genuinely feel like a part of this circle, and I think—no, I *know* they can feel me too.

Like when we were all on the prayer mat earlier and we all laughed at the memory of Grandad's farts. Or when Mamma Mia burst out laughing when I was so amused by her histrionics. I can accidentally project my feelings into the room, and we can all share them.

It's like I'm here, but so much more than here. Like a guru's higher plane of enlightenment, when you can start affecting things around you. Taking over the power of your body's health, your mind's mood, and even inanimate objects or other people.

This is the sense of complete—

Oh fuck...

Here he comes...

11.11 p.m.

I can't believe he had the audacity to come to my funeral.

Well, yes I can. As an uncle, he is culturally bound. His igno-miny should have kept his arse at home, but duty surpasses deed in this Family, I guess.

I am about to test my limited power, and I focus really hard and I manage to make the lights flicker, weakly at first, as he walks past each one down the hallway to the back bedroom.

It's fucking working!

Everyone's reaction as he passes fills me with glee. They all gasp and whisper *SubhanAllah* (Glory to God) as the lights flash on and off supernaturally. We believe in jinn, in angels, in things we don't understand. And although no one comprehends why the lights are flickering, or even that it has anything to do with him, the fact that it's filling HIM with dread makes me... I don't know...

Vindictive.

Vindicated.

Powerful.

Poltergeist!

Mamma Mia is standing at the end of the hallway as he walks toward her. She is completely still. She sees the lights and she knows it's me causing them to flicker. Everything in her mind goes dark along the corridor, all the mourners disappear, the Quran reading fades into silence, and all she sees in the lights that dim and illuminate, is Uncle B's face coming toward her.

She knows.

•

It was the summer holidays of 2000, after my dad announced our move.

I was sent ahead of the rest of the family from England to Oman, to stay with Baba's youngest sister, Aunty Zaina, her husband, and their two daughters.

I don't blame my parents for sending me away. My dad had to see out his contract in England, I had to start a new school term in Oman, and my aunt and uncle were the perfect choice as temporary guardians. My dad doted on his little sister, who in turn doted on me. She had studied in England, which made her perhaps a little more sympathetic to the huge move we were making. Her daughters were around my age and would attend the same school in September.

It was a good choice really. In their position, I may have made the same choice for my daughter.

And then there's Aunty Zaina's husband.

Uncle B was kind and funny. He told corny knock-knock jokes and took us for ice cream. In a culture where children were to be seen and not heard, he had an air about him that made me feel that, unlike most adults, he remembered what it was like to be a child.

He was an artist and an amateur photographer.

He would take me into his office slash studio where walls and easels were filled with his framed watercolours of Omani scenes, palm trees against burnished horizons, clouds bleeding into the sunset; whispery colours of mountains in mist, blending into the sky.

Also on the walls and scattered on desks, tables, and the sofa were his photographs of *wadis*, oases in the desert valleys, with late afternoon light streaming through palm fronds and dappling on the water like a Monet painting. There were tender, candid portraits of his children looking pensive, and black and whites of local old Omanis with creased faces and toothless smiles.

I knew every detail of the paintings and photos. I would lose myself inside the landscapes, imagine the coolness of the water, the thick afternoon sun on my back.

There were shelves of paints and coloured pencils, and rows of blank canvases on the floor behind another cabinet that held all his photography equipment, lenses, light boxes, reflectors, tripods, coloured gels.

I was absolutely fascinated by it all, and he allowed me access any time I wanted.

He also had a darkroom in his house, and I was intrigued by the solutions, the trays, the dim, red light. No adult would usually allow a child access to such grown-up stuff.

His daughters weren't at all interested in his hobby, so I felt like I was the protégé he had always wanted.

And so he becomes my mentor, taking me out to the garden to take pictures of the flowers and trees teaching me about light and composition. He flatters my photographs, my eye and my talent, even when I suspect him of being disingenuous. He encourages me and suggests adjustments. I love the attention and the admiration while so far away from everyone I love. He thinks I am very witty, and we giggle at his jokes and at my jokes. He tells me how clever I am, and how pretty. Especially how pretty. We spend more and more time together; teaching, learning.

And then he turns off the lights in the darkroom, where he touches my fingers in the developing solution and links and intertwines his fingers with mine, stroking them, sloshing liquid around in the tray. He comes closer from behind me and presses his chest onto my back gently yet urgently. He breathes hot air on my earlobes and nuzzles my neck while we examine the photos, which makes the baby hairs stand up on my arms, and he whispers conspiratorially, saying that I love it when he does that, don't I, and tickles me when I reply that it feels funny and tingly.

He wipes the solution off my hands and kisses my fingertips, slipping my fingers into his mouth and sucking on them, asking me to do the same to his fingers. He rewards me with little, sweet kisses on my shoulders, my forehead, my nose, my cheeks, my lips, slowly easing his tongue into my mouth. His tickling fingers start searching into my panties. He lifts me up on to his lap and massages my tiny body over my clothes, under my clothes, and sits me astride him pulling my baby hips against his crotch. Against him. Hard. Harder. It feels strange down there. He has taken control and I don't know what to do, so I just sit there until he groans, quietly – then louder – but never loud, and then he jerks a little and squeezes me and when he's still again, breathing hard like he's just run a long way, he says that I make him very happy. This new game seems weird, but I'm glad that someone likes me and is pleased with me, and that I make someone happy. I'm someone's favourite.

He never threatens or forces me. He is gentle, never mean or scary.

Everything seems like an organic idea. A natural part of our unique friendship. Our unique love.

And just like that, he created something he could never undo. An unbreakable bond between us.

He took a seven-year-old girl as his mistress.

He cheated on his wife with a baby.

And he made me complicit.

Yeah, this is really hard to think about, but I fucking had to live it. And what many will never understand is that I didn't know it was wrong at first. How was I to know? I was six when I was sent to his house! I don't remember what I was aware of when I was that age – did I even know how to spell properly, braid my own hair, make my own bed?

And oh, how seamlessly he slithered from innocent games to abuse. Where was the line? I didn't know at what point it stopped being fun and became a crime. I didn't know the difference and I thought it was all part of a game and I enjoyed it.

Yes, that sounds awful, but I enjoyed the affection, the attention. I felt special and wanted.

That's why I tried to make sure that we had "photography days". I designed it so that we went into his darkroom, where the photographs were quickly forgotten. And I essentially orchestrated my own abuse. Made it so easy for him to have me. Made it so easy to betray his wife, betray his kids, my parents.

Me.

I was barely seven, alone, lonely, invisible; yet he saw me.

And he would say,

'Don't tell your aunty, you know what they're all like,' and he would wag his finger and mimic their voices. 'Don't do this, don't do that!' and we would giggle.

Yes, I knew exactly what they were like.

My aunts were colourful and giving. And loud and crude. They were glamourous with their satin, shoulder-padded dresses, outdated by a decade. They were inseparable as siblings and yet envious of each other's small successes, like a son's graduation, a daughter's marriage to a wealthy man, a holiday or a promotion.

I admired them and feared them. Nothing was too much effort for them; they would give unconditionally but humiliate you in front of everyone with a tongue lashing. They would take someone else's child into their own homes and treat them as their own child, and also beat them for any wrongdoing, as they would their own child.

They were fierce like divas and spiteful like snakes.

I was terrified of their sheer magnitude.

They belched as they sat around babbling in Swahili over a confusing card game of *wahid wa siteen* (sixty-one), sipping sweet cardamom tea. I would look away embarrassed as the King and the Queen in the deck got "married" and the aunts ululated (not Word of the Day, part of my DNA) wildly, or when someone dropped the Jack with a dramatic flourish and it would "rape" the Queen from behind as they whooped and told the loser to enjoy the big cock.

Then they would laugh at my mortification and scold me.

'Don't be precious, little mzungu. What you have is no different to anyone else. Don't be proud of that young body, you will start drooping and farting uncontrollably before you know it!'

And the cackling would resume.

At other times, they would poke fingers near my face and then toward my crotch.

'You'd better keep your legs crossed. Good girls keep their legs crossed.'

I wasn't really sure why. Maybe because there were *dudus* in this new hot climate, insects that would crawl into your panties, so I should make sure they couldn't by crossing my legs.

Fuck, why couldn't they have just explained it? In our culture we are just not very good at talking about subjects that they consider taboo. Their half explanations were more dangerous than silence.

They go from calling your pussy your *susu* when you're potty training, to calling it something *e'eib*, shameful or forbidden, that should be hidden. Why??

Women are instructed to conduct themselves conservatively around men, because men's lustful nature is expected. But we aren't taught about their lasciviousness, and we aren't taught when to expect it. No sex education, no honest chat.

I wish they'd explained how much power there is behind that mighty, meaty triangle.

The Power to bring men and empires to their knees. The Power to launch a thousand ships.

I wish they'd explained how much potential regret.

The ecstasy and the disgrace.

I wish they'd explained why I would bleed one day. No one explained the point of it and sex ed was woefully absent.

I wish I had understood the reason behind the clitoris and its ONLY purpose.

I wish I hadn't felt the taboo and the weight of almost two thousand years in me. Or I wish that someone had told me the real truth. That it wasn't Eve's fault. That original sin was a Christian construct and that the patriarchy was man's fragile ego's attempt at retaining power. That would have made sense and may have allayed my guilt.

I didn't know that by "crossing my legs" they meant that I shouldn't let anyone—even a trusted husband, my trusted uncle—crawl up between them.

And then, years later, the chilling thought occurred to me: What if she knew the whole time? I certainly would be very suspicious of my husband spending hours in a darkroom with a little girl. Maybe she turned a blind eye and allowed him to continue having an affair with her niece, afraid of angering him, afraid of upsetting the order in her life, thrusting her and her daughters into the world to fend for themselves.

And so it remained Our Little Secret. Me and Uncle B.

And at first, him saying that we shouldn't tell anyone was A-okay by me. I liked having someone to bond with. All the Secret Stuff felt like inclusion, like a private gang of two. The secrecy actually made me feel more special. For several months.

When my parents arrived with young Sara, I'd try and ask to go back to his house, to "take pictures", but he'd always be shifty, be busy, pretend we didn't have a bond, and we lost our time together.

I felt rejected. And I felt bad about myself. The mixed messages were so confusing; flavour of the month and suddenly persona non grata. It could only be because I had done something wrong, and I couldn't get close enough to ask him what. What had I done? It must have been something awful.Unforgivable.

I blamed myself. And I became less sure of myself, withdrawn, a shrunken version of me. But that was just the start.

I guess I was around ten when I was watching a film and there was some kind of soft sex scene, and my parents freaked out, telling me not to look at the TV and that it wasn't for little girls, and things started to slowly dawn on me.

This had something to do with what the aunts had been saying about closing your legs, and your body, and your beauty. That only dirty girls open their legs, and not because insects had crawled up between them.

I pieced it all together with ever-growing horror, like an ink stain blotting out the clean space I had in my soul.

I realised what he had been doing to me. What *I* had been doing with him.

I have angels on my shoulders, but the devil between my legs.

And I hated them all. My aunts, for lecturing me instead of protecting me. For talking about bodies in abstract code but never explaining the real dangers. I hated my parents for sending me into a lion's den at the age of seven. I blamed them for not seeing that something wasn't right with me as I got older. And, of course, I hated him. For... fuck... everything. For his disgusting lust, for his gross tongue, for his illegal fingers, and most of all, for making me hate myself. That was the worst part. I hated myself for liking it. For wanting it. For instigating it. For being the youngest little slut to have ever lived.

I felt dirty. I felt so much shame. I felt more remorse than any ten-year-old should ever feel.

I cried.

I cried a lot.

I hid and I cried.

I used to wait till I could hear Sara snoring lightly at night, and then I would sob into my pillow until my body was so exhausted, it was dragged into slumber.

Then the tears stopped and the anger came. The bitterness and disdain.

I helped him do it to me, and I liked it, so it must mean that I was bad, dirty.

I wish I could cry now. I want to hold ten-year-old me. I want to tell her it wasn't her fault. I wish I could have known that then.

Everything might have turned out differently.

Suddenly, as this ten-year-old kid, I wanted to be rid of everything. I hated myself. I hated Oman. I hated photography. I stopped wanting to be the smart girl, whereas before I had strived for approval and admiration. I now knew that my desire for attention had landed me right here.

I stopped trying to learn Swahili and Arabic, languages I had started to associate with Them.

I didn't want to be around any aunts or any Family gatherings, in case he was there.

I hated it if anyone called me pretty! Fuck my looks! Isn't that what he liked? Isn't that what got me into trouble in the first place?

Even when I felt horny, I felt guilty. Did other pre-teens want to touch themselves and then hate themselves for allowing the lust to creep back in?

How about seventeen-year-olds? When they wanked, did they fantasize about inappropriate men—grotesque men—fondling them, groping them, fingering them?

I didn't fucking think so. I was an abomination, and I prayed literally until my dying day that I would be okay. That I would be forgiven.

In Islam, we believe that children go to heaven even if they have done wrong, since they were too innocent to know better. I would desperately pray and pray that I would die before I grew up, before puberty, before I became an adult.

The day I saw blood in my knickers, I mourned for my soul.

•

But now, thirteen years later, I can finally see it as it is. It wasn't my fault. Even the memory of his cloying, salacious whispers telling me that I wanted it, that I was such a sexy little girl, that I was irresistible, can't convince me now that it was my fault.

I feel powerful admitting this, there are no more secrets, and all I can hope for is that the abuse that I endured will be put on the Scales when I am being judged.

I lived life hating parts of myself, resenting my Family, the abusers and the protectors.

I wanted to be a good girl, but I had lived as a sinner and a liar.

And it lay heavy on me.

I have heard about people who self-harm. And I understand why they do.

Some people cut off their emotions so effectively and make themselves so numb to everything, the only way to feel again is to slice into themselves.

Or everything hurts so much emotionally, the only way to drown that out is to hurt physically.

But it was just never for me. I didn't want to hurt myself. I didn't want to *cut* out the part of myself that caused me anxiety.

I felt everything so keenly that I just wanted to numb myself.

So I turned to weed, and for that short time, heroin. I didn't panic when I was high; I didn't think, I didn't feel. But it didn't solve anything.

When I was around twelve, I heard the term "the wolves at your door", which was a terrifying image, especially after a childhood diet of fairy tales: large, shaggy-haired wolves towering over little piggies' houses, huffing and puffing, hungrily demanding to be let in, snarling lips curled over salivating fangs, swallowing grannies up whole only to be axed open by a woodcutter.

The wolves at your door...

But I wondered what you do when the wolves aren't at the door but are in your *head*? Where do you hide?

When the phone call is coming from *inside* the house, when the murderer is in your safe space. Where do you run?

What do you do when the enemy is your own voice? That Voice that kept telling me I was filthy and no good. That it was my fault.

What do you do when the nightmare is part of your body? The corruption that multiplies.

Cut it out.

Numb it.

Shut it the fuck up.

Every Family function became torture, facing them all, having to kiss his hand in greeting, knowing what we both knew. Knowing where that hand had been.

When he looked at me, he looked at me squarely, directly, defiantly denying it ever happened. Either that, or he was cleverly spinning me into his web of duplicitous guilt, like we still had

Our Little Secret. It was almost as though every time I saw him, he was winking at me in collusion.

He knew I wasn't going to tell anyone. He KNEW.

Or he would pinch my cheek lecherously and call me beautiful, and I would run to the closest bathroom and wash my face.

If I had to see him, I would look at his ear instead of his eyes when he spoke to me, and if he placed a hand on my shoulder, I would duck and pretend to scratch my leg. I couldn't bear his eyes on me. Or his hands. I couldn't bear him knowing I still lived.

To everyone else, he was just a jovial, good-natured uncle giving his niece a compliment. And to everyone else, I was an insolent, spoilt girl.

Why didn't I tell anyone? At first because it was Our Little Secret.

But when I figured it out, I felt so stupid and ashamed, and then so guilty, tainted by my enjoyment of it.

I couldn't tell anyone then. They wouldn't understand. I would get beaten. I would get told off. I would be accused!

And so I adapted, as children do, and I became a skilled little liar before I had even started secondary school.

I lied. And I evaded.

And when my parents lectured me, I tuned out, because their advice didn't apply to me, because they didn't KNOW me or what I had been through. I only listened to my own stupid advice and regularly emotionally self-flagellated.

And they thought I was surly.

I resented them for not being there for me, for sending me away, for not guessing that I was hurting, for not seeing the signs.

And there it is, Our Little Fucking Secret. Safe forever with me. Pinky Promise. Cross my heart and hope to die, taking it to the grave with me.

I hated myself for protecting him. Why should he get to face no consequences?

But as far as I was concerned, he was protecting me. I was sure that if I told anyone, they would blame ME, for instigating it, for liking it, for encouraging more trips to the darkroom.

My dad couldn't bear the fact that I didn't want to be around his beloved siblings. And I could never tell him, because I was terrified that he wouldn't take my side.

Children who live with shame grow up with guilt.

Once, Mamma Mia set homework for me: to read the book *Perfume*, by Patrick Suskind. I loved it, and we talked about how evocative writing can be to conjure smells. His mastery of synaesthesia. We were repulsed by the fish market of Paris and intoxicated by the scent of the virgins. Not by smelling them, but by just reading about them. It was genius.

What she said that night made me hint to her about what had happened.

By the way, SPOILER ALERT...

The novel's protagonist murdered the women to capture their scent. Their purest essence. He couldn't get their perfume without killing them. They were all young, innocent, and beautiful. They were all virgins.

It was a metaphor, Mamma Mia asserted...

Innocence is irresistible for some men. That's why some men fuck naïve, trusting, sweet girls—to capture their innocence. Some want to seize the purest innocence: virgins or children. And they can't seize it without fucking them. And they can't fuck the girls without fucking the girls up. For life.

It's a big sacrifice, but it's a sacrifice *they* don't have to make.

She looked sad and I instinctively knew something had happened to her as a young girl. NO! No, not Mamma Mia too?

Without thinking, I blurted out that something had happened to me. Her expressive face went through all the emotions (curious, searching, heartbroken, loving, and protective) and settled on furious. Her anger scared me. I know Mamma Mia. If I had told her any details—when, who, what—she would have driven straight to his house and told Aunty Zaina and their daughters what a sick fuck he was. Mamma Mia would have caused a fucking family mutiny, and I was terrified of being outed.

It would all come back on me. Why did I allow it? Why did I enjoy it? Why didn't I tell anyone back then, when something could have been done about it? It would all somehow have been my fault.

So I told her that I might have imagined it and that I didn't really remember.

But I remembered everything.

2 September 2016, 4.34 a.m.

It is now the early hours of the morning. When it is the darkest. Before dawn.

The hour when the most pious wake to pray to their Creator, kneeling on their prayer mat in reverent supplication.

The hour when revellers stumble home, kneeling at their porcelain god or watching the ceiling above their head spinning round.

I have been both those extremes.

Crying in the dark for forgiveness from Allah. And tears streaming from my eyes as the tequila made its way back up.

Don't judge me. I am well aware of my imperfections.

And I have also witnessed, first-hand, people who prayed five times a day, people who had returned from Hajj, people who covered every inch of their body, and yet who pay witch doctors to summon jinn, cheat on their spouse, and beat their house help.

I refuse to be lectured. Everyone should mind their own flawed business.

My Faith is a deeply personal thing for me. It was something that helped me *inside*, in the place that hurt, and it prevented me hating myself too much or giving up. It helped quiet the voice that told me how filthy and bad I was.

I didn't flaunt my beliefs and I didn't preach to anyone else.

I love being a Muslim.

The mercy of God, upon which I always relied, and which I'll need more than ever now, I guess. I love the rhythmic recital of the Quran, words I vaguely understood but which seemed to mean everything to me. The message of peace and belonging. The tolerance and the equality. I love my religion in its purest form (i.e., not what some people have made it).

I also loved the reactions from people abroad, if they ever asked. I loved the way it challenged everyone. Because they all had prejudices and notions of what Muslims looked like, and I loved watching them having to accept that all 1.6 billion of us are going to look different.

Since 9/11, suddenly everyone "knew" what a Muslim was and hated us all. Neighbours, doctors, and colleagues were now the enemy, and their previously barely noticed hijabs or beards now became beacons of warning. Attacks on Brothers and Sisters soared. Waves of hatred against people they had lived next to for decades.

My aunt in Texas had her hijab ripped off her head in a supermarket car park and was spat on. Two men and a woman carried out the attack, which confused me. Not that women are immune to bigotry; it was more that she stripped another woman of a garment so other men could abuse her. She must have really hated what that scarf represented.

The point of covering your hair is to be modest and therefore not draw attention to yourself. If the hijab is attracting not just attention, but *negative* attention, it's having the opposite effect.

After that incident, I heard my dad telling his sister not to wear the hijab in America, which must have been a painful day.

For her, of course, but *really* for him.

4.35 a.m.

They arrive.

My parents.

And like the parting of the sea, people move out of the way, making a theatrical path from the front door. The remaining scattered mourners who are taking the night watch scramble to their feet, move coffee cups and tissues from the floor, and tuck the Qurans under their arms.

Mama and Baba.

They have arrived with Uncle Mo.

Some people stand aside awkwardly, staring at the parents who will have to bury their firstborn.

Some people attach themselves to the growing grief snowball that rolls from the front door, up the stairs and to the back room where my body is waiting for their farewells.

Uncle Mo is holding up his sister, helping her put one foot in front of the other as she screams my name with a gargling anguish. She sees everyone as she passes them, as they hold on to her scarf, to her fingers, saying *polé* (sorry, in Swahili), and reminding her to invoke God's name, but she looks through them all. A few try and stop her for hugs, and a few others push those people off her.

Everyone wants a piece of her. They want to attach themselves to the grief. To remind themselves what it feels like to hurt that keenly. To remind themselves that they are lucky to have dodged a bullet this time. But Uncle Mo guides Mama single-mindedly, straight toward Bibi who is standing at the door of the guest room.

My Baba walks mutely behind her. He, on the other hand, sees *all* his family. He looks everyone in the eye, he accepts their condolences, he thanks them for being here, he hugs his sisters, he hugs his oldest brother, Issa, who lost his twenty-four-year-old son to a brain aneurysm years ago. Baba now understands his brother's pain. He's gracious to everyone. He really is so loving, caring, and considerate to them all. He is the perfect brother. He thinks of them first, before himself.

Before me.

As Mama walks into the room, I feel so light that I think my soul might fade to nothing, or float away like desiccated skin.

That Wall of Death in this room hits her and she falls to the floor, reaching out to her mother, crying out to her, 'Mummy, Mummy, help me! I'm going into labour!'

This is some kind of witchcraft! I'm dead, yet she feels like she's giving birth to me! It's like my life is coming full circle now that my mother has entered the room. It's like the pain of giving me life has returned now that she has seen me dead.

I will never know what it's like to have a child. And I will never know what it's like to lose one.

She curls up next to me in agony, one arm around her womb, one arm around me.

•

Witchcraft is not an alien concept to us.

Ask anyone in the Middle East: Oman is known for witchcraft, for juju, the harnessing of the jinn. In Zanzibar, the only thing that would make the local witch doctors shudder was the strength of the magic from the Congo.

Everyone in Oman has a story of their brush with juju.

Like the friend of a friend, Aliya, who had been possessed by an evil jinni all because of another woman's jealousy. The jinni was instructed by the witch doctor to not stop tormenting poor Aliya until she had lost everything dear to her. She was so mentally troubled, she did insane things like pick fights with the wind and shout at gravity, and subsequently she lost her job and her husband and was sent back to her parents' house to live out the rest of her life, to slowly lose her mind.

And there was a man we all knew who made a contract with a witch doctor, asking to be rich and revered. He became both very wealthy and powerful. But his son died not too long after, which was the proverbial small print that this power-hungry asshole didn't read. (Worse still, I'm not sure how upset the man was. Maybe he did read the small print and found his son's life a fair price to pay?)

Witch doctors are not your friends. It is an evil contract you enter. Like Ursula from *The Little Mermaid*. Even as a kid I could see the disastrous outcome a mile off. It's a deal with terrible caveats. You'd have to be desperate or stupid to enter into a deal with an agent of the devil.

4.50 a.m.

I'm not sure if witchcraft is at play now, or it's the devastation of losing her firstborn child and phantom pains from when she first met me, but Mama is freaking out and I can't help her and I can't comfort her.

Mamma Mia runs into my room and upends her bag, rummaging through the detritus, finally finding a small bottle containing pills.

She runs back in, where my mum's breathing is erratic through her sobs. She is lying next to my body, trying to hold it, grip my corpse, grasp on to it while people are holding her back so she doesn't knock me onto my side.

She is fighting these people, saying that she wants to hold her FUCKING DAUGHTER and to LEAVE HER THE FUCK ALONE! My mum never swears. She sounds like Mamma Mia.

Or me.

They are bruising her, and she is kicking anything she can come into contact with.

Mamma Mia presses something into her mouth and gives her a glass of water to sip. She doesn't know what's happening, but Mamma Mia's whisper in her ear cuts through the noise of women wailing, men calling for her to 'Remember Allah!' and aunts wrestling to make her let go of me. I come close to Mamma Mia. Uncle Mo kneels with her, and we whisper together, soothing her. Mamma Mia's purr makes the surrounding noise melt away, and Uncle Mo's arms protect her from everyone else. And suddenly the chaos subsides and disappears outside this circle and the siblings look at each other, hold each other's faces, and break down.

My Death. Her Grief.

Two jinn that will remain her constant companions till her dying day.

•

The fact that both Mama's siblings are here together is splendiferous serendipity.

Mamma Mia could have driven or flown here from Dubai easily enough, but Uncle Mo shouldn't even be reachable. He's supposed to be halfway up a mountain right now, climbing Everest. How come he's here? God is good.

Growing up, I knew Uncle Mo the least in the family. He was like a birthday balloon in the wind, floating around, celebrating, bobbing gaily, unable to ground himself. He spent some time with us in Oman and he took me under his wing and then he floated away again. With his father's intellect, he was head boy at his prestigious school and sailed easily into university, where they had high hopes for him to follow the academic path forged by Grandad.

There, however, he skipped classes and joined every society he could: salsa dancing, astronomy, art history, and then there was camping. He went into the English countryside, spent nights in tents and hiked up hills, went to the rugged coasts enduring British biting winds and sideways rain. And he loved it. He started spending money on proper hiking boots, expensive backpacks, and windproof clothing. He began to train at the gym, climbing on ridiculous little bobbles nailed into high vertical walls, strapped into harnesses upon which he relied less and less.

His body was changing, and his laser focus was now set on anything that could give him a rush.

Rowing, cycling, skiing, climbing, diving, and travelling to do it all. And then, of course, telling everyone about it, in his easy, entertaining style, recounting close brushes with death with breathless, nail-biting tension, and bringing to life the wonder of watching sunrise from above the clouds on a Borneo mountain. I'm sure there was plenty of hyperbole thrown in, but he'd laugh and tell me never to let the truth get in the way of a good story, especially if you were getting paid to tell it.

He got his degree and I feel bad not knowing what he studied, although it clearly wasn't important to him either. He somehow just managed to scrape enough money together to go backpacking and climb, swim, sail around the globe and live to tell the tales.

He realised three things quite early on.

1. He would never work in an office.
2. People loved hearing his stories.
3. He wouldn't break any records doing these things as a Brit.

Having made these realisations, he came to Oman, spent some time living with us, training to become a dive master, and eventually saved some money teaching it. In the meantime, he became a naturalised Omani, which required more than a little help from some vitamin W, since his father is a Brit and not an Omani, and in true patriarchal fashion, that's what matters.

While he stayed with us, Uncle Mo passed on to me his Wanderlust, which he says is German and gave him the idea for the tattoo on his arm that he got in Thailand that read,

Not all those who wander are lost.

Next to the words are three birds silhouetted in flight, representing, he told me, him and his two sisters. He promised one day to get one each for me and Sara.

(Tattoos are totally not allowed in Islam, which he hadn't realised when he got it. He hid his arm from his parents for ages.)

He couldn't stay still for very long, and Muscat city life bored him to distraction, with the same Family functions, the same faces and same stories. On the odd weekend, he would take me camping under the eruption of stars in the desert, or on hikes through rocky wadis, to swim in freshwater pools, or on the Dive Centre's boat to remote bays along the craggy coast. We went fishing and snorkelling, driving on dunes and spending nights in the chilly mountains.

Around campfires on the beach at dusk or on one of our long rides in his 4x4, he'd tell me about living in the back of his modified camper van as he drove around the South Island of New Zealand, or the time that a gorilla tried to grab him by the leg in the Congo. He told me about the time he was forced to cut his hair, which was long and unkempt from months of backpacking, before he was allowed to cross the border into the Nation of Brunei. Or the fishing boat that took seven uncomfortable days to reach the island of Flores where he could see Komodo Dragons.

I swear, his stories were as good as Mamma Mia's fairy tale bedtime stories. Jungles, waterfalls, forbidden cities, and dragons!

Baba said that I was too young to learn to dive at the time, but Uncle Mo told me that I would love it. It was so peaceful down there, the fish moved so gracefully, in coordination, like choreography. I always worried about being clumsy, but he said I would be weightless (oh, the very idea!), and my breath through the regulator would be the only sound I would hear, and that the blue light was like a dream sequence. I would be able to leave Muscat and everyone in it behind.

I loved getting out of town and getting away from everyone. With Uncle Mo, I felt like the old me again; free, curious and wide-eyed. He, in turn, could never understand why I was doing so badly in school. After all, I listened and learned, asked all the right questions.

He was just asking all the wrong ones.

They all were. They tried to reach me, but my parents didn't know how. Mama, who had become more than a little frustrated with my moods, was delighted that Uncle Mo had found a connection with me and could take me off her hands so that she could start focusing on her master's degree.

As a naturalised Omani, Uncle Mo was an adventuring novelty. He did things no Arab had done: He became the first Arab to row across the Atlantic, the first to walk to the North Pole, and the first to cycle the length of England. And the first to attempt to climb the highest mountain on each continent.

I say attempt, because he climbed Mont Blanc while still at uni and Mount Kinabalu while backpacking in Borneo. He then set his sights on the world record and conquered Kilimanjaro and Mount Vinson and was preparing for Everest as of yesterday.

The amazing thing is that he was breaking all these records. And the ironic thing is that Omanis set no store in such things. They didn't care about walking for miles in the cold. Or rowing across an ocean when one could get there faster and drier in an aeroplane. These were mad endeavours. No one understood. When the Oman football team won the Gulf Cup, however... now that was big news! No one cared about an Omani doing White People stuff.

Between adventures, he gave talks in schools and at corporate events and conferences, speaking engagements that paid surprisingly well. He also did life coaching, NLP training, and learned how to hypnotise, not just to help people improve their lives or stop smoking but also as an irresistible party trick. He was charming and fun, unconventional and trailblazing.

And he still loved to salsa.

5.01 a.m.

Everyone has quietly retreated from the room, leaving the three siblings to cry and hold each other.

Maryam, Mohammed, and Mina. Best friends, all completely different. Far-flung lives, united today in grief.

Mama sits up, her eyes never leaving my body, and they sit on either side of her, holding her hands.

They take it in turns telling each other the stories of their day, how they found out the horrible news. Their incredulity, shock, sorrow.

Uncle Mo was in London dealing with some really shit news about the weather patterns around the Himalayas, and waiting to get the all clear to join his team to take the flight to Nepal.

When he got The Call.

Mama was staying with some relatives near Windsor. Baba was more or less living from one relative's house to another, suitcases always in his car, and had followed her to Windsor to try and talk to her, much to her annoyance.

When they got The Call.

This is how it went down for Mama:

Grandad makes The Call and calls her Maryam when she answers the phone. They never call her Maryam. They always call her Mary (or Mother Mary, or Mare, or Nightmare, or Western Supermare if they were being sillier than usual).

She knows immediately from the gravity in his voice that something is wrong, compounded by him asking her to sit down.

'I don't want to, Papa.' She's scared.

The dread in those interminable moments.

I can't even imagine.

Belying his own grief and tears, he says with gentle composure that there had been an accident and that I am 'no longer with them'.

Mama's vision darkens, her stomach shrivels, her mouth dries, and her heart crumbles. The next awful endless breaths elongate into years of empty pain, as she silently shrinks into herself and then finally shouts, 'What about Sara?'

Great.

Thanks, Mother.

But I know she knows that we are inseparable, so if something had happened to me, it might easily have happened to us both. And both would be too much to bear.

(Or maybe Sara is just her favourite...)

She must have screamed coz my father comes running to see her slumped on the ground, her hand over her mouth, eyes wide staring at the phone that she has thrown on the floor across the room, as if to distance herself from this—a parent's most dreaded call. He grabs the phone and sits next to her, still wanting to protect his Little Bird. He sees that it is Grandad calling, and despite every instinct, lifts the phone reluctantly to his ear and hears the news that has him growling like a wounded animal.

The next hour is a blur. Neither of them will ever remember it properly, coz neither of them is really present.

He shifts to robot autopilot and gathers my mum's clothes from the laundry, hanging on the back of the door, from the closet, collects her toiletries from the bathroom, packs them all up in her suitcase, places it next to his matching suitcase in the boot of his flashy hire car (old habits), picks his trembling wife up in his arms (oh yes, they are still married), and drives them, without blinking, thirty minutes down the road to Heathrow.

They manage to get on the next flight, some woman at the airline's desk trying to charge them practically a year's salary to change their existing bookings.

'I understand sir, but without proof of your daughter's death...' she begins, before her supervisor hurriedly and apologetically intervenes.

They walk, trance-like, through security, not talking, not touching, not even acknowledging the other parent or the pain they are individually sharing. Yet they never physically separate more than a few inches.

Suddenly, my mum looks up in the waiting area and sees Uncle Mo, who is supposed to be shivering against the legendary ascent, running toward her. Finally, the tears flow as her grief finds an outlet, and she howls in his arms as my dad stands mutely by.

They babble over each other, as she sobs and folds herself into his incredulous hug. They thank Allah for the coincidences that meant they would be here together, the bad weather over the Himalayas that kept him here and not unreachably thousands of metres above sea level, and the fortuitous timing of their flights that had them reunited when she needed him the most.

They share what little news they have, and they try to call someone, anyone, for news on the burial time. Will they make it? Muslims usually bury their dead within twenty-four hours, so they pray that they make it.

Mamma Mia sends a WhatsApp message back that nothing will be done until they arrive. They thank God again.

Mamma Mia tells her older siblings about the needle and tells them that no one else knows. They discuss what that could possibly mean? 'Needles? Summer is scared of needles! Remember, when we were planning the family trip to Zanzibar, but didn't go? She could barely get her Yellow Fever without fainting!'

They both giggle at the memory of me acting a complete wuss, and then a grouchy shit at the clinic, embarrassed by my little hissy fit.

'Mare,' he says gently, 'we have to mentally prepare ourselves that this could involve drugs. After the Edinburgh Episode.'

'No, Mo, she learned her lesson then. No one would be that stupid, to do drugs again after that.' She pauses. 'Right?'

Baba is on his phone too. With his own siblings. But he's also listening to Mama and Uncle Mo, trying to figure it all out.

Uncle Mo doesn't let go of his sister's hand for the entire flight. He tries to distract her by suggesting movies they can watch together to pass the longest seven hours of Life. He doesn't sleep, even when she passes out on his shoulder from emotional exhaustion; instead, he watches over her. He's not a sentimental guy, but he waits till she's asleep before he sheds his own tears for his funny, moody, inquisitive little niece.

I feel sorry for my dad as I imagine this eternal flight. My parents are supposed to be going through a divorce, so they don't know their boundaries anymore. Mama is trying to get away from him, but he wants to be close to her. Shouldn't they be holding each other? Or is that reserved for lovers? People who love.

He was brought up not to allow or accept defeat, so he's followed her twice to the UK to convince her that divorce isn't the answer for them.

Both times have gone horribly wrong. Edinburgh and now this...

And now, on the loneliest of a million lonely days with her, Uncle Mo is physically sitting between them, along with countless hurts and incalculable regrets.

5.15 a.m.

Now that my parents have arrived, Bibi gently asks anyone still left to please go home and rest. Although everyone considers themselves close family members, only the closest family stays behind to clear up silently.

Bibi asks them to leave my parents to grieve, and to come back later. The burial will be at midday.

The burial.

So final.

Will I still have all these thoughts and memories to mull over when I'm buried?

I suppose now's the time to place the Edinburgh Episode on the conveyor belt of memories, and evaluate what it meant to the rest of my life: the impact, the implications, and the embarrassment.

•

I was so excited to get to university. I studied my ass off with the single-mindedness of my female ancestors, and the ridicule and doubt of the Family goading me on. I had caught up enough to get decent grades at GSCE, and was laser focused for A levels, and aced them.

Being accepted into uni was my emancipation! It was women getting the vote, it was the divorce papers coming through, it was American soldiers walking into Paris! I was freeeeeeeeeee.

And what a fucking anticlimax.

I strutted onto campus in Edinburgh enthusiastically anticipating my Life to begin (picture, if you will, a wide-eyed, fresh-faced virgin twirling onto the scene in the opening credits of a musical à la Julie Andrews).

I knew the world was exciting and extensive, with so many different types of people. And yet I had no idea who I was. I wanted to try on different personalities to find out which fit best. Would I be a mysterious intellectual? Or an infectiously joyful friend? Maybe someone whose aura would inspire.

I envisioned faculty soirées sparkling with witty repartee, mind-bending conversations, and life-altering encounters. Gorgeous intellectual men, weekends in Amsterdam and Paris, parties that started at midnight. Sex, drugs, rock 'n' roll!

Perhaps even Love.

Instead, Freshers' Week was filled with nervous teens, rambunctious kids away from home for the first time, acne, over-eager society recruits, predatory third-years, dizzying orientation, and lots of fucking puking Brits.

For the first time since I was six, I was homesick. The emotion took me by surprise.

This Whole New World that I had been dreaming of, made me feel claustrophobic.

There I was, carrying the naïveté and the burden of a privileged expat life. For the last thirteen odd years, I had known big cars on smooth eight-lane highways, huge houses cleaned by housemaids, international schools with international friends, and above all, good weather. Most people I met in my first month had not been further than Spain, had never heard of Oman OR Zanzibar, and assumed all Arabs were terrorists and / or rode on camels.

It always struck me as ironic that some white people call us savages, even though we've travelled farther afield than them and are often better educated and more civilised. And they didn't use bum hoses...

I waltzed in, expecting uni to be more cosmopolitan than my former life, but it was more parochial, more limited. I came in ready to embrace life and everyone, but I wasn't greeted with the same open-mindedness. Everything had changed between the ages of seven and twenty-one. I thought I remembered the UK. I thought I spoke the language. At the very least, I thought I had kept up to date with trends and music on the internet.

I found myself Other yet again.

It's a funny (not haha funny) thing, being mixed race.

When one of your mixes is dark.

Especially when you live in a predominantly white country, like England. I couldn't say like America or Australia, coz they were clearly originally brown countries. (Okay, off my soap box now.)

Anyway, being even *half* brown, Mama was always an outsider in her own country, England, the only country she'd ever known. They were never going to accept her as one of their own, not in the '70s and '80s.

When you're mixed, no one ever refers to you as white.

I did kinda feel bad for Tiger Woods when he said he wasn't *just* black. He wasn't denying his blackness; he just wanted to ALSO celebrate his Chineseness (damn, that's definitely NOT a word).

Or Barack Obama. The first black president. I wonder if his white mum, who raised him on her own, thought, Ummmm ex-CUSE me!

When a country has something called the One Drop Rule, you know you're in trouble if your lips are full, your nostrils spread a little wide on your face, or your hair curls too tightly.

And so Mama and her siblings were never really accepted in the country of their birth. In their father's country. They learned to resent the ethnic side of their blood, from years of teasing at school, from growing up with only blondes on the cover of *Just Seventeen*, from only white-girl makeup in Boots, from never being considered one of the Boys on the rugby team. They tried to be as English as possible, rejecting their Zanzibari and Muslim roots in front of their English mates, and emulating instead their way of talking and acting, pretending to smoke at school and sniggering about which white kids from the neighbouring school they fancied. Embracing Christmas and downplaying Eid.

It must have been worse for Bibi and Grandad, who, in the '60s, got untold abuse walking arm in arm or embracing each other in public. I say 'untold' abuse, because they literally wouldn't tell us. They didn't want any of us to be prejudiced. They didn't want their children to see the eggs broken on the back of their coats, and they shut their doors quickly against shouts directed at Bibi, of 'Wog' and 'Paki' and the oft-repeated chorus of 'Go back to your country!'

They didn't want us to resent these people or think of ourselves as Other.

And yet, when we went to Oman, essentially going "back" to our roots, "back" to a country Sara and I had never even *been* to, we were Other again. We all were: me, Sara and especially my mum. Mama, with fair mzungu skin and a straight, fine nose. Hair that didn't need to be relaxed but fell in gorgeous soft curls around her face. She had the almond eyes that Bibi got from her Malay granny and a cute spattering of freckles, like someone had sneezed on her. And she had those green eyes that reflected the envy of every petty bitch who caught her gaze.

And just like my Indian friend Nehal's mum who used Fair & Lovely to lighten her skin to be like the higher castes, the Family valued Mama's fair skin, they valued straight noses and straight hair. Her green eyes were such a rarity that everyone talked about my dad's new bride for months. They talked about her behind her back and called her mzungu to her face, teasing her for her risible grasp of Swahili (which she had stopped learning in England, rejecting it in favour of being as English as possible). She soon started regretting not embracing her roots in her youth, because it had left her such a stranger to her "own people". She now resented the English part of her, which here in Oman made her an awkward anomaly at best, and always an outsider.

She was "exotic" to these women in Oman. And they hated her for it.

She had been exotic to acquaintances and colleagues in London too. And it had kept her separate from them.

Mama hated that word. Exotic.

As a result, Mama never felt like she was with HER people, wherever she lived. Even in Zanzibar, she said that she didn't look like the people there, especially since many people who were mixed were murdered or exiled. She was exiled from her mum's country and a foreigner in her dad's country.

And now, this unfamiliar place, Oman, where people looked at her as a stranger, was this her new homeland?

The other word she hated was Diaspora. She didn't understand it; it always confused her. She just never felt that she came from anywhere, or fit in anywhere.

•

I did work hard at uni. For a while.

I kept my head down at first, conscientiously attending all lectures, handing in homework on time, researching extra modules and reading the second-year curriculum books just so I could be prepared. I worked so hard to get there and I wasn't going to waste the opportunity.

My grades were exemplary, and I was well liked in my department.

At night, from the ivory tower of superiority known as my third-floor dorm room, I looked down (physically and metaphorically) on the kids stumbling out of the pub, singing rugby songs, throwing up in bushes, hassling girls, and kicking over dustbins. I bemoaned the lack of civilised life and sophisticated companions. I longingly lamented the silly broken Swahi-nglish jokes my cousins would tell.

And I missed Sara so badly it hurt. I missed her easy companionship and dissecting with her everything that went on in our house, in our Family and our lives. She would always calmly try and make me see another point of view, a more generous, empathetic, measured point of view. Mostly, she put me to shame, because she was right, but since she didn't know everything about me, she would never be able to make me see

Aunty Zaina's point of view. Or Uncle B's point of view. Or even Baba's point of view.

I missed spending evenings shut in our room putting Jolene bleach on our upper lips while singing Dolly Parton songs. She'd Epilady my fuzzy legs and I'd braid her hair while talking girls, talking boys, talking dreams. Talking a Whole New World.

I wondered what Sara would make of this place. I suppose she would have looked to me for my opinion, in which case she would have found Edinburgh cold and intimidating, with its Gothic spires and windowless castle. And she might have found it dark, in the same way that Bibi found London dark, after the swaying palm tree–framed open skies of Zanzibar's coast.

Or would she? Maybe she would have been positive and optimistic. Maybe she would have told me that this is what I had always wanted, what I had spent the last few years working really hard toward. Maybe she would put me to shame again by telling me not to be ungrateful and go and *carpe* the bloody *diem*! And, of course, she would have been right.

She would tell me that I was finally on the right track, and not to go the wrong way on it.

Mamma Mia pulled me aside the day I left and gave me a Little Black Book. She wears the love-tinted glasses of a favourite aunt when she looks at me, so she thinks I'm gorgeous. I don't know if she was just trying to boost my confidence, but she contended unequivocally that the boys would go nuts over my stunning face (she made no mention of my figure) at uni and that I'd have to beat them off with a stick.

'But if you do beat them off, don't use a stick; it will hurt,' she added, giggling, and then had to explain the joke.

So, after settling into my course and into my tiny dorm with the single bed, with Mamma Mia's and Sara's voices egging me on, I decided to go and put myself out there. After all, how would I ever discover the real me without testing myself?

I didn't mean to go buck wild. I didn't want to deny my roots or stray too far from the path forged by my culture. At the end of the day, it was MY culture.

But I wanted to try something else on, something other than Oman. I wanted to try on new hats, new skins, new MEs. Who am I? I had no idea! I never had the freedom to find out back home.

If I didn't swing to the extreme ends of the pendulum, I would never find out who the real me was. I had been waiting for years for the opportunity to find out.

So I vowed to experiment. I promised myself that I would oscillate between extremes to find my rhythm, my tribe, my vibe.

Each betrayal of my strict and restricted upbringing would be a step closer to finding out. Each rebellion meant a new venture into becoming a new me.

I was betraying my father's rules, my mother's footsteps. Betraying the foregone conclusion of being a good daughter and becoming a good wife and mother. Betraying all those expectations of me gave me the freedom to move country, to complete MY education, my emancipation, maybe even to try alcohol, a fake accent, new drugs, maybe lovers (but not pork!). And answer to no one.

No one knew me here in Scotland; it was time for reinvention.

I wanted to suck the marrow out of life and find out who Summer really was.

I wanted to live!
I wanted to feel ALIVE.
Even if it killed me.

And it nearly did.

•

I had no idea of the emotionally complex minefield dating was at
uni. And when I say complex, it really is enough to give you one.

Overhearing boys that you know and like, talking about girls
only in terms of "hot" and "tits" and numbers out of ten, and
whether a girl had already snogged / blown / shagged one of their
group, was terrifying. Mamma Mia would be horrified how little
we had advanced in taking the "boys will be boys" out of boys.

And smart girls that I knew, tearfully regretting a Fresher's
Week shag because she now fancied a friend of aforementioned
shagee but didn't want to seem like a slut.

Complex minefield.

It reminded me of a documentary of some poor people who had
been smuggled into Europe in a shipping container, many of
whom had died en route. The survivors were given counselling
to try to alleviate the trauma of their ordeal, but they only wanted
to talk about who they fancied and how another woman had
taken their man and other relationship problems.

I guess we'll always just be animals who want to bonk.

How was I going to navigate in this unfamiliar world? I wasn't
about to shag just *anyone*—I wanted to wait for love, although
the Virginity thing was starting to become an Entity unto it-

self. People would actually ask me if it was true, like I was a freak. Word had spread. Surely it wasn't *that* uncommon to be twenty-one and with hymen? (Yes, twenty-one. I was kept behind at school, coz of bad grades, and my birthday is right at the beginning of term.)

From listening in on the boys, I also gathered that I was not what they considered hot, so it might be a while before I would find a charitable volunteer.

Plus, being desired thoroughly freaked me out. The idea of being sexualised as a twenty-one-year-old, when inside I still felt like a seven-year-old, really gave me the creeps, and I had a bitterly nauseating taste in my mouth from being coveted before.

Uncle B's illegal lust had made me the delightfully sarcastic bitch I am today (was yesterday). How would I even recognise if someone my age fancied me?

I can only associate my snog with the sweet Norbert with getting humiliatingly whipped with a belt in front of people, which isn't the best association.

And at this point I was almost six years deep into my unrequited obsession with Fido Dido, who, at the end of the day, was my heroin supplier.

I only had my parents' example as a less than desirable road map to relationship territories.

Basically, if I had lived, I may have turned out to be a junkie, sadomasochistic gerontophile.

The dating game was not therefore something at which I was an expert.

That's why I fell in love with people who would never like me back! So that I wouldn't have to actually deal with a relationship.

Surely I didn't do that self-sabotaging nonsense on purpose. Did I? I fell in love with two men who would never love me back: Fido and Sexy MotherFuckin' Mike (more on that to come). I briefly fancied a married professor too; another man who was definitely out of bounds and wouldn't fancy me back.

Yes, I was clearly avoiding dealing with real love and a real relationship.

And then of course there was my darling Semen...

Most of my uni friends were gay. I didn't know they were gay when we became friends, and in Simon's case, even he didn't know he was. Simon Jones, whom I eventually affectionately nicknamed, was my dear friend and Halls of Residence mate. We met on the first day as we were moving in; we helped each other with suitcases and blu-tack, and a welcome cuppa, and the mandatory questions of where are you from, what are you studying, what did you do for A levels, what did you get for A levels, and was this uni your first choice?

We nicknamed everyone with a middle name: David "First Floor" David, or Julie "Pukey" Julie or Ben "Great White Shark" Ben (he had a reputation).

(Was I Summer "Virgin" Summer?)

Semen was so handsome that he was pretty, with steely blue eyes and a clean jaw and eyebrows that looked like he'd visited Blossom, the best threader at our local salon in Muscat. Quite dreamy!

When he came to uni, he was in the stages of planning to get engaged to his girl back home, but every time he was drunk (most nights) he would pop into my room after the pub, say cryptic things about not being sure, about not being true to himself, then apologise for bothering me and leave.

Being the astute expert that I am, I was convinced that he was trying to tell me that he loved *me* and not his girl-next-door-mousey-shop-assistant from back home. I was sure of it!

When he was tipsy and therefore suggestible, I would try and coax it out of him, coz I was sober and *knew* what was in his heart (Mamma Mia was right, I AM desirable!), but he would say that he was too drunk and he'd leave me alone with thoughts of how I would finally make him admit it and we would eventually live happily ever after. The next day he would sheepishly ask me to forget what he had said, which I knew was a textbook sign of his affection and undying love.

Nope. He was trying to get the courage to ask for my advice, because he was as uninterested (disinterested?) in his future fiancée as he was in me. He was in the stages of admitting as much to himself, realising that his life was about to become a lot more complicated, and he had to figure out how to admit it to his girl, who, despite his penchant for penis, his desire for dick, his craving for cock, he loved very much. He was so confused, and helping navigate through his life's conundrum brought me and Semen closer together than any love affair could have.

It must have been hard for all these young men—Semen, Gerald, and Tom, still teenagers—to admit to their families that they were not the "norm"; that they were not the sons their parents had wanted or expected. That their mothers wouldn't have grandkids. That their fathers had to come to terms with the fact that they had sons who liked cock. It's a hard thing for most straight men to swallow. Pun intended.

These boys were trying to navigate their own sexuality AND deal with the potential disappointment of their parents, while also figuring out their place in a hetero society, and some of them would end up blaming themselves, getting depressed, confused and angry.

Just like me.

And that's why we gravitated to each other. An invisible magnet drew us together, and at first we had no idea why. On the surface we didn't seem to have anything in common.

I loved God, and most of them didn't believe in anything. Simon was in fact an atheist (this was a first for me).

I didn't drink, and everyone at uni was enjoying their first taste of freedom, aka binge drinking.

I was super hard working, and they wanted to skive off lessons and smoke weed by the water.

I thought I was a pudgy tomboy, but they treated me as their diva. My scathing wit and sarcastic cynicism got cackles from the bitchiest queens.

So suddenly I was a fag hag, sucked into a world and subculture I had no idea existed mere months before.

They educated me on their pop culture; they introduced me to the divas of the '50s silver screen and '80s pop music scene, the black-and-white beauty of the Herb Ritts supermodels of the '90s, and the tragedy and brilliance of Freddie (they LOVED that I came from Zanzibar, like him), George, and Elton, who blazed trails and paved ways.

And I mean, RuPaul?! Where do I begin? She was everything to us!

I was reintroduced to artists that I thought I knew and regarded as a little corny. But spending Thursday nights dancing down at The Hound, looking at cute topless boys on podiums, and dancing to cheesy disco, the music was reinvented, and a new life opened up before me.

This life included the time when Semen pushed a little pill into my mouth on the dance floor and we had perhaps the best night of our young lives, dancing to Abba, Kylie, Madonna, and Gaga and then repetitive house for hours (or it might have been one really long song), hugging strangers on the dance floor, touching the chests of the oiled-up dancing boys and giggling, feeding each other water from our water bottles as our bodies heated up, finally going back to my room, smoking cigarettes and professing eternal love for each other until dawn.

And Semen told me why he didn't believe that religion was a good thing, why he was opposed to organised religions in general.

He was brought up a Catholic, and I hate to think that this is going exactly where one expects this to go.

His priest had touched him and made him kiss things that weren't for kids to kiss, and when he told his parents, his father beat him for being so disrespectful to the church. Semen reported the priest and there was an investigation and a semblance of closure. Meanwhile he cut off ties with his father as soon as he could, which was fine, coz dad definitely wouldn't have taken the whole homosexuality thing very well. He didn't miss his dad, but Semen still wanted to conform and be "normal" and have a girlfriend, fiancée, wife, kids. But we are who we are.

He didn't use his experience as some kind of misguided reason for being gay. If anything, he told me, it should have put him off…

I was numb. My friend was my hero. So brave. I found depths to my love for him that drilled into the earth's core.

I also felt simultaneously liberated and stupid.

Liberated: I wasn't the only one!

Stupid: Did I think I was the only one?

And so I told Semen about Uncle B. He's the only one who knows the whole truth, all the horrible details. I told him, not knowing how anyone would or could take it. I felt so open, that I risked him looking at me differently, being disgusted with me, the way I had been with myself for years.

He didn't judge me at all, even when I said that I sometimes instigated it. He cried a little and held me. I couldn't believe he was crying for me after what he had been through and so bravely admitted to me, and I held him. And we finally fell asleep, spooning on my single bed, fully clothed.

Yes, that was a perfect night. I don't want to regret anything about it. I know intoxicants are *haram*, I know homosexuality is forbidden, but I refuse to taint anything about that night by judging it as wrong. How could something so beautiful, so real, so joyful, so liberating, and so touching be bad?

I'd found this bunch of people who were also misunderstood and felt alone. Who hid their shame, confusion, and pain behind a smokescreen of weed fumes, drowned their sorrows in the bottom of a bottle, and got high to hide how low they felt.

I had found a different type of family altogether, with nothing in common except everything that mattered.

These might be the best friends I ever had, Gerald, Tom, and Semen. We were fiercely loyal and we held each other's freak flags high.

I joined a few societies. The first, naturally, was Photography. It was quite enlightening, especially the art of editing, which became my new favourite magic trick. Scotland's dramatic skies and soot-coated buildings were perfect Gothic muses. It was almost worth braving the cold to capture the clock tower and spires against pale silver mornings, or the castle sandwiched between dark, craggy rocks and tragic clouds, or rain glistening on cobblestones.

Fuck, Scotland was cold.

And my Leica was a piece of magic.

I started zooming in on bricks and leaves, frost in the corner of the windowpane, even the curls in my hair, so close that you couldn't tell what they were. I was obsessing over shapes and shadows, to make abstract art. Spirals and sharp edges, contrasts and light. I was finding my voice, my style, my eye.

But the most beautiful thing I could see was Mike. Sexy MotherFuckin' Mike. A fourth-year languages mature student, who was a mix of Harry Styles and a Pierce Brosnan's Bond. When I say mature, don't worry, he was twenty-nine, not Uncle B's age. I wasn't manifesting my childhood trauma into the people I fancied.

(I think.)

He was a handsome, cheeky, artistic English gentleman slash scoundrel and I would never have had a look-in with him. I guess that made him safe for me to set my romantic sights on. Guys like that liked blondes with slim legs. Personality optional, but definitely blonde hair and slim legs. Bond girls don't come in larger, thigh-chafing, potty-mouthed sizes.

It was a shame because we got on really well. We were assigned as partners for the first term and then chose to remain partners for the following two. He admired my eye, while I was losing myself in his (I know—so corny!). He loved my black and whites, which had become my signature style (everything else in life had so many shades, sometimes I wished everything were simpler, just black and white). He would lean over them, commenting, and I would stand stalker-close to him, examining his tousled waves and trying hard to sniff him without getting caught.

And, bonus, he loved to smoke weed, which we did sneakily on our walks around campus or the city. We stopped often at cafes for munchies and to talk until it was dark.

He was fascinating and deep, with unconventional opinions and experiences for a regular middle-class English boy. He realised that his path in real estate in a London suburb was going to send him to an early grave or insane asylum, so he came to Edinburgh, then spent his year abroad in Ivory Coast, which then became five years, learning French and building houses. There was never any small talk; neither of us could stand it. Talking to him was exciting.

He was almost killed once in Cote D'Ivoire. He'd made friends with a hooker, who waited for johns near his house and was always hungry. He used to hand her little parcels of food and some change whenever he had some, then they started talking. He's only human, and he wanted to save her from her wretched life, but I guess her pimp didn't approve of that and threatened him with a knife (he let me run my finger along a small scar on his neck) and he never saw the girl again, even though he tried for months to find her.

My mouth hit the floor. I'd never met anyone here who had stories like that! Since I'd arrived in Scotland, I'd become used to being the interesting one. People here had never heard of the places I was from (apart from South London) so there was always more to conversations than the obligatory five small talk questions. There were misconceptions to dispel and ridiculous stereotypes to dismiss.

But SMF Mike and I were fascinating to each other.

And the way that he slipped into French accidentally as he got more passionate was amazing, not just coz it was devastatingly sexy, but I loved that his mind worked like that, the train of his thoughts slipping from one language track to another so seamlessly. I would watch his hands, the inside of his index finger, slightly yellowed from nicotine, as he waved them around with animation.

Sometimes I even forgot how much I fancied him as we stuffed our faces, talking over each other, with so much to say.

He was genuinely interested and amused by my anecdotes of home, and the characters in the Family, since he had always wanted to go to 'the Oman' (he'd actually heard of Oman!). I found that telling stories of the Family's foibles and hypocrisies eased my homesickness and reminded me how wonderfully ridiculous they were.

His favourite stories were about the wild female cousins. He thought it hilarious that girls were sneaking phallic vegetables into hostels, until the house mothers would only allow cucumbers into the kitchen if they were already chopped.

Or cousin Noora, who was accused of sleeping with a married man, by his famously jealous wife. Noora had absolutely no interest in said husband until she realised that her reputation was being ruined by the vicious rumours. So she slept with him. May as well fuck him, if she was being accused of fucking him, was her rationale. Noora was savage!

He'd ask questions: 'Aren't you supposed to be virgins till marriage in your religion?' Or 'Aren't you supposed to stay away from adultery in Islam?' 'Don't these women cover their hair?' It didn't occur to me that he might have been internally judging them for hypocrisy.

SMF Mike was also fascinated by stories of the jinn, but I think he treated them like fantasies or fairy tales. I told him that Yes, jinn really *do* exist, and No, you can't see them coz they're made from smokeless fire, and Yes, I suppose, they *could* reside in a lamp. And Yes, they can grant your wi... Until I realised that he was just taking the piss out of me.

I got out a *shoki shoki* once to nibble on when we were out and about taking pictures. He was totally intrigued, and the name shoki shoki gave him the proper giggles. I didn't know the English name was rambutans, although I actually think that may be the Bahasa name for them. So we called them hairy balls, which made us spit with laughter at the back of the bus. I'd seen them in Sainsbury's and they were a little piece of home, so I had to have them, despite being crazy expensive.

From then on, I made it a mission to buy passionfruit, mangosteen, or jackfruit before we saw each other, despite being next to impossible to find and way beyond my student food budget.

Fuck, I didn't know what I was hoping for. I guess I was trying to buy his affection. Or trying to get to his heart through his stomach. I can see now that I was just trying too damn hard.

Semen always told me that I shouldn't have to try, that I was amazing just the way I was, and Mike should see that and appreciate it. But it just sounded like the kind of pep talk a true best friend would say to an average-looking girl.

SMF Mike's sister came to visit and Mike flattered me by suggesting that the 'best photographer he knew' take some artistic portraits of her by the castle. I couldn't believe that we got on so well, had such a laugh together, AND that he admired me. And I was head over heels with him. Surely that was the making of a relationship! Why couldn't he see it?

Anyway, after dropping his sister at the train station, we decided to get something to eat. We stopped at a wine bar, where the low lighting prompted him to take some candid pictures of me while I was trying to get him to STOP taking pictures of me.

He took my hand away from my face and held it. He stroked my thumb with his and said that I looked really beautiful.

I swallowed hard.

I had to swallow hard, because my heart was in my fucking THROAT, blocking all the words, allowing only a silly gurgle to come out.

I love him! My stomach is in knots, my veins are throbbing, my basement is preparing for a flood. I hear fanfares in my ears.

This is the man to whom I shall offer up my virginity in both hands!

He ordered a glass of wine and he ordered one for me.

And so I drank it.

My first alcoholic drink.

The other society I joined was the Muslim society.

I met a smiley, inky-haired girl from Dubai. Nada. She was my Muslim friend. As much as I wasn't looking back over my shoulder at Oman, I gravitated to something that was familiar to me; something from home. She got my cross-culture jokes, my experiences, and my Islamic references. She understood how homesick I was, even though I was conflictingly so happy to be this far away.

And of course, I finally met someone who had been to Oman, and she loved it and the Omani people.

'The nicest people in the Gulf for sure!' she enthused while I swelled up wistfully for a place I had been gagging to escape just a few months prior. 'So friendly, humble, and kind', which is the general consensus of people who had visited and met the locals, even including my Family.

I had to look inside myself to identify this unfamiliar feeling.

Intense pride in being Omani...!

Nada asked me to go to the Muslim society with her. I was hesitant, but she said that we would be Muslims wherever we were in the world, and we might need our Brothers and Sisters at some point, and they might need us. Which made total sense and made me feel foolish.

My hesitation wasn't because I didn't want to be around Muslims.

Actually, correction. It was.

But I have to try and explain that.

I love being a Muslim and I'm proud to be a Muslim.

I suppose I was worried that people who felt like *they* were Muslims wouldn't feel like I was Muslim enough. Their perceived perfect piety made me uneasy and paranoid.

Muslim sisters wearing hijabs would look disapprovingly at my hair, and devout brothers would try *not* to look at it. Probably not a soul among them had tried a glass of wine, or been so stoned that they couldn't move their arms.

I mistrusted religious preachers with long beards. I had to question whether it was an effective campaign by the media, of association with terrorism. But no, it was more than that for me.

I felt that I was going to be judged by them. I already judged myself, and I was certainly no authority. I felt that they were going to look at me like the filthy degenerate I was, even though they had no idea what was in my heart, what was in my past.

I felt that it was their job to tell me how dirty and impure I was. I'm quite sure they were, in reality, lovely people. It wasn't them—it was me. It was my guilty conscience.

And as for the beardy men, shouting and spewing hatred and vengeful rhetoric from pulpits in Saudi and madrasas of Pakistan? Well, I felt like the Quran *they* were reading had all the bits about Mercy ripped out. They made my religion look like a foreign land, somewhere I didn't recognise at all.

And I resented them, for making Islam a household name for all the wrong reasons. For making me an apologist for my religion, suddenly feeling the need to defend it, and in doing so, coming under scrutiny for how well (or otherwise) *I* was performing as a Muslim. I begrudged them, because how was I supposed to credibly defend a religion that I wasn't following religiously? If

I wasn't living an exemplary existence, then who the hell was I to safeguard the Faith against its many critics?

Instead of the accepting, open-minded prototype I had known growing up, *these* men had become the new poster boys of my religion.

And I felt, despite sharing this beautiful faith with these men, that I had less in common with these fanatic zealots than I did with "sinners", pill-popping, disco-dancing, bum bandits. These "religious" men weren't flying any freak flags; they were just looking disapprovingly at mine.

So, there I was, finally at university, dividing my social life between the Gays and the Muslims.

I hadn't seen SMF Mike for a couple of weeks, which in and of itself wasn't so strange. It was more an uneasy feeling that I got.

When I finally caught up with him, he told me about Jenny.

True to form, he had seen right past me, and predictably his gaze had landed firmly on Jenny. She had naturally long lashes and slim legs.

(Of course she was blonde. Did I HAVE to specify?)

She was, in reality, a very pleasant girl. Sweet disposition, decent photographer, and pretty.

All the bland adjectives.

Frankly, I was stunned. It occurred to me that men were ridiculous.

Like Uncle B: They take what they want from little girls who can't talk back.

Like Fido: They can share hobbies, a smoke, and a common life philosophy with one of the gang but want to marry the subservient child bearer.

Like Mike: They never run out of things to say with someone they find interesting, but they want to date the pretty, bland, and pretty bland English Rose.

Bibi was right. Men didn't want an equal who could challenge them philosophically and intellectually. They wanted someone pretty to look at, who could cook and wouldn't talk back.

I knew that I was young and completely inexperienced, but it seemed to me that, East or West, men were led, against their own self-interests, by their dicks and their egos.

I was deep in my dazed and confused reverie, but he was forging on and enthusing about his new girl, despite my silence. I felt that he wanted me to enthuse too, but I couldn't even manage a fake smile.

At the risk of sounding self-absorbed, all I could think was *What about me?*

Oh, lovely! Mike said that we should all meet up for a drink sometime, him, me, and his girlfriend. We would get on really well, maybe become fast friends.

Mike knew she'd love me, coz I was great, and talented, and fun, and smart.

And it was so considerate that I always brought him fruit that was exotic.

You know, just like me.

I snort when he says 'exotic'.

He asks what's so funny and without realising that I'm doing it, I spit out, 'Really, "exotic"? Fuck that word!'

The funny thing is that he was telling me about Jenny the way you'd tell your mate, giving me details about their dates and her sense of humour and her bloody figure! Which made me recognise that he didn't see me as a potential girlfriend at all. I was a MATE. He looked right through me as a woman. Which, I realised, was just as horrible for me as being desired. Had I done such a good job at being undesirable, of avoiding being looked at sexually?

It was so frustrating.

Or was it something else about me?

Namely, ME.

Omanis like Fido didn't want someone like me. Mzungus like Mike didn't want someone like me.

I was too ethnic for some and too mzungu for the others.

Maybe it wasn't MY avoidance of a relationship. Maybe relationships were avoiding me.

Mike clearly doesn't understand why I'm upset about the word 'exotic'. I say that it's typical of a mzungu not to get it and call me something insidiously racist like that. If Omanis don't get me, how could I ever expect someone like him to get me?

He asks why I'm so upset and what I expected of him.

I fidget and chew the inside of my mouth.

As it dawns on him slowly, he gets agitated and starts speaking spitefully.

'Wait, what were you expecting from me?' he scoffs. 'Wait, you thought, You and Me? For us to get together? And then what? What was I supposed to do? Convert to your archaic religion and marry *you*? Move to Oman? Haha what, live in a world of genies in bottles?' I feel my face burning. 'You can't blame me and you can't blame your culture. You don't even fucking know who you are!'

He's swearing at me now.

So much venom.

'You say you're an Arab, you're an African, you're English. You don't even fucking know who you are! You say you're a Muslim, but you just pick and choose the parts you want!' he spits out.

'You know what you are?' He narrows his eyes to deliver the fatal shot. 'You're a fucking buffet Muslim!'

I stare at him, my shame turns to rage, my rage turns to shock, and my shock turns to a little mouse face, twitching to stop the tears from spilling out of my face.

We look at each other for the longest seconds known to mankind.

Should I storm out? Should I try and explain myself?

BUFFET?

I wasn't hurting anyone! Was I a hypocrite? I never ONCE pretended to be pious or tell someone to do what I wasn't doing. Isn't *that* the definition? I didn't pretend to preach or to have any moral high ground.

BUFFET??

I should shout back! But say what? I shouldn't have to justify myself to someone I thought was a friend. Someone I thought I loved!

He hadn't done anything wrong really, until he spoke to me like a King-Size Prick.

All he did was not love me back. And judge me for things he would never understand.

He never thought of me like a girlfriend. Is he upset that I thought of him as a potential boyfriend because the notion is so repulsive to him? Or because of a hint of guilt at letting me down, and then the guilt turning pretty speedily into resentment?

I realised that the line between love and hate was very fine indeed.

Yesterday he loved me. He introduced me to family, and he knowingly and purposely elected to hang out with me. And enjoyed it! He loved spending time with me, swapping stories, and he couldn't wait to tell me about his new girl. But now he was spewing the vitriol I expected from ignorant Islamophobic strangers at best, and someone who truly hated me at worst.

I had also crossed that fine line. I thought I was in love with this interesting, interested, well-travelled artist. But I found myself sitting across from a stranger. An ugly-hearted stranger.

And I hated him.

I sat across from him, my little mouse face metamorphosing into a fucking lion with the adrenaline thundering through my body.

FIGHT? FLIGHT? NEITHER? BOTH?

I stood up, leaned in close to his face, ignoring the smell of his hair for the first time, and as I tipped his drink into his lap, whispered in his ear, 'Buffet this.'

For months afterward I wished I'd said something cleverer.

·

I'm going out on a limb to say that I'm not a bad Muslim.

And I'm not a good Muslim.

I guess I had an ongoing, questioning, growing, breathing relationship with my Faith. As if we were still figuring each other out. I felt that Islam was trying to evolve in this fast-paced internet world, without losing its pure heart. And I was trying to stay true to it while trying to deal with the voices in my head and simultaneously satisfying my curiosity for a broader life. It's a delicate path to tread. Especially for cross culture, Muslim millennials who grew up with tantalising freedoms and grounding discipline in equal measure. With paths, both righteous and slippery, calling out to us with their own equally and opposingly appealing qualities.

And it was especially tricky for women who think. And since education for both boys and girls is mandatory in Islam, what was a girl to do?! Once educated, some of the patriarchal rules seemed anachronistic and hypocritical to us.

Why do some men frolic on the beach in shorts and make their wives swelter under abayas? (Both have to cover their bodies.)

They used to check a woman's bedsheets after the wedding night, and yet boys are never told to keep their virginity. (Both have to wait for marriage.)

Since Islam was the original feminist movement, if rules *now* seem particularly convenient for men, it is no mystery why. Clearly these rules, as with all rules, were modified by the ruling class: men. And I was always challenging them! This often did not make me popular. With my father, with his brothers, even with his sisters, who no longer cared about their own virginity or ever sitting on a beach again. My fights held no interest for them, and they thought I should just behave.

How much easier life would be if you didn't believe in something. If you didn't believe in God, Heaven, or Hell, you could do what you wanted, guilt free.

But I was a Believer, and nothing would change that. It wasn't a choice.

You have to have faith to believe that, even though bad things happen to good people, it will all work out in the end. A Greater Power will even the score and balance the scales. You have to be strong to believe that everything happens for a reason.

Even famine, wars, and grown men who touch little girls.

•

I think that's what upset me so much. SMF Mike ridiculed me for something he would never understand.

How could an atheist ever understand that Faith can talk you off the ledge, a ledge you've been pushed to against your will? That despite straying from The Path, the very fact that you know The Path is there will save you every time you are lost.

How could someone like him understand this truth: That piety is sometimes harder for those who have seen ugly things. Being saintly doesn't come naturally to those who have been exposed too early to too much sin.

He judged something he was completely unequipped to judge, because he was clueless of the subtleties, and despite that, I let it devastate me.

Mike had essentially chosen someone totally predictable over me. He found me too complicated, too much like hard work to try to understand and love. He'd chosen someone like himself, from his culture, and rejected me. After realising that he'd had basically done a Fido on me, I started getting drunk.

A lot.

With increasingly mortifying results.

I drank at The Hound with the boys and practiced flirting with some cute, completely un/disinterested homosexual patrons.

I got pissed with my photography friends, making sure to avoid Mike and Jenny, and yet talking about them to anyone who would listen (and even those who had stopped listening).

I got wasted at the subsidised student's pub, The Stumble Inn, and told everyone that I was still 'A BLOODY VIRGIN!'

I got wankered at the Summer Ball, annoying everyone by repeating "It's MY ball! Summer's Ball! Hahaha!"

I got sozzled at the faculty party and tried to snog the campus slut, Richard, or Big Dick as he was known among all the girls, because... well, big dick. He was also known to snog ANYONE, but he must have looked at me, wondering if it was tantamount to date rape to even kiss me, so he chivalrously walked me back to my room and left me there, certain that I was about to throw up and glad he had dodged a projectile-vomit bullet.

I got trousered at the student union, made the best of friends with some random girls in the toilets, danced till I was dizzy from swinging my hair around like helicopter blades, bumped into the same girls from the toilet earlier (my new best friends) and threatened to fight them on the stairwell when they started calling me a Paki and telling me to go back home to Pakiland. I told them proudly that I was an African Arab and was greeted with chants of 'Terrorist' and 'Monkey'. I shouted and screamed back and got thrown out on my ass by the bouncer who said that I SHOULD go back to where I came from. I got home and puked, cried over my destitution, and called my parents, sobbing my heart out.

So, it's really my own fault that they came to Edinburgh.

•

Mama used my blubbering, late night phone call as an excuse to get out of Oman and come check up on me. She informed my dad of this trip after she'd already packed and had booked her ticket, and she escaped with no more ceremony than that.

Baba didn't take this very well.

Remember, when Baba took Mama to Oman to live, he found her sudden dependence on him quite intoxicating. It was the feeling that he wanted when he married her. He wanted to be the provider to his Little Bird. He *needed* her to need him.

He even sneakily changed her surname to his surname on her new passport, ID, and licenses. (Women keep their name in our culture; you don't change clans just because you marry a man). He wanted her to have his name. Like a label.

She handed more power over to him than she ever expected to. She needed him to help her find a job; she needed help with orientation, with directions, even with new friends.

She spent several years living his life. The only parties she ever went to were hosted by his Family, the only holidays she ever went on were with his Family, the only connections she had, the only friends she made! Everything, until she started resenting it. And him. She realised that he had moulded her into what he wanted her to be, defenceless and dependent on him, and that was not the person she wanted to be.

When she realised that she had to reclaim her independence before she no longer recognised herself, she got an online master's and started her own company. She rushed out in the morning in business suits, pored over contracts in bed at night, lunched with clients, and laughed on the phone with colleagues. This is where she found her true happiness, her real badass power.

Baba had been bewitched by her initial dependence on him, and then addicted to it.

And as anyone knows, an addiction is a weakness.

She no longer needed him.

And the less she needed him, the more he needed her.

She was no longer a naïve twenty-one-year-old with incoherent dreams. She had her degrees and her own business, and she was still young and energetic. Initially she hadn't been able to figure out what career path to follow, so she opened a recruitment company to help others find *their* ideal career path!

But most of all, she didn't want to be owned any more. She was unhappy and told Baba as much.

Baba was getting older and was therefore more adamant than ever to keep her into his old age. He didn't want to be alone, and he was too old and stubborn to start looking for another wife.

He'd spent quite a lot of energy trying to break in the foal, and he wasn't going to let his prize mare just walk away. Besides, he loved her. Or at least, the idea of her.

People just get stuck in love with an idea, even though everything about the relationship has fallen apart.

More misunderstandings.

By the way, Bird, Foal... I'm not sure why all the animal analogies with my mum? (ANAL-ogies haha! This, by the way, is a Semen joke.)

I had forgotten that I called my parents bawling my drunk little heart out. When Mama turned up at my Halls of Residence without any notice, I was speechless. I had no recollection of summoning her. And I wasn't happy to see her.

The main problem with Mama is that she couldn't get it into her head that we weren't friends. I was hiding so many little secrets from my mum that a surprise visit wasn't a pleasant surprise—it was fraught with Fuck! What have I left out on the table? I have to watch what I say! Shit, do I smell of smoke / weed / booze?

However, now that it's too late, I regret not telling her about Uncle B. because maybe I wouldn't have kept quite so many secrets from her. Now that I'm dead, I actually think she would have been a good ally.

I don't know if she would have had the strength to stand up to Uncle B though, to stand up to Baba and the whole Family in my defence, against one of Their Own. She was new to Oman in the days when it happened, and she would have been the intern taking on the huge corporation. They would have crushed her.

But she always tried really hard to talk to us like friends.

She tried to advise us about schoolwork, about boys and love, about university and the issues we might face with racism and culture shock. But because I knew that she didn't know the REAL me, how could her advice resonate? The advice meant for regular daughters wouldn't fit someone like me.

So I didn't listen.

That was weird for her, because she always listened to her parents and valued their experiences, advice, and warnings. Everyone said that I was 'too-much-know', which I assume is some loose translation from Swahili for know-it-all, because I never listened and thought I knew best. I had to navigate my own childhood riddled with guilt, shame, and oppressive secrets, and no one knew better than me how that felt or how difficult that was.

If I weren't so unreachable, if I weren't Too-Much-Know, we might have had a good relationship. Now that I look back with less selfishness, I think sadly that my mum didn't have any real friends, and that's why she tried so hard.

Mama tried hard until she didn't.

She took an interest in school and who our best friends were, encouraging us to invite them home, where she offered to help us bake cookies. But like some little emo millennial Wednesday Addams, I didn't relate to the kids at school, who still played with abandoned innocence, so I didn't invite anyone home.

Mama offered to take us to the material shops or the tailor (yes, that was the extent of the Muscat shopping experience), but I wanted to hide behind baggy t-shirts, so I always declined.

She would excitedly suggest that the 'three girls of the house' get all dressed up for weddings together, including a little rouge (who still calls it rouge?!) and some kohl, but I had absolutely no interest in prettying myself up for Family functions.

She would sit at the end of my bed and try to communicate, but I averted my guilty eyes, in case she could see in them what I had done. And what I had seen.

And, eventually, she gave up.

Mama was gracious. That's a good word for her. Despite being married early, denied the glamourous life of her daydreams, and tricked into a life of dependence, she did not resent in me or Sara the youth that was now behind her. She didn't hate our clear skin and boundless energy and limitless potential. She didn't lament the small pouch at the bottom of her stomach, the mark of motherhood she would never lose. No snide, sarcastic comments or side glances.

Quite the opposite. She poured all her hopes for her life into us, hoped that we would travel solo and wait deep into our thirties before settling with one man. She prayed for fulfilling, flourishing careers, after mind-expanding college and travel years.

Whether it was going to be the weight of her resentment or the weight of her hopes, they both amounted to the same potential to disappoint.

There she was, Mama at my Halls of Residence door, bright and early and a little flustered, having rented a car, forgotten about driving on the left side of the road, and almost crashed into someone at a confusing roundabout. Luckily, her distraction meant that I was able to grab my bag and a coat and take her for coffee, stopping in at Semen's room to give him my keys and beg him to clear up and fumigate my room for me.

I had a bit of a hangover, so the coffee was great; the news of my parents' ongoing turmoil was a little harder to swallow.

I don't know why. After all, they had been clashing for most of my formative years. I guess it has something to do with one's ego: When the problem isn't in front of you, you think the problem has gone away. If there's no one in the forest to hear the tree falling, maybe your parents aren't fighting anymore?

Quite the opposite was the case. My emancipation had inspired my mother and she had decided now was the time to explore her own life. She mused that perhaps she'd move here to Scotland to be closer to me. (What the FUCK?!)

After my initial horror, I gathered that she was staying in a serviced apartment in Old Town and wanted to look around and catch up and have a tour of my university and meet my friends and see the castle and dip a toe in a loch.

Her return flight ticket was open ended, so she had all the time in the world.

Great.

It was the weekend, so she asked me to stay with her in her apartment, and I obeyed immediately, in order to buy me some excuses when I really needed them.

To be fair, we had a nice time.

It really hit me while she was there that Mama and I never spent any time one on one. It made me nervous, and I felt an overwhelming pressure to think of topics of conversation. At home in Muscat, I evaded both parents as often as possible, and if we did happen to eat a meal without blessed distractions, there were always loaded comments about my hair or my future, both evidently equally important.

When you're a student in a city, it is clearly unacceptable to do touristy stuff, unless someone from out of town happens to visit. She was my excuse for long strolls in the Botanical Gardens, a tour of the castle, a Hop-on-Hop-off bus tour and plenty of art gallery visits. I had no idea she had such an artistic eye. When she actually started speaking with some authority and insight, I was condescendingly impressed, until she told me she studied Art History, and then I felt like a tit. I guess you forget that your parents were people with knowledge and passions long before you came along.

I timidly showed her some of the photos in my growing portfolio.

And she genuinely loved them.

I took her to the places where I shot the photos, so I could explain why I chose those particular angles, and the contrasts I'd selected in Photoshop and the moods I was trying to create. I made her guess what I had taken close ups of, the details of my curls, of leaves and frost and shadows.

Mama said she was so proud of me and my talent.

I warmed from the inside of my semi-defrosted soul. She had been so busy for the last few years I'm not sure she even realised how hard I had been working to get into university, or how the girl who couldn't spell was now quoting Jean Paul Sartre. She had rightly moved on from focusing solely on us and Baba, to her own life, her own company, and her own career.

Maybe women reach a point where they decide to step back from sullen kids and unhappy marriages and start making sure that *they* are happy? Maybe MORE women should do that.

With the relief that comes from a slow fart, I began to release the blame I'd placed on my mum for not noticing and attending to my changes when I realised what Uncle B had done to me. Of course, I wish she had tended to me, asked me questions, asked Uncle B questions, figured it out and helped me, but parents are humans, just overgrown, clueless children really, and despite her best intentions, she's not clairvoyant. I had to keep reminding myself that Mama was already the mother of an infant when she was my age, and I can't keep a bloody cactus alive!

And so she went from dealing with shit from her husband and his family, to trying to deal with me, and getting more shit from my direction. No wonder she looked elsewhere for some satisfaction.

It occurred to me, as I released this blame, that Mama and I did the same thing, really. I escaped my depressingly limited options by running away from my family and running to university. And she escaped her small, unsatisfying life by unplugging from her family and logging on to her online university.

Huh. Turns out we were exactly the same.

Weird.

Still, we were basically strangers...

I arranged a dinner with Semen, who was very much Simon that night. He showered her with attention and compliments, and they were suddenly allies, lightly ribbing me while I sat feigning betrayal in the corner of the restaurant. He thought she was an absolute goddess—gorgeous and glamourous at forty-two. I thought he was just inveigling his way into her good graces, but he genuinely thought she was fabulous. She was well dressed, knowledgeable, threw her head back in laughter at his jokes, which became increasingly off colour with each glass of wine (at which she did not bat an eyelid), and she was equally risqué in her retorts. He whisked her into his arms as we left the restaurant and waltzed with her in the streets, singing "I Could Have Danced All Night".

She knew all the words.

She could harmonise with him.

She didn't need alcohol to be uninhibited enough to dance in the streets.

He called her 'My Fair Lady' as he kissed her hand, bowing low, and then hugged her good night.

Was she this Fabulous Creature? I had never seen her in this light!

I was re-evaluating truths I thought I knew to be self-evident. Look how free and happy she was!

It was good for her to get out of Oman and flex her liberated muscles.

It was good for me to see her as a person. She was a woman, not just a mother.

In the blur of her carefree twirls, I saw a movie trailer of her other life. The life where she didn't get married young and move to the other side of the world. A life where Sara and I weren't born. And suddenly the family photograph started fading, and our faces were replaced by interesting professors and exciting lovers.

It was a bloody good weekend.

Apart from, of course, when she wanted to complain about my dad.

'He's so controlling!'

'He has such antiquated ideas of what a woman's place should be!'

'He wants to own me!'

I knew all this, and I had my own opinions and struggles with Baba; it would take a miracle before we would ever be close again after the Norbert Nonsense, but I certainly didn't want to hear her badmouthing my dad.

Maybe the burden of Familial Duty was too deeply entrenched in my DNA, where duty and loyalty overrides resentments, guilt, and sins.

My mum and I weren't bosom buddies, and this wasn't some scumbag boyfriend she was venting about. Why didn't she get it? This was Mama shitting on Baba. And I was his *daughter*. Plus, I had my own dramas and heartache to deal with.

Mama walked me back to my dorm on Sunday night.

Edinburgh was showing off that evening.

It was the summer term, the word Summer so loosely bandied about in Scotland. The days were longer and the sun was out, sure, but it was still bloody chilly to me.

But students were buzzing lazily around the town like fireflies, released from the anxieties of exams, kissing on the grass in ever-extending twilight, sitting in beer gardens, sipping pints. Buskers, laughter, life. So weightless. So unburdened.

Mama was in love with the city and the way it made her feel young and light, like a student again, free from scrutiny and obligations. She felt like an artist and she felt beautiful, admired and complimented by my gorgeous, hip friend. She had her slightly outdated "Europe clothes" that, despite years in storage, somehow made her look effortlessly chic. And she loved the hum of life around her—real people with tattoos and piercings, all different hairstyles, and clothes that told you more about their personalities than an hour of questions; what music they liked, whether they were body-confident, if they were conservative or creative.

We discussed the idea of dress codes. I thought it was good for people to express themselves through clothing; actually, through any means they wanted to. Life was expression, said the girl who never expressed herself to her parents!

Mama agreed. She loved seeing all the different personalities expressed on one street, but she then asked me to consider that when people dress the same, as they do for Hajj, they are solely being judged for what is in their hearts. Imagine if people didn't spend time and lots of money on what they showed the world, and instead spent the time and resources on improving their character and their community? What if we weren't judged for our appearance, and everyone's loose apparel hid their figures, so no one could take excessive pride in their looks? We wouldn't judge or be judged, there would be fewer eating disorders, perhaps even less lust and violence.

'Who would we be as a society then?' she mused.

I looked at her and internally shook my head at how ignorant I had been of her quiet depth.

It was almost the end of the scholastic year, my first year abroad, and what had I learned?

Some stuff about business, yes, that's true.

I had met some wonderful friends, who taught me a whole world of new, potentially useless information.

But I hadn't found myself yet. In fact, despite having tried on a few hats, I was even more confused.

I was homesick.

And this place was no Home to me.

Was I always going to have a restless spirit? People like that never find peace.

Mike's comments had cut me. Great, just what I needed; something else to feel insecure about. Something else to agonise over, to feel shit about. Something else to need to shut out and dull.

I had also found my Soul Mate in the most unexpected place, somewhere I had always been told was haram. Another reason to question everything I knew! I figured I would probably end up marrying Semen; at least we would always laugh. And bonus, my mother already adored him.

And I learned that love just made you feel bad. That's what Mike, Fido, and my parents had taught me.

Mama and I strolled slowly through the streets amicably. She linked her arm through mine, like she did with her friends at her school in London, bold girls confident in their youth and numbers, raucously laughing down the high street in uniforms, she told me wistfully.

We had found a delicate balance of talking about relatively superficial subjects, backing off warily from getting too close to a potential confrontation, like encountering a snake in your path. We laughed about Mamma Mia's antics and talked about how well Sara was doing at school and avoided the subject of her unhappy marriage to my father. And also why I had called her, sobbing my heart out.

And we smiled and sauntered, almost like friends.

Despite this, I got a really uneasy feeling as we approached Halls. She insisted on coming up to see what I had 'done with the place'. It was a fair request. Why would I want her to just go back to her apartment?

Since Semen still had my key, I texted him asking him to be there too. Plus, he would charm her to distraction in case there was still a pack of fags or rolling papers lying about.

We walked up to my room and Semen was there in the doorway looking dramatic.

It's Semen, of course he was looking dramatic.

I should be more specific.

His eyes were wide and he was trying to mouth something to me. But since I haven't used my lip-reading skills since, ummm EVER, I kept shrugging and whispering, 'What?!'

He moved out of the way and there, sitting on the edge of my single bed, sat Baba.

Well, after around three minutes of Mama shouting like a cornered harpy and Baba trying to calm her down in patronising hushed tones, I ushered an open-mouthed Semen out of there. He thought of my mum as his emerald-eyed Salma Hayek; he didn't need to see this and shatter his illusion. She was about to go from Dusk till Dawn.

I took him to his room, had half a fag with him as we stared mutely at each other, and then I went upstairs again.

As I approached my room, I heard it.

Tears.

The word Divorce.

And someone being slapped.

I honestly don't know who was crying or who had slapped whom. I didn't fancy hanging about to find out, so doing my finest ostrich impression, I grabbed my handbag, my gay best friend / future husband, and a bus to The Hound.

I was in denial, in retreat, in flight, in need of getting utterly fucked up. I wanted to shut it out! I wanted to escape. I wanted to forget, to get blotto, to get completely, sweetly annihilated. I didn't want to remember anything. It was exactly what I set out to do. It's exactly what I achieved.

Which is why I can't really be sure how I woke up in hospital.

When I woke up, Baba was standing over me like a thundering question mark. He had aged several years since last night.

Wait, was it last night? A few days ago? I had no idea what day it was, where I was, or what had happened.

What was going on? I felt terrible.

I strained my brain to think... It hurt.

Think, what was the last thing I remembered? A club. Throbbing music, throbbing dance floor, throbbing head. Semen. Fighting with him, animosity. More fighting, raised voices, shouting, slapping, divorce.

FUCK. Yes, divorce.

But how did that bring me here, and where was here?

I started panicking. My breathing started stalling and I couldn't catch my breath properly. No matter how hard I tried, my lungs felt shallow, like I couldn't fill them properly. I tried to sit up, but something was holding me down. I needed to bend forward so I could take a deep breath. I panicked.

My father ran out, calling for my mum.

Was I dead? Was this some kind of purgatory? Like a waiting room for the Next Step, like in *Beetlejuice*?

Mama ran in with a nurse.

Fuck. I'm in hospital.

Semen filled me in. (That sounds bad.)

We had taken a bus to The Hound, and there, Semen tells me, we had a vertiginous cocktail of cocktails, pills, fags, and a weed chaser. I was furious and frustrated, and therefore this particular visit to our favourite haunt was already doomed to be a little less fun than on other occasions. The pills weren't having the desired effect of joy and love, release and inhibition; instead blurring my vision, making me sweaty and nauseous. I was bumping into irritated revellers on the dance floor, walking into the fetid walls of the toilet stalls, unable to hold my head up properly. The pills had loads of speed in them and I started getting really antsy and anxious. I didn't want to go home and I was about to get thrown out of the bar. I was unsure if my parents would still be in my room, and I was completely unable to face them. No one was listening to why I couldn't see or talk to them. I started having a panic attack...

Semen did try and talk me off the ledge and away from the bar several times, but I was having none of it and even tried to pick a fight with him. Self-destructive mode ON!

He didn't leave my side, though, even as I called him names and shouted that he would never understand a girl's impossible duties or what was expected of me by Society. I was shouting incoherently about jinn and fighting parents. About marriage and hijabs. About shame and hate and identity. Lashing out with my arms and my tongue.

Oh, the drama.

I must have looked and sounded like a complete knob.

He walked with me, by my side, preventing me picking fights with homeless people minding their own business on the edge of the park, and stopping me from tripping over my own feet. As we approached Halls, I was sobbing, snot running down my face, and clutching my chest, coughing and wheezing. He was amused by the histrionics, taking mental notes to tease me with the following day, until I looked up at him and squeezed out of my twisted throat that I couldn't breathe.

He told me that he'd never seen my face so contorted. After he emptied the contents of my bag onto the street, he realised I had left my inhaler in my room.

He flagged down a taxi and they raced me to the closest ER, where he pushed me in the door and fled.

He didn't stick around because of all the drugs in his system, and I don't blame him.

Several hours passed before my parents received a call to come to the hospital. Had they noticed that I was missing? How long before they stopped fighting in my room? Did they move the fight elsewhere?

I had suffered a sudden onset asthma attack, exacerbated by my creative mix of stimulants and extreme emotional anxiety. I had only been out for a few hours. The doctors used a breathing tube to open up the airways. I was mostly unconscious for that, although I woke up with the comedown hangover headache from hell and an excruciatingly sore throat. And even when the drips sorted out my dehydration, I was still left with The Fear, that dread of someone letting you know what got you into this position.

My days in hospital were a mixture of exhaustion and humiliation.

Mama and Baba visited at all hours, alone, together, and treated me like a wounded kitten, bringing my favourite chocolates, flowers, jokes, and books. Suddenly the parents felt like they were united—in their grief, but also in solidarity with each other.

I felt so foolish. I had almost killed myself in a self-destructive rage binge. I could have caused so much pain for everyone that I loved so much. Between my sheepish humility and shame, I was meek and respectful, loving and appreciative. I felt terrible for putting them through such an ordeal, and I was determined to make it up to them.

I silently vowed that I would support their decisions regarding their own relationship and stop making it about me.

With the end of term approaching, they tenderly sat by my bedside and convinced me to change my plans for the holidays. I had wanted to stay in Edinburgh and get a summer job to save some money, but they reasoned that no one knew what toll the attack had had on my heart, on my lungs, and on my stamina. Mama insisted that I had worried her half to death and she wanted to be close to me to keep an eye on me. Rightfully playing on my guilty heart strings.

Why don't I come home? they asked. I had to move out of Halls anyway for the summer, so where would I stay? What if I relapsed? Who would be there for me?

I could return to Muscat with them, to recover and convalesce. I'd have Sara there with me, she'd missed me so much this whole year (more guilt), and best of all, it was Ramadhan, my favourite time of year. Mamma Mia would come to Oman for half of it, as usual, and we would play cards and binge watch TV shows.

From my NHS bed, it all sounded perfect.

The entire flight back to Muscat was spent in silence. Baba was unreachable and Mama was melancholy.

I wasn't imagining it. I felt really uneasy, like they had some inkling of what I had been up to that night. What if the doctor told them about the drug cocktail I had consumed? Nah! That was my business. I was an adult.

He would have no right.

Right?

But surely I was stressing unnecessarily. If they'd known, they would have shouted at me, humiliated me in front of the doctors, Semen, and the other patients. And they would have punished me. They were just worried parents. I'd put them through a bloody intense ordeal. Seeing your daughter almost die. Again, I sank into shame.

Maybe they'd been shocked into a silent prayer of gratitude and renewed appreciation for me! Maybe they wouldn't pick fights with me and just accept me for who I am now. Maybe the close shave would give us a new lease on life together?!

Why, then, weren't they smiling at me, loving and relieved, touching my hand to reassure themselves that the nightmare was behind us?

As for me, I swore to myself that I would swear off alcohol. It just made me messy and loud, crass and annoying. I silently promised this to God on the flight back to Muscat. If they don't bring up the whole ER Episode, I won't drink again. How does that sound?

As if God needs deals from me. I'm an idiot.

We landed in Oman. The aeroplane doors opened and the dusty heat slammed into us as we walked to the top of the steps. Like opening the oven door to check on your slow roasting life. The hairdryer wind blew my hair away from my face without any of the relief that a breeze usually affords.

With the fiery blast, the memories hit me too.

I hate the summers here.

Give me a crisp Edinburgh evening, please.

There's nothing to do. The sand on the beaches burns the bottoms of your feet. You can't sit outside, you can't walk, or swim. The humidity is unbearable, fogging up your sunglasses as soon as you step out of the house and soaking through your clothes within seconds, even when you're simply standing still. The steering wheel of your car burns your hands, and the air conditioners everywhere drone all day, drying up your throat and lungs.

It was dusk when we landed too, and I always found sunset to be the saddest time of day. It reminded me of sitting in my room as a remorseful and disturbed ten-year-old. It was the loneliest time of day for me. Bibi says the heavens are open at dusk so prayers can ascend directly to God. Maybe that's why I felt so tortured. There was no veil between us, and God knew exactly what I had done, and He was disappointed. Sunset was when darkness began to creep into my soul.

I didn't know if I could bear the whole season here before going back to Scotland for my second year. Two months of oppressive heat and the scandal and scare.

In the car from the airport, I stared out of the window at our small capital city between the mountains and the sea. I barely recognised Muscat. It felt like going back to your junior school and finding that the halls that you thought were huge and the classrooms that you found intimidating, are in reality Lilliputian. It was like finding an old piece of clothing and putting it on only to realise that it was now two sizes too small. I was now a different size, a different person.

I didn't recognise myself in Oman.

I could feel hot tears falling down my cheeks and I turned my face farther away from everyone so they couldn't see how sad and lost I felt to be Home.

I fell into my sister's arms and wept when I got to our room. She hadn't rearranged anything. Her clothes and possessions hadn't crept over to my side, like overgrown plants in abandoned ruins. She had left my side intact, like some sort of shrine. I would have turned her bed into my clothes horse, her dressing table into my desk, and removed all her toiletries to make room for mine, the minute she'd left.

She held me while I cried. She didn't need me to explain my misery, and I didn't need to tell her how relieved I was that she was there.

Ramadhan came and went, and as I started preparing for my return to Scotland, the parentals came to my room, asked Sara to leave us to talk, and sat me down. A thousand wings flapped inside my belly like a Hitchcock nightmare scene. A confrontation was a-coming and I desperately wanted to flee from it.

Well, turns out the doctors DID tell my parents about the assortment of drugs in my system.

And the copious amount of alcohol.

And the cigarettes I'd been smoking for years that had affected my lungs.

I didn't know it at the time, but there were harsh, hushed words hissed between them at the hospital. Baba said that I was losing my culture, losing my religion, and that the whole Edinburgh Experiment just proved that I was not ready for the evil influences of the West. They could not afford to lose me to the loose morals of the mzungus.

Mama, although not so dramatic in her prognosis, had to agree. This was not what they raised their little girl to be or to do. They could accept me being a moody teen, but not a debauched young woman.

So they finally agreed on something.

And they came into my bedroom in Muscat. Muscat, to where they had convinced me to fly back with them for the summer, under the guise of guilt and concern.

They sat in my room, the walls of which seemed to be claustrophobically closing in around me.

And Baba told me that I was never going back to Scotland.

I screamed. I cried. I swore. I threatened.

I freaked the fuck out.

It didn't matter. Baba had taken my passport and even Mama didn't know where it was. At one of his siblings' houses, no doubt.

They had tricked me. They had planned this, and I had unwittingly agreed to my own capture. They had lured me back to Oman with promises of protection, my sister, home cooking and care.

I heard the words Culture, Alcohol, Religion, Drugs, Upbringing through the ringing in my ears and my protests.

I was trapped.

All my limited options ran on the computer screen of my brain, like the opening credits of *The Matrix*.

I couldn't escape if I didn't have a passport.

Could I get a new passport?

I couldn't bribe anyone.

I could ask Bibi to intervene, but she wouldn't.

I could ask Mamma Mia to intervene, but Baba would pay her no mind.

I couldn't burn the house down. (I went through ALL my options.)

I had nothing to lose, so I let rip.

I accused them of being shitty parents, of fighting constantly, of being selfish, of having no idea nor caring what their daughters were actually like, or how their pernicious relationship had affected us.

And in an unprecedented display of disrespect, I stood up, my head higher than theirs, looked down at them, and said that the reason I had taken drugs was BECAUSE OF THEM!

It's all a little blurry after that, but I know that when Baba jumped up to hit me, I swung my leg up in defence and my foot connected with something disturbingly like cock and balls.

I fell into a pretty long depression after that. I washed, sometimes, when I couldn't stand the smell of myself.

I barely ate. I lost seven kilos in the first fortnight and twelve in total over a year. I have to admit, I enjoyed the more concave feeling of my stomach when I lay down in bed, but it didn't really matter. I never really got dressed.

I ignored Sara's pleas and would rarely touch the food she brought up to the room, once the parents had gone out.

I ignored Semen's increasingly worried WhatsApps, wondering when I'd be back.

I ignored Cousin Adel's messages, asking if I was in Oman and coming over to get baked.

I ignored the university's emails, enquiring after fees.

I ignored messages from Nada asking whether I would like to share accoms with her for our second year.

I ignored Mamma Mia's assurances that everything would turn out okay.

I didn't really give a fuck what anyone had to say.

Any guilt I felt for worrying anyone by my hospitalisation was so far behind me, I couldn't remember the feeling underneath the filthy bile taste of contempt.

Of course, Baba had no intention of reaching out to me. It was a child's place to reach out, to initiate the peace-making, with an offer of apology and admission of guilt. (Or avoid all contact till everyone forgets about it.) It was not the adult's job, especially as he was the one righteously punishing me.

Mama, on the other hand, had seen me in Edinburgh. She had yearned for and tasted that life, and she had naively convinced herself that my attack was brought on by an accidental use of drugs, like maybe someone had spiked my soft drink. She thought it was probably an unfortunate one-off situation that had caused my airways to shut down.

She didn't want to deny me finishing my degree. She didn't want to deny me the freedom to walk through the park and to dance with Simon in the streets, to graduate or simply to live.

So Mama made two promises. It was a dirty deal but she made it, and she stuck to it.

She promised to get me out of Oman if I could prove to them both that I was responsible, that I could get back to my roots, and convince them that I was no longer doing drugs. If I promised that I could be a good daughter, she would write to the uni and defer me for a scholastic year.

It was a distant light at the end of the tunnel.

This was her promise to me.

I held her hand and put my head on her shoulder, in silent and deep gratitude, tears rolling out the side of my eye and onto her shoulder.

But then something occurred to me. How had she managed to get Baba to agree to that? He was unyielding and uncompromising. There was no way he would have admitted that his punishment was too harsh. How did she get him to capitulate?

She asked me to trust her, and I had no choice, so I did.

She told me the only way to get out was to use this year to exhibit obedience and compliance. Don't complain when Baba told me to cover my hair or go to Family functions. Answer the first time I am called and do errands with a smile. Don't stay out late and don't touch cigarettes or alcohol or any other kinds of drugs (she couldn't name any). The best thing to do was get a temporary job.

I agreed to all terms.

We started talking about what kind of job I'd like to do, what my interests were, what kind of basic salary I could expect with my qualifications, and what bonuses I should ask for from an employee, as a single woman living with her parents.

We went to her computer and Sara joined us.

There were jobs at all the big places: oil and gas companies, PDO, Oman LNG, and telecom companies Omantel and Nawras. Entry-level, low-skilled jobs for school leavers. And plenty of more interesting jobs for people with degrees.

I tried not to get disheartened at my lack of qualifications and the slim career pickings. Arrogantly, I felt like an entry level job was beneath me, but looking at it objectively, I was a school leaver who really only spoke one language. Mama and Sara were so encouraging though. I suppose they were fearful of me slipping back into my depression-stained pyjamas.

Delving deeper, we found an interesting job at the Opera House, and another at a local art gallery that needed someone to help with admin, no real experience necessary but fluent English a must. I applied for the gallery gig.

Mama showed us how her job worked, matching people in her data base with vacancies. And how she had managed to secure exclusive seconding rights with certain companies, without relying on Vitamin W.

She showed the difference in pay grade and perks between certain level of jobs, for those with a master's versus a bachelor's, and those with fluent Arabic and the perquisite-heavy expat packages.

She showed us a few CVs to demonstrate how to and how NOT to.

We found a particularly funny one that had clearly been written in formal Arabic and Google translated without anyone to proofread it.

*To the director of the employment matters by company of the respected gazelle (*the name of Mama's company was Ghazal, meaning Gazelle*)*

The subject – he looked for a job

A honour of the might of a twist has he that I lay a my letter these between your two hands and by the senior of the hope by preparing carefully the kind person identified you.

I am from postgraduates of the scholastic year 2010, I walked is where they endeavoured for the search from job I attain the salary's month a part from to need her. But the good luck does not enter into a federation with me, then all the doors had come by night but without use. A muzzling that I am obtaining the sessions in the computer and the English language.

The hope lays my chest in that you will aim the sides by any job you look at it as the opportunity of a twist, and this for reply be near a simple favour and the charity for the homeland they compromised his foot be slow, and I work diligent with and a sincerity of the service's nationalist.

With my best regards and estimations.

Suddenly, for the first time in three weeks, I was laughing with Mama and Sara, bent over double, crying, reading this CV cover letter to each other like a Shakespeare soliloquy, competing to see who could bring the most gravitas to the nonsensical prose.

It was such a relief to think that I might actually make it through the year.

Oh.

The second promise Mama made was to Baba.

On the condition that I was an exemplary daughter, he would allow me to go back to study abroad.

If she agreed not to divorce him.

The gallery was in an old bungalow in Muttrah, the ancient port city of Muscat that stretches along the coast. The city starts at the beautiful Al Bustan Palace Hotel and sweeps past the marina and the fish market, where vendors peddle fresh lobster and tuna daily. It then stretches to our "famous" souq, ominously named *Al Dhalam* (The Darkness) for its labyrinthine alleyways bustling with haggling tourists and locals alike, and vendors hawking beautiful silver artifacts and Made-in-Taiwan tack.

The old city is watched over by a sixteenth-century Portuguese fort and surrounded by a wall, the gate of which used to be locked every night after dusk as recently as forty years ago. The narrow merchant houses with ornate balconies were built close together in odd shapes, punctuated by minarets piercing the sky, all lining crooked lanes not built for cars. The Palace, its gold and turquoise pillars reaching up, sits on the water at the edge of the town, observing the rows of lights on the sickle-shape Corniche.

I loved driving to Muttrah. It's separated from modern Muscat by a circle of coastal mountains and as you burst through them, a triangle of bright turquoise sea beyond the hills beckons you away from the malls and McDonald's to something older and purer.

I had to park quite far from the gallery, illegally no doubt, and was more than a little sweaty when I walked up for my interview. The outer walls of the gallery were swallowed by flaming bougainvillea and the building was protected by a heavy rusted gate. The courtyard, with its wrought iron tables littered with overflowing ceramic ashtrays, and its water feature, was reminiscent of being on an island in the Mediterranean.

The eccentric, elderly Greek woman who owned the gallery opened the door in wide trousers and a flowing cream abaya and chunky jewellery around her neck and wrists. Her silver hair was long, tapering into wisps by her waist, which made me wonder why most old ladies cut their hair short.

This was Alex.

She ushered me in. The old city, the rusty gate, the quaint courtyard all belied a high-ceilinged, well-lit, modern open space that would not have looked out of place in a chic New York gallery. She had installed some skylights for more natural Omani sunlight to stream in. There was a reception desk, which was no more than a soulless white upright rectangle with a streamlined lamp. With so much light, you could hardly see the corners of the room or any shadows. It was like Heaven. Not metaphorically; it was SO white!

The back office, on the other hand, had two messy, paper-strewn desks, a variety of comfortable sandals under them, and smelled like fags. She smoked skinny menthol cigarettes. Often.

And she swore so much it made even *my* ears hurt!

It was love at first 'cunt'.

I presented my CV, prepared to explain and make excuses for my disjointed university career.

She tossed it to the side and asked me what I thought of art.

I told her that I thought it was the only way to tell the truth, for people who didn't know how to otherwise.

And she replied that I had the job.

Alex was a fag-stained breath of fresh air. I hadn't met anyone like her in Oman, although the truth was that I had barely socialised outside of my Family before.

She had been married to a supplier to the Palace in the very earliest days of modern Oman, who had died of lung cancer. (That didn't scare Alex; she wasn't a 'fucking quitter'.) Her husband had been invaluable to the people at the top, so he and Alex had been granted permanent residency. She had lived here so long, she was treated like one of the locals, spoke fluent Arabic, and had started the gallery to give something back to the community.

'Fucking pearls before swine to be honest, darling. Excuse the pig reference. Omanis are the best people I know. But do they care about art? Do they, fuck!'

Her gallery therefore remained an ignored and forgotten oasis of culture in the perfect setting of historical and abandoned Muttrah. She had had a grand opening with several ministers and royalty attending out of respect and in the hope of supporting the arts. The newspapers covered the inauguration, and the gallery had remained empty from then on.

She insisted I call her Alex. Just Alex. No Aunty or Mrs. Here I was, calling an older lady by her first name. Casual as school buddies.

'I may have lived many years, darling, but I'm not old,' she'd say, offering me a fag every time she pulled one out of a silver case. I wasn't smoking. It wasn't hard to quit, to be honest. I'd kind of lost the taste for it, as well as the lung capacity.

I think Alex hired me more for company than for any actual assistance. I did a little paperwork, but otherwise we drank coffee and she told me about her colourful past and we discussed Oman, how she came with her husband in the '70s when there was nothing here but a tiny airport and a vision. They had been so happy. They planted the seed of their life here and couldn't be happier with the way it had grown.

She couldn't believe I was so ungrateful. How could I hate being in Oman? A country that maintained a peaceful, neutral stance in a world of hot-headed and dangerous religious politics.

We were so blessed to have a leader like our Sultan. So lucky to have the kindest locals. So fortunate to have the wealth of nature, some of the best diving in the world, a beautiful coastline, green mountains and verdant oases, intimidating deserts.

It pissed me off that she was right, and I started to open my ears, eyes, and heart to listen to a story about a country that I didn't know.

She told me of the expats that came dribbling into Oman in the '70s and '80s, with hardship-post salaries that afforded them houses back in their home countries, paid off within a few years. They worked hard and they played hard. They had to be creative to entertain themselves, so they spent weekends camping in the deserts or on the untouched beaches. They would find a boat and would congregate at one house or another after a long day at sea, to BBQ and get pissed. They threw wild parties in their small incestuous compounds, and they had a young community that helped build a nation of which they were proud.

It was tough. Everyone was cutting their teeth and learning to cope with very little, but it was a simple and genuine existence. The shops were pretty bare, and many young couples were starting families far from home, far from family support, in a country that started with only three schools in 1970. But they loved it, they loved each other, and they thought of Oman proudly as their country.

I told her about uni, how much I was enjoying it and about my hospital debacle and my dad and how I had ended up trapped here, to give her some background to my story and not make me look like a total spoilt brat.

'It's all perspective, my little grasshopper,' she explained, although it was no explanation at all. What had grasshoppers got to do with the price of fish?

'This could be the work experience you need to complement your degree! Think how valuable a year of paid fucking work experience is. No one else on your course has that luxury. And as a bonus, you lucky bugger, you get to spend it with me! Now let's get some use out of that useless fucking degree, eh? How about you come up with some business ideas to get some asses in this place?'

Oh great, I was now expected to do some work...

Although, I was quite excited about this prospect, because I had an idea.

In Edinburgh, the bars always wanted student bands to play in their venues, because they would bring in a big crowd of all the band's friends, students on their course, roommates, teammates, all spending money on subsidised beer. And the venues only had to pay the bands a paltry fee. It was a win-win. For the bars and for the bands who got an opportunity to play their forgettable, angsty punk tunes to a packed room, and possibly get laid. We just needed to apply the same business plan.

Approximately.

Exhibit an Omani artist with lots of family members. Maybe even a royal, or a minister, so people would not only be interested, but obliged. Wouldn't matter what we thought of the art, while we established ourselves. And when we had real patrons, real buyers, we could be more avant-garde, fussier and truer to the art we admired.

I knew exactly who the first victim / artist would be.

A second cousin, who was second-tier royalty from her father's side, used her time and above-average artistic talents to turn old Omani / Zanzibari coins into jewellery. She used semiprecious stones and a deaf Indian artisan to make necklaces; some dainty wires holding a single coin, and some chunkier twisted ropes of gleaming stones holding a large silver box, originally used to carry messages. Rings, and droplet earrings, and bracelets in lapis lazuli, deep garnet, sparkling cut aquamarine, and 3D-looking tiger's eye.

Alex put me in charge of procuring her, getting the collection together, and using 'those bloody hashtags' to spread the word. And Alex herself pulled some strings with the papers, the high-end magazines, and some of her old friends in high places.

We framed some pieces that were too heavy to wear but looked beautiful mounted and lit up. And we displayed everything else in cases without price tags. I took pictures of Sara wearing the collection, in late afternoon sunshine, for the catalogue we produced for the gallery, and then we Instagrammed the shit out of it.

The exhibition was a success. A who's who of Muscat (which I joked was like the sanest people in an asylum) sipped sparkling date juice from champagne flutes. The media covered the event in true sycophantic style, and we managed to create a vibrating buzz. The framed pieces sold immediately; everyone wanted some Omani history on their walls. The jewellery sold well too, and we collected a tidy profit and the start of a reputation.

I also met and courted two very popular artists at the opening: one an Omani man known for his bold Islamic themed and very pricey oil paintings, the other a Ukrainian ex-cabin crew from whom the wealthy commissioned art.

Our next exhibitions were sorted.

Alex was very happy and I fantasised that maybe soon, when I got the confidence, my photographs would be exhibited on those wide, white walls.

I had the beginnings of a sense of pride in my existence, like a tiny pilot light warming me from within. Not since I aced my A levels had I had a sense of achievement or satisfaction. I had handled something. I had created something, and I hadn't fucked it up.

The pay wasn't great, sure, but it didn't matter since my overheads were minimal, considering I was living at home, being fed, and driving one of the family cars.

(This sounds like a luxury, of course, especially when I found out that some of my mzungu friends had to pay rent at their parents' house! It was, as with most blessings, double edged. Even if I wanted to, I COULDN'T leave my parents' house until I moved into my husband's house. Mamma Mia was the only person I knew who got away with it, but she lived with another lady, called Jazz, who was a bass player, so it wasn't as frowned upon as a woman living alone. Plus, she was in Dubai, so, out of sight, out of mind.)

I didn't spend any of my salary because I rarely went out, instead choosing to spend time at home, mostly in my room, making sure the door was open to make a show of reading, studying, and performing my five daily prayers.

Going to Family functions was a necessary evil, but they were part of the deal and I was nothing if not focussed. Harnessing the dedication I employed to catch up with my floundered education, I swallowed my anger with Baba, threw a scarf over my head, and greeted all his siblings with deference and smiles, even when their snide comments about me being back in Oman made my lips curl. I made some saccharine comment about being homesick but planning to go back and complete my degree next year, *insha'Allah*.

My eyes were constantly darting around the room, looking for Uncle B. There was a limit to my Oscar-worthy performances, and he was where the show ended.

The jewellery cousin, Nadine, had some friends with boats, Omani friends who had come back from university in London and Boston, come back to join their family businesses and determined to enjoy everything their land had to offer. They invited me and Sara out with them, on Nadine's recommendation.

It was strange because I was actually nervous. I didn't know these people, and I worried about who they were. Would they gossip about me and tarnish my reputation? In my experience, the people I had always mixed with here could be petty and jealous, backbiting and bad-mouthing others out of boredom and envy.

I didn't want anything to ruin my chances of going back to finish my degree. I didn't want my father to take something from this innocent outing and use it as an excuse to keep me here longer. I couldn't afford any bumps on my road out of here, but a day on the water with the sea breeze in my hair sounded like the closest thing to freedom I had had in a while.

I needn't have worried. As the boats pulled away from the marina, the music came on, the cooler came out, a couple of them grabbed a beer, and outer garments came off as they held on to the rails of the boat, bumping over the waves in bikinis as if we were in the South of France.

And no one batted an eyelid.

There were guys and girls not related to each other, and they laughed with abandon and let their laughter get carried away by the wind. I was once again surprised at how little I knew about the different kinds of people here.

We took all three boats to the empty, hushed coves and bays of Bandar Khayran, accessible only by boat. The mirror-still waters of the Arabian Sea lay settled and silent in their cradle between mountains.

The bay came alive with music and jet skis, squealing and splashing into the water. Beer and sandwiches for lunch and jokes all day. Sara and I wore t-shirts over our one-piece swim-suits, totally unprepared for the unselfconscious carefree attitude of these Omanis. They were well travelled, and fascinating. They chatted all day and not once did they talk idly about anyone who wasn't present. Not once did they stir shit! They discussed the latest technology, music they had just been introduced to, movies, environmental issues, travel, books.

One of them had gone diving in the Galapagos Islands and got a mild case of the bends going too deep following hammerhead sharks. They compared the diving there to that in the Maldives and concluded that Oman was still world class.

Others had gone to boarding school in Switzerland and were planning a ski trip in the winter.

They tried to come up with creative ideas to inject life into Oman's tourism sector in general and specifically how to improve the nightlife in Muscat.

They collected all their cans and fag butts and cleaned up the beaches of others' trash, so proud were they of their country's natural beauty.

They included me and Sara in their circle, explained old in-jokes to us so we wouldn't feel left out, so that by the time we pulled back to the marina before sunset, we all felt like old buddies.

Talking to these young Omanis who were sent abroad to get degrees and work experience from the West, I learned that it never occurred to any of them to NOT come home. Quite the opposite; they looked forward to their return. Sure, there were restrictions and familial duties, but this was no cruel dictatorship or third-world backwater. This was a young country, and as the next generation, they had a chance to shape it. How many other twenty-somethings can say the same? They thought a brain drain was a waste of natural talent at best, and ingratitude at worst.

They didn't judge my enforced "gap year" at all. They knew better than most how tough it was to marry the two diametrically opposed cultures. Sara showed them a couple of my photographs and Nadine said, "You see, the new artists of this country of ours! You are another one of Oman's rising stars!"

All my life, I had only hung out with my cousins; they were at my schools, at every social gathering I ever attended. I'd never really fraternised with anyone who didn't share some genetic code.

I had never met these guys before, but they insisted that we were welcome back on the boats any time.

I hated to admit it, but occasionally I felt glad to be here and not in Edinburgh.

I kinda lost touch with Semen. It takes some real effort to lose touch with someone, considering the myriad ways to stay in contact these days, but I purposely hid from him. All these ways to connect and yet I felt isolated.

I think I was humiliated by my ridiculous display of self-destruction, at forcing my friend to drop me at a hospital and run away like a criminal.

I was ashamed that I was some kind of university dropout.

I was mortified that I was fitting into a clichéd stereotype of an overbearing, dominating Muslim father effectively imprisoning his daughter.

I would sometimes look at Semen's pictures on Instagram, and he would look at mine, generically double tapping them as if we were nothing but acquaintances. He would periodically give me the gossip, scandalous titbits of who was sleeping with whom, news we would have revelled in only eight months ago, but I couldn't bear it now, knowing that I easily could be the topic of others' ridicule. 'Did you hear about Summer Virgin Summer? She was kidnapped by her own father!'

I was embarrassed that Semen was moving on with his degree and I wasn't.

I also kinda stalked SMF Mike on Insta. I can't really pinpoint how I felt when I found out that he had broken up with Jenny. Some vindictive vindication, I guess. But Jenny was hardly the obstacle to our love, so why gloat?

I still got butterflies when I looked at his pics, and my face would glow hot with anger and shame, so I scrolled past them quickly, as if he could see out from under his rogue curls and out of his photos and catch me, phone in hand, staring at him.

How silly my crush was. I only fancied him because he would never fancy me back. It was the safest way to experience all the butterflies, the daydreams, the fantasies, without having to open my heart.

It's the same reason I'd fancied Fido for so long.

So, I could be in love without being in a relationship. I didn't really want a relationship. I was too afraid of them. A relationship would mean that I would have to communicate! That I would have to be honest about what I was hiding.

And why I was lying.

And why the fuck I was the way that I was.

Being married meant that you had to tell your partner exactly who you were and what you had been through.

And it meant being honest with yourself.

Well, that was the kind of marriage I aspired to, but I wasn't able to be entirely honest. I didn't know how. I had been lying for so long that I could no longer distinguish the truth from my own excuses. So best to avoid the whole messy scene.

Obviously, most people, like Fido, didn't think that was what marriage was about at all. I bet he never told his coquettish bride that he smoked weed, let alone dealt heroin.

If I had lived, it could easily have been another twenty-two years before I lost my virginity. I couldn't imagine the thought of letting someone in. (And I don't just mean "country matters".)

I just couldn't imagine myself being that vulnerable, that authentic.

So, logically, falling in love with the *idea* of falling in love was the safest way to feel something, without offering anything.

·

I wonder how Semen, Nada, and SMF Mike will react when they find out I'm dead.

I wonder how long it will take them to find out.

Poor Semen Jones. He will be devastated.

Summer "Dead" Summer.

•

In the meantime, the story of how I had made a complete tit of myself and been fooled into returning to Oman had been passed on to Bibi, Grandad, Uncle Mo, and Mamma Mia.

At first, they felt bad for me and then of course, in true White style, they found it inappropriately hilarious.

Not that I had nearly died, of course! But that I had been so ridiculous. That I had got so wasted, ended up in hospital, and ended up back where I had started.

They weren't devoid of sympathy, but they did find it, and me, ludicrous.

And so, to prevent me taking myself too seriously, they always referred to my year abroad—laughing the whole time—as the Edinburgh Episode.

That's because they don't know what happened last week.

Which was no laughing matter.

•

"But if you pardon and overlook and forgive – then indeed Allah is Forgiving and Merciful" The Quran 64:14

Forgiveness is a universe in its scope. Mercy is everything. It can change the landscape of a relationship, of a life. Even of an Afterlife.

To forgive someone is to release them from chains, from prisons. From Hell.

You can resent someone forever and keep ingesting that venom that insidiously spreads from your belly, expecting them to die, but in reality, killing yourself from within with malignant hate.

Forgiveness is freedom! You have the power to free someone with your absolution.

And you can liberate *yourself* from your own caustic self-loathing. Or you can hate and blame yourself forever, shrinking yourself into a shadow, cowering from the voices in your head.

It is a gift. You can withhold it or give it generously and hold the power to alter the entire world for someone.

It is a blessing. You can desire it, require it, and be denied, and the denial will squeeze the joy out of your soul until it resembles a shrivelled date, rotten and black.

Mercy is everything.

I am relying on Forgiveness.

I didn't know how to forgive myself for what I had done. I didn't think I deserved to be let off the hook.

I *should* have gifted it to myself. The greatest gift of all.

But I never gave it to my dad. And I never gave it to Uncle B.

Someone wise once said, if you want to guarantee Forgiveness from Allah, you need to pardon all those who have wronged you. And if you can find it in your heart to forgive someone for the worst thing they have done to you, perhaps God will forgive the worst sins that you have committed.

I so desperately wanted God's Mercy.

But what a heavy caveat!

How was I supposed to forgive my uncle? When I thought of him, I could feel acid burning my brain, searing my veins, so toxic was my hatred for him and what he had made me. How could I ever release him of the guilt that he had himself earned with his own fingers, with his own tongue?

I could *say* that I forgive him, in order to gain God's Mercy, but it would be lip service. I wouldn't mean it, and God, being The Omnipotent One, would definitely know.

My whole existence, since the age of ten, I had been secretly hoping that God would punish this psycho sicko in this life and the next. If I forgave him, then I would have absolved him of his sin, and maybe God wouldn't punish him.

And I couldn't risk that.

As for Baba, he was my father, and inside I forgave him. Of course I did. I understood him. I didn't like him sometimes, but do we really like everyone that we love? I know that he didn't really like me either. He didn't understand the women in his life—nor was he trying to—but he did love us, in his own clumsy, heavy-handed way.

I resented him for beating me, but I forgave him.

I was still bitter about the way he handled the Edinburgh Episode, but I forgave him.

The fact that I had landed on unexpectedly happy feet in Muscat was a lucky coincidence that had nothing to do with his malicious move. I loved my job. Alex was an inspiration. I was saving a little money too, so I would be the only student not struggling on a budget when I returned in the autumn.

Nadine and her friends often invited me to hilariously themed parties at their homes, where everyone made an effort with their fancy dress, and what happened at the party, stayed at the party.

I stayed clean. I didn't drink at the parties, and even though Adel invited me to his basement a few times, I used work as an excuse to avoid it, and him, and all the associated distractions.

My year off was proving quite bearable, quite enjoyable actually, and so my heart had softened toward my father.

You can imagine, then, my feelings when, as the year was coming to an end and I started to prepare for my departure, Baba said that I could go but he wouldn't buy my ticket, pay my tuition, or finance me in any way to return to Scotland.

I fucking knew it! I had let my guard down, finally relaxed my trust sphincter muscles only to be shafted again!

I would like to say that fights and tears ensued.

But all I could do was look at him and narrow my eyes. 'Even with the lowest of expectations, I would expect nothing more of you, Baba.'

I think the double negatives threw him off, and he began shouting about 'his daughters, his house, his rules'.

Mama moved over to the bed where Sara and I were sitting, firmly and physically entrenched on our side of the house and the argument. They had made a treaty. She had sold her dream of the life of an independent divorcee, and he was reneging on his part of the bargain.

Sweet Sara was trying to reason with her daddy, but he was immune to her pleas.

I would have killed him with my words, so sharp and venom tipped and aimed directly at his heart. Spears of spite. Bullets of blame. I wanted to wound him. But I had no energy left for him.

Getting nowhere, I left them to their cyclical fight and stormed out of the house. Aimlessly, I walked to the stupid excuse for a mall at the end of the road.

I called Adel.

He picked me up before I could finish my frozen yoghurt.

We went to his basement and got baked. I can't elaborate because I don't really remember anything. I didn't speak to him much, even though we hadn't caught up in months. I just sat and closed my eyes and listened to music. Loud.

Sara picked me up at 4 a.m. because, having been clean for a year, I had accidentally got so stoned, I could barely move. She held me and cried with me when we got home.

She told me that when I walked out, Mama had demanded a divorce. Sara said she'd never heard so much profanity from her mouth in all her years! They used to sling the arrows of outrageous, unfortunate enmity behind closed doors, but now there was no shame in his defiant betrayal nor in her bare-toothed, snarling animosity.

The next day she flung some possessions in a suitcase and flew to England to start the divorce proceedings, since their marriage had been registered in London.

Baba followed her the very next day to try and change her mind.

I never had the time, the chance, or the inclination to forgive Baba for this, his most recent dick move.

This was last week.

5.29 a.m.

So here we are in my parents' house in Muscat, full circle. My mum is on the bed, a little spaced out from the Valium.

She looks up at Mamma Mia, turning her head first and her eyes following a millisecond later, and sleepily asks, 'Did you give me alcohol?'

Mamma Mia giggles and gently lowers her big sister down on the bed, and then lies down next to her. The chaos in the house has subsided. Most people have spent an afternoon or evening shift with us, but because they won't bury me until midday prayers later, everyone has gone home to sleep for a few hours.

It's 5.30 a.m.

The two sisters lie back on the bed and hold hands. Tears fall out of the sides of their eyes as they look up to the ceiling, slivers of sunrise showing through the gaps in the curtains, knowing that everything was going to be different from now on.

They don't speak, each engulfed in the grief of losing their child.

Meanwhile Baba has seen all the mourners out and is sitting downstairs in the living room with his brother, Issa, whose son died of a brain aneurysm. They are doing their own version of comforting each other.

They don't hold hands; they don't compare the perverse, unique grief of surviving a child; and they definitely don't cry. Communication is unknown territory to them, and raw, vulnerable emotions, a foreign language. They don't know their way around this unfamiliar land, so, like arrogant tourists, they talk loudly in their own tongue. For them, that means jokes, making light of the situation's gravity, ignoring the pain, teasing each other.

Uncle Issa teases Baba for his undying and foolish devotion to my mother.

'So, you chased her all the way to England again, eh? (Last time was Scotland, and Scotland isn't England, Uncle.) Ah, you're a fool, Yousef! Why do you keep following her if she doesn't want? She doesn't want, she doesn't want! You love that woman so much, and she doesn't appreciate you. Get another one, a younger one! A better one!'

'What do you know about love, stupid?' scoffs Baba.

'Who, me? I know everything! Ah, who needs love anyway? You want a woman, not love! See, I went and got a young one. Wow! But that one, she keeps me on my toes. Aiiiish, so fiery, always has an answer for everything! Sometimes I wish for the old, quiet days of Safiya. Except no one wants a wife who just lies there like a spatchcock chicken!'

They laugh.

I burst into Mama's room. (God, I wish I could make a proper dramatic entrance!) I want to explode.

The spatchcock chicken. Baba's own fucking brother? So *he* was the arsehole who tried it on with Mamma Mia? She is sensual, exciting, dangerous, the complete opposite of a spatchcock chicken, and certainly not like the meek and sanctimonious Aunty Safiya. This is all true.

But Mamma Mia must have only been a teenager at the time. Thirteen or fourteen, for fuck's sake. I'm trying to scream! Or flicker the lights!

I can do that.

But I can't. It's not working. I want to tell Mamma Mia that I know. That I'm sorry!

I want to tell Mama that her brother-in-law is another sick fuck.

I want Baba to know about his sick fuck brother!

What did Mamma Mia say to me all those years ago when she told me the spatchcock story?

She said that she didn't tell the wife, because 'it would have ruined her life. It would have ruined a lot of lives'.

She meant Aunty Safiya's life: How awful to know your husband is a paedophile! Such shame on him, or would some of the shame rub off on her? Would she leave him? And go where? She didn't work and her parents were dead. Who wants to be a forty-five-year old divorcee in this town? It would ruin her.

She meant Uncle Issa's life: What a horrible scandal to face. His wife would leave him and he would be shunned by the Family. Right?

She meant Baba's life: How would he ever confront and punish his brother? Wait! *Would* he confront and punish his brother?

Maybe she meant Mama's life: If Mama had stood up for her little sister, they would have crushed her for her audacity, this new mzungu addition to the Family.

She meant Sara's and my life too: We would somehow get caught up in the scandal and used as pawns between Mama supporting her sister, and Baba supporting his brother.

She probably meant her own life too: How could she have stood up to the wall of support that is the Family? They would have ridiculed her, maybe called her a liar or a slut, names that would follow her always.

Maybe they would have believed her, but I think her instincts were right. Not saying anything was the only way to guarantee only ruining *one* life.

Her own.

5.55 a.m.

Bibi and Sara walk into the room to join Mama and Mamma Mia. They look tired. Mamma Mia tells them to sit down on the bed in a row. She stands up in front of three generations of women in our family like she's about to make a presentation or an announcement. She has her very earnest face on. We usually take the piss out her when she takes herself too seriously like this, ever the overdramatic thespian, but this time everyone, including me, is silent.

She tells them, with theatrical gravitas, about the flickering lights in the hallway and, as if they are amateur actors in a play, she waits impatiently for their stunned reaction.

Mama is drowsy and overwhelmed. 'I don't understand. Something is wrong with the lights?'

Mamma Mia explains. 'Mare, the lights would only flicker as Uncle B walked past them.'

BEDROOM INTERERIOR, DAWN

Mama:
So? I don't get it, Mina.

Mamma Mia:
Years ago when we were ston— when we were talking, Summer told me that someone had touched her, sexually, as a child, but she

got scared and didn't elaborate. She never
told me who it was or when.

Mama and Sara (unison):
Someone touched Summer?

Mamma Mia:
Yes, and when I was standing at the end of
the corridor, as Uncle B walked toward me,
the lights flickered, every time he passed by
one. She was trying to tell me that it was
him!

Mama:
Someone touched Summer?

Mamma Mia (impatiently):
Yes, Mare! Uncle B. That's what I'm trying to
tell you. That's what she was trying to tell
me!

(It's really hard getting through to everyone today, through their shock and their
thoughts and their Valium.)

Mama (hurt, confused):
But why didn't she tell me?!

Sara (quietly echoing):
Why didn't she tell me?

Mamma Mia (gently):
She didn't tell anyone. Lots of people don't
tell anyone.

(Is she going to tell them about Uncle Issa
trying it on with her?)

Bibi:
Wait a minute, Mina. The lights were
flickering and now you're accusing B of
abuse? How do you know? That might not be
what she was trying to tell you at all!
We're all tired and upset. These are harsh
accusations you're making. You have to be
sure, before you say things like
that.

(Please note that no one questioned that
I was sending signals to them as a ghost.
That part of the story was totally credi-
ble, no question. The abuse part, however,
was harder to swallow, because it meant some
very uncomfortable truths, memories, and
confrontations.)

Mamma Mia:
Do you think it's so unimaginable? This kind
of thing happens all over the world every
day! Why shouldn't it happen right under our
noses? To any of us!

(Is she going to tell them NOW about Uncle
Issa?)

Mamma Mia continues:
Think about it. She said it happened
years ago, right? When has she ever been
alone without any of us? (She lets them
think about it.) And who was she with,
when she was without any of us to
look after her?

Mama (dazed):
She was here, in Oman, in B's house.

Mamma Mia:
In HIS house. That's what she was trying to
tell me years ago, and again tonight!

Mama (replaying a faded home video
in her mind):
And when we arrived here in Oman months
later, she was… (what word to choose: sad,
weird, moody?)… she was different.

Mamma Mia (encouragingly):
Yes, she was different. And then she
just got (what word to choose?) sadder,
weirder, and moodier as the years
went on, remember?

Sara (numb, piecing things together):
She used to cry herself to sleep. I had to
hold her. She was always so sad.

Mama:
I mean, from London to Oman, it's true, she
became a different person. And then it just
got worse.

Mamma Mia (starts crying):
We let her go. She left me and came here and
into *this*! Into his arms. Why did we let her
leave? Why did you send her here?

Mama (defensive):
We didn't know. How were we supposed to
know? It's not my FAULT! It wasn't even *my
idea*! That's her uncle! That's Yousef's sister, for God's sake!

(Mamma Mia wasn't actually blaming her
sister for sending me into the lion's den
intentionally. Mama became immediately defensive because as a Mother, your weight-
iest job is to protect your child. In her
eyes, she hadn't done that, and therefore
she felt that she had failed as a mother.
She needed to defend her position as fiercely as possible in order not to make her
life meaningless, which on top of her grief

would have been too much for one day.
One lifetime.)

Mama:
She should have made him stop!

Mamma Mia:
What? She was just a baby! Even women can't
make men stop! How can you make a grown man
stop anything, least of all an uncle!

Mama:
Or she should have told an adult then! She
should have told Aunty Zaina.

Mamma Mia (horrified):
Do you think she knows? Aunty Zaina? You
know we have to tell her!

Bibi:
We can't tell her! We don't have any proof!

Mamma Mia:
We have Summer. We have her whole life! Look
how she became the shadow of herself, after
she was here alone. After whatever he did to
her at SEVEN years old!

Sara (barely a whisper):
God, why didn't I see it?

Mamma Mia (talking over her):
You've seen her at Family functions, if you
could ever get her near one. We have to say
something!

Sara (to herself):
C U Next Tuesday…

Bibi:
We can't say anything now. It will ruin
a lot of lives. It will ruin Zaina!

Mamma Mia (in dangerous answering-back
mode):
Ruin ZAINA? How about Summer! What about
other girls he might be doing it to? Huh?

Sara (world of her own):
She wouldn't let him touch her.

Bibi:
You can't just do something like that, dis-
rupt lives like that! How do you think their
daughters will feel when you announce to the
world what their father is?

Mamma Mia:
He should have thought about his own daughters, before he touched mine.

Bibi:

Think about all the people who will be hurt!

Mamma Mia:

Why do I have to be the considerate one? Why
didn't he consider his *own* family?

Bibi (shaking her head):

Well, that's the problem with men.

Mama:

What do you mean?

Bibi:

Men don't think of anything but their
penises.

Mamma Mia:

That's it? Is that supposed to be some kind
of Get-Out-of-Jail-Free card? Their penises,
so we should just accept it?

Bibi:

I'm just saying that's what men do. She's not
the first, and she won't be the last.

Mamma Mia (clearly lost her mind and
will to live):
What the ACTUAL FU—

Mama (interrupting just in time,
trying to keep peace):
Mina, DON'T!

Mamma Mia:
No! We can't let men get away with this! He
touched my BABY! (crying)

Bibi:
This was years ago. Nothing can be done now.
She should have told us then, when we could
have done something.

Mamma Mia:
Sure! What would you have done then? Would
you have confronted him THEN?

Bibi:
Maybe…

Mamma Mia: (at Mama)
What? You would expect your husband to turn
against one of his own?

Mama (shaking her head, admitting it):
He wouldn't have.

Mamma Mia:
I KNOW! No one would have done anything then
and no one wants to do anything now!

(So, was I right not to tell them? What good
would it have done? If I was worried that
they wouldn't believe me, I needn't have
been. They know it happens. If I worried
that they wouldn't do anything, well, I have
my answer loud and clear.)

Bibi:
There's only one thing we can do now. We
have to forgive. If we want forgiveness for
her, then we have to forgive him.

Mamma Mia (shouting):
STOP! Stop siding with him! Side with her!
Side with our SumSum! I'm sick of this culture protecting the predators, coz we're too
scared to oust them.

Mama (placating):
We're not siding with them! But they are our
Family too. We can't upset the whole order
of things!

Mamma Mia:
Yeah? Just watch me. I'm not going to just
let him get away with it!

Mama:
Get away with what? We don't even really
know what happened!

Mamma Mia:

I know what happened! And he has to PAY!

Bibi:

Pay what, Mina? Pay whom? Summer is DEAD!

They all shut up in shock.

Except for Sara whose face falls with Bibi's last echoing sentence, and, as if the truth has irrevocably registered, finally shatters.

They all scramble to apologise to her and try to hold her in comfort, but she runs out of the room.

They try to follow her, but she slips into the room with my body and barricades the door, her back leaning against it, racked with heavy sobs. They knock, apologise, and beg her to come out, but she just tells them to leave her alone.

They look at each other with guilty expressions, but they agree to give her some space to grieve for a while, in her own way.

When they eventually start preparing for people to arrive for the funeral a few hours later, they find my baby sister sleeping next to my dead body, spooning me from behind.

9.07 a.m.

The morning comes and people start trickling in again. Some are fresh from a night's sleep, some have swollen eyes from little rest and many tears. They arrive armed with boxes of small water bottles, bumper packs of tissue boxes, and platters of *halwa*, sticky and sweet and decorated with chopped pistachios.

And the whispering continues, behind my back and my parents' backs. It's the latest rumour, and it couldn't be juicier. It has all the best ingredients for a tragic soap opera drama: drugs, a young girl, and death. They are flies around roadkill.

They are as addicted to the gossip as their kids are to heroin. They're just shooting up other people's misery, enjoying the scandal coursing through their veins. And who is to say which addiction is worse?

I wish my parents would just talk about it. Admit it! Yes, she was found with heroin. Demand to know where I got it and who gave it to me! I must have got it from somewhere! And from someone I knew.

They should ask each other these hard questions, and they, in turn, should ask their children. Maybe they should discover that it's more of a problem among their kids than they realise or want to admit. Maybe their kids are unhappy.

And WHY?!

Maybe by confronting this, they can prevent another death. Maybe the government can figure out where it's coming from and stop it.

I wish they would stop sweeping our problems and pain under the rugs of customs, traditions, and religion. This is the reason that this culture and these people won't move into the twenty-first century, because they won't adjust and admit to the fact that their kids are already there.

And the landscape is different from the world that our parents enjoyed in their youth. Times have changed. Discos, cocktails, and perhaps the lure of Free Love were the extent of their temptations.

It's a completely different circus now.

We have the internet, the unattainable beauty standards of Instagram posts, a head-spinning news cycle, false information, judgment, and peer pressure, and the threat of everything you say, wear, or do being immortalised in someone's cloud or on their Facebook page, poised to humiliate or emotionally blackmail you.

That's our circus.

All while walking the tightrope of a split personality culture, juggling the expectations of our parents with our own limitations, and swallowing the double-edged sword of a confused religious identity.

No wonder so many of us lost our footing and fell, without a safety net of honest advice or experience. (Too much circus ANAL-ogy?!)

And speaking of clowns, here is my dear Cousin Adel...

Poor guy looks dreadful, pale, in shock. I only just saw him, last night. I was just at his house. I've been at his house every night this week. It must be tripping him out. It's the case of, 'I JUST saw her! How can she be dead?!' It must have happened a few hours after I left his house. Maybe he's wondering what he did, if he contributed to my demise.

And as I have now recalled, Fido Dido was there, at Adel's, last night.

And here he is, in my parents' house, with Adel this morning. He looks even worse than Adel. Shock. Hangover. Agitation. Something else. Dread. Fear? He kissed me last night. He's feeling guilty.

The kiss of Death.

He knows he has something to do with this. He can sense his culpability. I can sense it, and I'm dead. What did he do? Why is he acting so shifty? Shady, sweating and shaking.

They walk uncertainly through the house, Fido hiding behind Adel, up the stairs, ignored by mourners in their own worlds, young people helping elders find seats, people handing out drinks, tissues, Qurans.

They walk past them all and stop when they bump into Sara on the landing upstairs. Adel wraps her in a hug and starts blubbering a little into her hair. My sweet cousin.

She is quite still inside his shaking hug. She is numb, A.I.-Sophia-perfect, but broken and leaking, tears flowing down her cheeks.

Fido remains behind Adel, whispering and nudging and urging him nervously, until Adel finally asks Sara if they can see my bathroom.

She obliges, looking askance from one to the other. They go in, with trepidation at first, gingerly picking up the glass bottles on the shelves, opening up the mirrored cabinet over the sink and rummaging, then pushing things aside on the counter, tearing the shower curtain back, ripping up the pink rug (which hasn't yet been removed for some reason, considering I died on it). Sara has stepped back out of the bathroom and is watching them. They then ask to see our bedroom.

Sara is sizing them up and piecing it together. She can tell they want to tear the bedroom apart now. She can see that they're looking for something, but she would rather slit their throats than let them rummage through my possessions.

"What are you looking for?" she finally flatly asks.

Fido nervously tells Sara that he's looking for a Transformer's pencil case. Has she seen it? It is very, very important.

Shit.

I remember what happened.

31 August 2016, 10.22 p.m.

My Last Night Alive

It's my last night alive and I'm spending it getting baked at Adel's, for the sixth time this week.

Mama left five days ago, and Baba followed the day after, like a pitbull puppy unable to let go of a toy and unable to comprehend why it is time to do exactly that.

I haven't been great company, but Adel rolls the joints and plays music and makes me laugh when he can. He understands why I haven't visited him all year since I was grounded in Muscat, and he doesn't blame me for it. He knows he's a loser and he wants me to be successful. He's a good friend.

Unannounced, without knocking, and taking my breath away with his entrance, Fido Dido walks in with a cheeky fedora hat pulled over his slightly stoned eyes. His shoulders have broadened over the years since I've known him, his voice has deepened, and his face is a little more serious, but his smile is still lopsided and he still giggles like an eight-year-old girl when he's high.

I haven't truly resolved my teenage crush, so the butterflies having a carnival in my belly almost makes me sick.

He does a double take and is incredulously ecstatic to see me. He shouts my name, drops his fag in the closest ashtray, rushes over to my crack in the sofa (always between the same two cushions), picks me up effortlessly (somehow), and holds me close. I feel his heart beating from the rush and sudden movement, and I wonder if he can feel mine, which would mean that my boobs were really pressed up against him. I hope he can feel my boobs. I hope he can feel how I have morphed into a woman.

It's been several years since we talked, since I decided not to hang out with my stoner buddies in order to focus on my studies, and I wonder if he can sense all the changes in me. All the changes and new emotions I have experienced since then. How going to university had matured me, how I had lived on my own, studied, made friends outside my own Family, how I had had another crush and been crushed by it, been punished by Baba, got a job, and almost died.

That's a lot of living, while these guys were still getting stoned in the Basement That Time Forgot.

He pulls away from me, studies my face, looks me up and down, and wolf whistles in admiration. I guess the loss of weight and the gain in experience is really noticeable.

I know it's frivolous and shallow, but I perk up considerably.

Fuck, it's just something to take my mind off everything else, isn't it? A temporary reprieve from my misery. A way to feel special for a fleeting moment.

He declares that it's an occasion to celebrate and demands Adel bring out whatever cheap booze he has stashed away, and we all chink glasses to toast our reunion, and shoot back straight vodka.

I haven't had a drink since Edinburgh, and the liquid burns a harsh reminder down my throat, an acidic souvenir of that night at The Hound.

And then at the hospital.

I know I probably shouldn't, but what the fuck... I did what I was supposed to do all year, like an obedient daughter, and yet here I am, where I started all those years ago, unhappy in Adel's basement, fighting with my dad. That thought is so depressing that I pour another shot for us all.

The hours pass and Fido's body shifts closer, closer to mine on the sofa, head bending conspiratorially toward mine, knees occasionally accidentally grazing. I know I'm not imagining the sparks every time his skin touches mine. And he is definitely doing it more often as we catch up on the last few years.

I tell him about my A levels and getting accepted into uni. The transition to the UK, the unexpected homesickness, the friends, the course, the clubs, the weed. I don't mention Semen, and somehow I also censor the story about SMF Mike. I guess I'm just not sure how he feels about gay men. Or about me fancying someone, even someone who so flatly and humiliatingly rejected me.

I'm not sure I want to tell him.

He listens to my stories, giggling a little too hard at my observations and anecdotes. We smoke a joint and then do another shot while Adel plays video games, completely engrossed and seemingly glad someone else is cheering up his miserable younger cousin.

As I go into my wallet to find something to use as a roach, a photo slips out onto the floor.

It's a silly photo booth picture that comes in a strip of four, like the ones you see in the movies from the '80s and '90s. I was so thrilled to see a booth like it on one of my walks in town with SMF Mike, and insisted we climb in immediately and make funny faces. Mike humoured me, because he found my childlike enthusiasm endearing (at least he SAID he did), and when the photos slid out the side of the booth, I tore two off and gave them to him, and kept the two in which he looked particularly dreamy. I was sitting on his thigh, sticking out my tongue or cross-eyed in all of them, and he was looking at me and laughing. My pictures were worn from numerous wallet extractions and insertions, caressing and tears. I wonder if he even kept his.

'Who is this?' Fido almost *demands* to know. I find his possessive tone off-putting, even though I had found his closeness intoxicating a moment ago.

He's jealous!

Years of fancying my cousin's cool DJ friend with the tight flat abs and spiked-up hair, and now he's jealous of a photograph of a no one.

Fuck, if my fifteen-year-old self could see me now! I wish I could tell her that the reality is not worth the agony of unrequited lust.

In that moment, the spell is broken. Years of this silly crush extinguished in a moment of jealousy.

He likes me back.

And that will never do.

At around 1 a.m., he goes to the toilet and I pick up my phone to check a random Facebook notification. The letters look a little woozy. I go to my home page and write a status update:

I see you can't resist it,

My mind, deliciously twisted

and quickly put the phone back in my pocket as Fido joins me again on the sofa.

He tells me of his last few years, how he married his distant relative from Mombasa, the one with the come-hither eyes and round butt. He reluctantly endured the scrutiny that all young newlyweds are subjected to, and hated every second. I laugh at the thought of him sitting with his nervous bride on a plush satin sofa on a stage framed by faux Grecian columns dripping with plastic flowers and fairy lights, in a badly lit hotel ballroom, being stared at by all the guests and having to pose and smile for a thousand photos with family and strangers. And after the wedding, he complained, there was a constant stream of well-wishing visitors, inappropriate questions about their sex life from nosey relatives, unsolicited advice about interior decoration for their new house or how to cook the thickest coconut cassava, or how to train the maid.

She on the other hand, loved the attention. She loved being called *bi-harusi* (the bride), and being treated like a queen, all her whims catered to, unrequired to lift a finger for herself (until, of course, the next big wedding and next beautiful bi-harusi).

Then of course there were the pushy aunts demanding an immediate pregnancy. Offspring! Progeny! A bouncy baby! That's all that was missing! When is it going to happen?

After a year, his wife started asking the same thing.

He was still just DJ-ing, a kid himself, and wasn't ready to be a dad, so he kept pulling out, he confides in me, passing me the joint there in the dimly lit basement.

He would escape the house, the questions, and the nagging, and he would stay out late, even on the nights he wasn't working, just to get high. The drug use got more frequent. He would sometimes return home in the morning, disorientated and dismissive of her desperation.

Her distress at home got worse and turned into depression, despair, and then disdain. And finally came the interference of her mother and aunts.

And he moved out.

He tells me that he's divorcing her. He tells me that he should have known better than to marry the *idea* of someone. He should have married someone like me, someone who liked to smoke up, who was his friend, who knew who he was, so he didn't have to pretend. Someone who could talk back and laugh with him.

What the...?

Oh, this *really* pisses me off. I seethe inside. I could have fucking told him that years ago.

What is it with men?

They think they want the girl with child-bearing hips. And then they get annoyed when the woman wants to bear children!

The concept of marrying your equal is so off-putting to them because they don't want an equal. They want to be the MAN!

He hands me a shot. 'Drink with me, Summer! I'm miserable. Maybe you were the woman of my dreams this whole time?!'

I don't want to drink more, but I feel the pressure of not wanting to leave him hanging, with his shot glass poised and angled at me.

Why do I do that? So *what* if he's left hanging? It wouldn't kill him! And I wouldn't have started to feel a little queasy.

I read an article once that said many women who have been sexually assaulted actually felt the pressure of not letting someone down, with familiar pleas like:

Please, you can't leave me like this!

Look what you've done to me!

Please, just a little kiss, where's the harm in that?

We're brought up to be kind, gentle, considerate of other's feelings. Even so far as to feel grateful that men find us attractive. We recognise in those pleas a responsibility on us to relieve a need, an obligation to serve; and we respond to them, no matter how it makes *us* feel.

I take the shot of vodka.

Adel helps stuff my drunk body into Fido's car and explains where my house is. We drive the twenty minutes to my house with the car window open and the hot, whipping air brings me round, making me feel less woozy.

I stick my head out of the window and pant like a dog, and we both laugh. I laugh at his schoolgirl giggle, which makes him snicker even more. I laugh until I snort, which makes him crack up!

My house is set back from the road a little and he drives past it.

'You Passed It!' I shout.

'Why?' He asks, feigning indignation.

'Why what?'

'Why did you call me that?'

'Why did I call you what?'

'A bastard!'

'I didn't call you a bastard, you idiot!'

'You just shouted at me that I was a bastard! Literally, just now.'

'I said, You passed it!'

'You bastard?'

'You passed it! My house. You passed my house!'

Fido guffaws so hard that the car swerves into the opposite lane and he has to pull over, bent over the wheel, convulsed in high-pitched shrieks of laughter, tears streaming from his eyes. I laugh too, wheezing with my head back, slapping his back.

We sit here for several minutes, in a shaking car, the butt of which is still in the empty, 3 a.m. road, laughing like drunk loons, like old friends.

As the hilarity eventually subsides, amid groans and gasping for breath, our hands are on each other's thighs and our faces are close together. We look up at each other for a million slow motion moments, until he reaches over, holds the back of my neck, and we collide in an uncoordinated, passionate, cathartic snog.

Eight years in the making.

He tries to pull me over to his side of the car, bringing me urgently closer to him, but my seat belt is still buckled and much fumbling and jerking ensues. Not the fun kind. We manage to undo it, and he reaches over to pull me closer. The roof of his sports car is low, and I bang my head. I also have nowhere to put my hands, so I'm leaning over to support myself on his door, while twisting to kiss him. I have been waiting to do this for years. I don't care that it isn't a little smoother, more romantic. I don't need romance right now.

To be honest, if I still fancied him, I'd be nervous. But I don't really even care that it's him. It could be anyone.

It's exactly what I need.

Right now.

It's a scream under a passing train, it's crying in the rain. It's release, a rebellion, it's a physical urgency, a craving that I can finally satisfy. It's an itch that I'm about to rip into with talons.

I'm panting again. I'm exploring his mouth with a demanding tongue, and biting his neck, gasping into his ear. I'm pulling his hair, pushing my body against his, digging my nails into his arms, rubbing my tits against him. I want him to crave them. I want him to tear my bra off. I want to be eaten, devoured, like prey being torn apart by its predator.

He reaches up under my shirt. Fuck! Yes! This is a first for me. My body is on fire for it! Begging for some touch, to be grabbed and groped. My body is starving for a satisfaction it has never known. The longing is self-destructive. It's primal, angry, and insistent.

I can feel my nipples straining for him. I can actually physically feel the heat of this need.

The heat is burning red, and throbbing. It's pulsating.

And it has a sound. Actually, a deafening wail.

Okay, this isn't right.

I open my eyes.

"Fuck, Fido! Police!"

The police could mean a few things for us in this situation, depending on their mood and whether we can convince them that we are either related or married.

And sober.

Although not a potential death sentence, like being black in America, being caught by the police could still effectively ruin my life. I could be dragged in front of my parents, or, in their absence and even worse, an uncle, and humiliated for being a slut. The shame I would incur for this lapse in any semblance of sense would be a Scarlet Letter forever branded on my face.

Oh, what was I thinking, kissing a married man in the car on the street like a hooker? Word would spread. That's all anyone would talk about for the longest time, and unlike the Edinburgh Episode, there would be no cute, alliterated moniker for this incident: the Adultery Adventure, the Ignominy Incident.

There would be no gentle ribbing and teasing from Bibi and Grandad, who would be so disappointed in me. My family would try to crawl out from under this scandal-rock, only to be humiliated and chased back under it.

Baba's siblings would tut and scold him for being so lenient with me. I would be a cautionary tale to all female cousins.

It could mean being dragged to the police station, being breathalysed and put in jail for being drunk and disorderly. That's what expats and tourists get. What punishment would Omani Muslims get? Everyone knows Omani men drink, you see them in the pub all the time, but not Omani ladies. Maybe they would want to make an example of me?

That would be it for Scotland. This could even mean the end of my short-lived scholastic career. The end of travelling. Maybe even the end of good marriage prospects, before I even got to the point of wanting any.

Wait, what if the police discover that we've been smoking hash? That's a life prison sentence.

Fuck.

I swiftly sit back in my seat and pull down my shirt, wiping my lips, freaking out. Shaking, I reach down for my handbag and wrestle my wallet out of there, ready to present my ID. Do I smell like booze? Like weed? Do I look stoned? I try and widen my eyes, shake some sobriety into my fuzzy, lust-soaked brain.

Fido is swearing and panicking. He's broken into a sweat. He's faring worse than me.

He grabs my handbag from my grip, tips it upside down, empties the compact mirror, lip balm, tissues, and inhaler onto the floor, reaches behind his back and stuffs something in my handbag, then chucks it back onto my lap before I can protest or ask what he's doing.

The police come to the window, and Fido greets them in the formal, exceedingly courteous and ingratiating traditional manner, wishing them peace, obsequiously (Word of the Day) enquiring after their health, their life, their job, their families, their goats (not really), and each time conveying the wish that God should continue to bless them.

And that's it.

That's all it took. Fido tells them that he passed my house while driving me home, and he was about to turn the car around, and they wish us a good night, continued peace, and that God should continue to bless us.

And that's it.

We are both numb. I feel like I've been holding my breath the whole time, relieved that the police didn't hear my heart thundering. I exhale, and when the police have disappeared around the bend, he turns to me, holds my hand, pulls me to him again, and tries to kiss me, pressing his lips hard against mine, searching for the passion that was so recently his. 'I think I love you, Summer.'

I shake my head no. I'm shivering with fear, shock, and leftover lust, and I can't reply. I get out, in a daze, ignoring him calling out to me, then, my breathing ragged, I sprint the 100 metres back to my house, heart thumping, fingers fumbling with the keys.

I stagger up the stairs and creep noisily into our room, where Sara is already asleep. I'm sure my pounding heartbeat and wheezing will wake her.

Trying my best not to disturb her with my inebriated stumbling and panting, I grab my camel bone hash box and lumber into the bathroom.

My hands are still shaking.

I take off my jeans and discard them bunched up on the floor. I try to replace them with the not-so-hot, hot-pant pyjama bottoms that are hanging on the back of the door, but I'm really struggling with bending, with breathing, with coordinating limbs, with balancing.

I feel faint after getting one leg in, so I lean against the wall beneath the extractor fan and slide down till my bum hits the floor.

My hands are way too jittery to roll a joint, so I get a cigarette out of my hash stash box. I've been beg-borrow-stealing fags these past few days—I need the tobacco to roll joints—but I decide I'm going to smoke this one, the first cigarette in over a year.

It's a night of firsts and renewed vices, after all.

With shaking hands, I search my handbag for my inhaler, but it's not there. I start to panic. No, not again! Not like Edinburgh! I tip my bag out, shaking it violently, to dislodge it from its hiding place in some crease or pocket, but instead all I find is a Transformer pencil case that I've never seen before.

I empty the contents onto the pink shaggy bathroom rug and sift through them.

What the fuck...?

No wonder Fido was so fucking nervous to see the cops. It's his heroin gear. A spoon, a little baggy, a syringe, a lighter.

His fucking heroin!!

I sit back, looking at it all, wondering what the hell he was thinking. The cops were less likely to search me than him, but...

What the actual FUCK!

I am freaking out anew as it dawns on me how fucking close I was to being caught with a handbag of heroin. He saw the police and planted his shit in *my handbag*!

He almost sent me to fucking prison.

Prison. That's a life sentence. Or is it a death sentence?

Oh God, he kissed me and then potentially condemned me. To life! To death!

He almost framed me and then tried to tell me he fucking loved me! That prize dickhead!

I'm furious. My fight or flight reflexes kick in, quickening my heartrate and turning my stomach.

Oh God! Oh God...

My veins are thundering and I feel sick.

I lean over the toilet bowl and throw up, vodka and bile, my head spinning and my chest heaving.

I take his lighter, light the cigarette with a shaking hand, try to take a drag between empty, ragged breaths, lean back, heart racing, put my arm down on the floor next to me.

And exhale for the last time.

2 September 2016, 11.28 a.m.

The mourners are reminding me over and over that two angels with eyes of thunder will come to me when I am in the Grave, as it begins to close in around me, when the darkness crushes me, when all the people have left the graveyard and I am alone. These angels, Munkar and Nakir, will prop me up, to ask me three questions.

The mourners repeat the questions and the answers over and over as they come into the room where my body is lying, limbs getting colder and stiffer, skin getting darker. They remind me of the questions and the answers, just in case I am petrified of these two angels when they appear. The mourners call out the questions to me, and the responses, because the angels will be terrifying and I will be scared stiff and might forget.

I will be scared stiff and I might forget.

The people remind me again and again.

Who is your Lord? *My Lord is Allah.*

What is your religion? *My religion is Islam.*

What do you say about that man who was sent as a messenger among you? *He is Muhammed, Peace be upon him.*

They repeat the questions and answers again and again as they lift my body. Only men—my cousins, my uncles, my father. People are wailing, calling to me, calling to God, reaching to touch me goodbye for the last time as I am carried through the room. Someone pulls at the sheet around my head and it slips. Some of my curls fall out. They fall onto my father's face.

The same curls that used to flop all over my face. The curls that hounded him, as if they spiralled and bounced in defiance of him. The curls he always wanted me to hide away, to cover under a scarf.

I swear it's some kind of poetry the way they have audaciously sprung free one final time, to tease, tickle, or torment him. To remind him of just one of the silly, insignificant things that prevented us being close. One of the things that he stubbornly held on to tighter than he held on to me.

Hair.

My relationship with him flashes before my eyes. The naps I took on his chest as he looked down at me with such tenderness I could feel his heart swell as I slept. The bouncing on his shoulders as he proudly walked me into a room. The Swahili lullabies he would tunelessly sing. The big, hairy Tooth Fairy who kept my baby teeth like trophies.

Then the drawing away from me as other relationships took over, female relationships like with Mamma Mia. He couldn't relate to those, not understanding women in any real sense, having only had one-year flings before my mum. He also couldn't understand bonds that looked different to the fierce and savage loyalty that defined his siblings' relationships.

Then his withdrawal from me completely after I turned ten and turned sour.

Then his desperation to fit in with his increasingly devout Family and trying desperately to make us do the same.

The haunting, persistent love for my mother, which I thought pathetic until yesterday, and today think could be the Holy Grail of True Devotion.

Then flashing before my eyes: the Cruise, the Leica, the Rules, the Fight, the End.

The curl flopping onto his face.

Baba unexpectedly sobs so hard that he drops my head. Two other pairs of hands cover for him immediately and wordlessly, and he rushes into his bedroom before anyone can see the tears fall.

He stands shaking against the door, hearing the chaos on the other side and hides his face in his hands.

'Summer, Summer, forgive me. Come back! You can do whatever you like to your hair. I don't care. I don't care, just please come back!'

He sobs for the first time, maybe the first time since he was a child. He breaks for me. It devastates me. To see the colour of his tears, just like mine.

I try to tell him that I would cover up my hair, my face, everything, if I could come back, just to tell him that I forgive him and that I love him.

But just like that, he has composed himself and he walks out of the room to rejoin his Family, leaving me midsentence. The only evidence of his grief are three tear stains on his immaculate white thobe.

11.38 a.m.

Sara hasn't stopped crying since the floodgates opened. She stands at the top of the stairs now, watching them take her sister away, inconsolable. I think the extra information about what had happened to me as a little girl has been too much to digest. It was enough to know that I had left her to fend for herself in life—*that* she could handle. But to think that I had suffered a persistent melancholy my whole life, caused by someone she knew, is filling her with the kind of rage that good people don't know how to process.

She can usually justify and excuse people's behaviour with her generous empathy and willingness to forgive. But she wasn't willing to lose me for it. The rage is burning her. And as they carry me away, she sees Uncle B near the front door, reaching his hand out to help carry me.

Without thinking, she leaps down the stairs lined with so many people that to me it looks like she's crowd surfing like a rock star. Without knowing what she's doing, she flies at him in a fluid motion from stairs to front door, and she punches him in the face.

He drops to the floor, and in their shock, my relatives drop my corpse.

Oh, the drama!

I hate to admit it, but I LOVE the ensuing kerfuffle. I love the melodrama, the tragicomic theatre!

Folks will dine out on this scene for a long time. I will live in infamy, as will Sara. They will speculate for years about what made young, amiable Sara punch her uncle out.

People pick up my body immediately. Shouts and shrieks are heard: *SubhanAllah, SubhanAllah*! Glory to God! People are crying and wailing at the horror piled on top of the bereavement.

Some people bend to help Uncle B, and some attempt to hold Sara back. Some feel sorry for her. She must be acting out because of her loss. How else would she have lost her mind enough to attack an elder?

But she's sane and ready to punch him again. She stands over him, willing, *daring* him to get up.

Mamma Mia runs toward the huddle, ostensibly to help her niece, and when she gets close, kicks him *really* hard in the side as he lies on the floor. There is a crunch and he yelps, inaudible over all the wailing.

Mamma Mia holds Sara's face tenderly. They look at each other and yes, you guessed it, burst out laughing through their tears.

Without words, they move two of our cousins out of the way and support my body on their shoulders to take me to the graveyard. Some people start to say that only men can carry the body, but the girls give them looks that wither the words in their mouths.

They walk with the men, sweltering in the blazing September midday sun. Mama and Bibi come to join them, walking by their side, knowing that I should be surrounded by those I loved the most.

Not just men.

I can't differentiate their sweat from their tears as they silently walk the ten minutes to the nearest graveyard.

As they approach, Bibi says quietly enough to us, so the men don't hear, 'In Islam, we believe that if you are murdered by someone, your sins go to that person. After all, they took your life, without giving you a chance to make amends for anything you might want to atone for. In the same way, Uncle B took Summer's life. He didn't give her a chance to choose her life. He will get all her sins, and our Summer will, *insha'Allah*, receive Paradise for the pain she suffered at his hands.

'Nice punch, by the way. Summer would have been proud.'

And with that they all relax, just a little bit, even smile sadly. Perhaps even surrender and accept the fact that God will balance the scales.

From now to eternity, my family will tell the story that Sara, in her rush to be near my body, happened to knock her uncle accidentally in the face. And Mamma Mia, in her rush to help Sara, happened to accidentally kick him and break one of his ribs.

Somehow, the secret knowledge that they had actually hurt him, and that he *definitely* knows why, was enough to sustain them.

•

One of my "famous" Facebook updates was: *One day your life will flash before your eyes. Make sure it's worth watching.*

I wonder what makes some people search, seek, and strive their whole lives. Why some people leave their villages to venture and adventure, to find out what else is out there in this Big Bad World. And yet others stay where they were born and just embrace what they are given, completely unburdened by curiosity, not even bothered by it.

And if someone is a natural Seeker with an innate need to move, discover, and suck marrow, are they Exploring or are they just Escaping? Are they really driven or are they just dodging? Are they poets and dreamers... or just cowards?

The Embracers, on the other hand, are the exemplary worker bees. They were born to stay put, work, marry, procreate, and they fear the unpredictability that comes with Seeking. So, are these people our anchors? Or are *they* the cowards?

I could see through the transparently mediocre life in Oman, like the only person laughing at the Emperor's New Clothes.

I wasn't satisfied there.

But I wasn't satisfied in Edinburgh either, where I had yearned and strived and fought to be. Maybe I would never have been happy anywhere.

Just like I had wanted Fido for years, and as soon as he wanted me, I was immediately repulsed.

Is this a curse of restless people?

Maybe it's arrogant to think that the Restless Ones are more intelligent because they are harder to satisfy, always searching for more. Or perhaps they are the unlucky ones, always doomed to be unhappy, unsatisfied. No one, after all, ever finds the end of a rainbow.

Maybe people become Escapers only because they don't have the strength or insight to stay put and face themselves.

It seems to me that I was born into a family of Seekers on my mother's side. It was in my DNA.

Perhaps my Destiny had been just around the corner, if I had lived, if I had held on a little longer. Maybe it was all just about to become clear. Maybe things would have become easier; I would have figured out how to deal with my abuse, I could have figured out a relationship with my parents, and where I wanted to live and who I wanted to be. Or perhaps I was always going to fruitlessly search and continue chasing the rainbow's end.

Perhaps the trudging wheel of mediocrity would eventually have crushed me—the ultimately insignificant, tiny pebble—in its cogs.

Perhaps Sara was right, that this death was my fate, because God could only see more heartache and turmoil ahead for me and wanted to save me from it.

Was I a Seeker? Or was I simply Ordinary?

I would like to think that everyone is extraordinary, but that's just what this mollycoddling, award-for-participation society likes to tell us. Everyone is *unique*, yes, but not extraordinary. Everyone has their own unique story, thoughts, and foibles, but not everyone is special, different, or phenomenal. Is it possible to feel in your heart that you're exceptional but in reality just be generic? That would be a cruel joke!

It would be devastating to think you were special and then find out you were just boring, uninspired, and uninspiring.

Just destined to die an uninteresting asthmatic virgin on the bathroom floor. Someone who made no difference to anyone, who wasn't butterfly-effecting anyone's life. Someone who hadn't even learned who she was yet.

What had I learned? Really. What had I learned in this life? About this life.

That growing old is a gift. And I took for granted that I would have time. Youth is wasted on the young.

That Mercy is also a gift, literally "For Giving". And I was not in a generous mood.

That we choose our path, and God knows what we will choose.

That everything is written. So I have not disappointed my future by denying it life. This was meant to be my legacy.

That I would give anything to be told off about my hair again, or to take the trash out, something so banal and ordinary that it makes me want to yawn just thinking about it. You don't realise that when you're rolling your eyes at being nagged to do such a menial task, one day it would be such a luxury. Life is wasted on the living.

That telling everyone my deepest darkest secret would have made no difference to anything.

The same Voice that told me in life that I was bad, and filthy, and not good enough, is trying to creep into my soul and reprimand me for not living enough while I was alive.

It's taunting me because I blamed this beautiful country, Oman, by association for the sin of one of its inhabitants. I was denying part of my identity because I couldn't separate the place from the deed.

The Voice is giving me a hard time for alienating my family because of something that happens to millions of girls every year. It's ridiculing me for wasting time, making a fuss, treating my circumstances as so unique and so awful, as if I am the only girl to suffer this kind of abuse. The Voice is even telling me that most girls who suffer abuse, have it much worse.

I don't know what to do with this information. I don't know if I could have done it any differently, if I could have lived with more appreciation of my abundance. It seemed too heavy for my young shoulders at the time.

Will my death change the way what's left of my family will live or talk to each other? Or will they all just get on with their lives, the same as before, only forever without me?

That might be even more painful than anything else I can think of.

2.07 p.m.

They lay me down gently, in the direction of Mecca.

It hits me. In the same way that my soul went to the hospital with my body, my soul will stay here with my body. I will no longer be a voyeur in the lives of my family. I won't be able to laugh with them or change the mood of the room. I can't hear what they're saying or check if they're hurting or surviving.

I notice a small, modest rectangular stone on the ground that they will place at the head of my otherwise anonymous grave. It has my name scrawled in Arabic, and my dates 03/09/1993 – 01/09/2016.

Yes, tomorrow is my birthday.

I'm trying to savour the last few moments with my family and not panic, but I can't help it. My vision is blurred. I can't see them properly. I want to look at my sister's perfect face again. I want to see Mama and remember her dancing in the summer streets of Edinburgh. I want to see the stains on Baba's thobe and remember him like that.

But I can't see. The sand, the sand thrown on my body, over my face, over the rogue curl poking out of the shroud. The weight of it landing on my body, with a thud that intermittently drowns out Sara's sobs, my darling, stoic sister who has finally broken completely, who is forever completely broken.

I can barely hear my mother's sobs as she watches her first-born being buried, covered in dirt. She collapses, holding her womb as labour pains once again pierce and penetrate her body.

My father holds back tears with such force that he won't be able to speak for three days.

Mamma Mia falls to the ground, and in a symmetry that I would expect from my artist aunt, regresses into the teenager at Heathrow and begs me not to leave her. Uncle Mo sits next to his sisters in the dirt, hangs his head, and tries to comfort them with his breaking voice.

Bibi and Grandad stand vigil over their small family, backed away from the men shovelling dust and small rocks on to their granddaughter. Hand in hand, tear after tear crumbling their sweet love story.

I can hear mumbled prayers. I try to say 'Ameen' at the end. I call to them. I call and call.

But they are walking away. I strain to hear the gravel crunch beneath their feet and their distant wails and calls for Allah.

And then it is dark.

And it is quiet.

ACKNOWLEDGMENTS

Firstly, praise and eternal gratitude to God, for thinking me worthy of this birth lottery I have won.

My family family – you may recognise yourselves in jokes, tender moments and personality traits. That's because you are my inspiration. I love you.

To my extended Family – any resemblance to you in this novel is totally your imagination! Maybe...

Love to my chosen families: the loves of my life - the OFs, to my mzungu family, to my DXB Fam from all over, for helping me grow (shout out to Turki and Gabs – thank you), and the MDB. And all those who touched my heart from LA to London, Muscat to Zanzibar. Enormous and humble thanks to RAK and TSA. You are really good friends, dudes. Thank you. And big, HUGE love to Joel, my left-handed right-hand man.

And to the Love of my Life, Karlito, who came and made everything better, funnier, safer, sillier and more organised.

And thank you to the whole team at The Dreamwork Collective. To Kira, who believed immediately. I am so grateful that you took on this novice novelist and took such care with me. Your passion is appreciated. Thalia, I have loved working with you. Your brutal cuts came with such wonderful encouragement!! (Two exclamation points, especially for you. Do with them what you will.) Thank you both for loving Summer as much as I do. I pray for success for her and for you all.

I wrote this book to try and make some sense of a death, to explore why we giggled so much between the tears, why I somehow *knew* he was at his own funeral. I wrote it for people with huge and ridiculous families. For cross- or third culture, diaspora or mixed race kids, growing up with customs that are theirs, but feel foreign. Or who are struggling to figure out which parts of each culture fits them best. For my cousins, my sistren, girls everywhere who have suffered in silence. For the rebels and black sheep and those who feel they can't air their secrets. Even though the world is getting smaller, doesn't mean we don't come up against resistance – even within ourselves. You're not alone. I see you. And hopefully you'll see Summer.

Resources:

If Summer's story is one similar to your own, please know there is support available.

While Summer's life was lived in the UK and Oman, the author has lived a big part of hers in Dubai where this book was published.

Below is a list of organisations that although not affiliated with the publication of this book kindly agreed to be included as a place you can turn to for help.

1. **Shuroq Al Amal Al Alamia** – Oman, +968 99381997, shuroq.amal.alamia@gmail.com
2. **The Survivors Trust** – UK, www.thesurvivorstrust.org, 08088 010 818, helpline@thesurvivorstrust.org
3. **The Lighthouse Arabia Center for Wellbeing** – UAE, www.lighthousearabia.com, +971 (0)4 380 2088

About the Author

Born in London to Omani Zanzibari parents, Salha has been daydreaming, performing, and creating songs, plays and stories since she was a child. As an adult, armed with a seemingly redundant degree in languages, she founded The Million Dollar Band, with whom she has travelled the world playing music. Family girl, proud Muslim, crazy cat lady, doting wife, shoe enthusiast and professional rock star, she has now added 'author' to the list with her first novel, *The End of Summer*. Having lived in Bahrain, London, Germany, LA, Muscat, Beirut, Dubai, she has finally settled (for now) with her amazing husband and two rescue cats in Zanzibar.

simplysalha

About the Publisher

The Dreamwork Collective is a print and digital publisher sharing diverse voices and powerful stories with the world. Dedicated to the advancement of humanity, we strive to create books that have a positive impact on people and on the planet. Our hope is that our books document this moment in time for future generations to enjoy and learn from, and that we play our part in ushering humanity into a new era of heightened creativity, connection, and compassion.

www.thedreamworkcollective.com

thedreamworkcollective

CPSIA information can be obtained
at www.ICGtesting.com
Printed in the USA
LVHW052250090523
746584LV00017B/213